MW01258547

Metro-Line

to

MURDER

by Jill Sawyer

Copyright © 2010 Jill Sawyer

All rights reserved.

ISBN:1456372246

ISBN-13:978-1456372248

LCCN:

For Jim,

my Companero and most discerning Critic

ACKNOWLEDGEMENTS

This author wishes to acknowledge the invaluable editorial assistance of Annie Abbott, Kristin Harvey, and Polly Tafrate, all members of a truly sophisticated and devoted writing group. Despite the advice of experts in the writing field who say to avoid your family's input, I have called upon them all to critique various stages of my manuscript. They avoided the all-out praise those experts had predicted they'd make and instead, provided me with truthful, on-the-mark editorial advice.

I am indebted to the willing assistance of The Darien Police Department who allowed me to interview three of their detectives. They advised me on valid police procedure for the various criminal predicaments that occur in my novel. I also wish to thank an anonymous FBI Agent, who was formerly attached to a unit for the Metropolitan Area, but is now working abroad.

Finally, thanks go to the exemplary staff at the Darien Library who provided me with ongoing support.

Corporate Game-Playing

Thursday - January 25, 2007 *Comp-Coordinates*:

Accounting Department

The intake of breath was so loud that she cast her eyes both right and left to see if anyone nearby had heard. Paula's hand jumped again to the middle section of the print-out she'd been proof-reading. He's manipulating earnings again. She could feel the anger rising. Damn it! Right here! The date's been changed. Paula ran her finger down the accounting transactions for October, checking once again. Those stock options were granted on the 24th, not on the 2nd. This meant trouble - big time. She wasn't going to allow him to pass over this one. On two separate occasions she had advised him of company misrepresentations. His manner had been gruff and dismissive. "I'll take care of it," he'd said the first time and then, turning his back on her, he picked up the phone.

Lazaro's office door was set ajar, so she could hear the

drone of his voice as it filtered through, and then fell silent. He must be off the phone now. Paula decided that she'd better confront him while she was still feeling the outrage. He wasn't going to appreciate her "meddling", as he'd called it last time. With files in hand, she stood up, and took a deep breath, as she made her approach to his office. Before entering, she hesitated a moment staring at the wall plaque next to his door: **Finance & Administration** and below that *Michael Lazaro*. Who knew where this would lead, but her mind was made up. She knocked lightly before entering.

He was riffling through some papers when she walked in. This was one of his ploys - in order to look busy. When you worked closely with someone long enough, you got to know his mannerisms pretty well. It had been almost two years since she'd signed on as his executive assistant. Paula was beginning to think that the salary it paid was not worth putting up with his conniving, surly temperament.

"I'm afraid I've found another mistake in our financial statement for October," she said when he looked up. Here it comes she thought, as he squeezed his eyes into slits - the "look". It was a scowl registering both scorn and resentment at being interrupted.

"What are you talking about now, Paula?"

"I'm going over our filings with the SEC. It's right here," she explained as she placed the report on his desk.

"We have discussed this," he said with his voice rising, "and I told you I'd handle it. I've approved that report!" With that he grabbed up the papers and pushed them into a group of folders next to his phone. "Now please let me get back to work."

Paula watched his body pull tight with contained anger,

but she knew that she couldn't back off now. "Mr. Lazaro I cannot permit this report to go out with improper disclosures. It's against the law. I just won't do it." He whirled back to face her, his eyes blazing with fury. Before he could say another word she added, "The other issue is with Comp-Coordinates failing to recognize a compensation expense. We can't risk being accused of misleading our shareholders."

"Let me tell you this, Ms. Metz." his voice took on a menacing tone, "Interfering with business affairs that you don't understand is not going to look good on your annual review."

Paula stood for a moment staring down at her new maroon, suede pumps. Here it is - the threat from on high. "In that case, I might have to take this up with Dennis Barkley." She paused, allowing him an out, "Unless, that is, you agree to make the necessary corrections." The two held each other in a stare-down. She watched as his lips pulled back baring two lines of yellow, stained teeth. She spoke quickly, "That is not what I want to do." Paula dropped her eyes to his desk, hesitating before saying, "but I see no other alternative."

Lazaro burst out of his chair, his fists curling into balls, "I warn you., Ms. Metz, such an act of insubordination means that you will be out of a job... by the end of the month."

"I'll be sure to take that into consideration, sir." Paula turned slowly, her body twisting with a tight mixture of anger and fear. She pulled herself upright before moving toward the door. It was only a matter of steps to get to her desk, but sitting down at it seemed pointless. She glided by her chair and continued down the aisle separating two rows of cubicles, only half aware of the general phone buzz and keyboard punching of Comp's auditors busily engaged in their work.

In the ladies' room she leaned on one of the sinks, feeling the strength flow out of her body. Thank God the place was empty. How was she going to proceed through the rest of the day? Was she really going to meet with Barkley? She recalled saying "she might" to Lazaro. She could still change her mind. Paula was surprised to feel her head shaking a refusal. Barkley's reputation as a tough nut didn't do him full justice. Surely Comp's CFO would force Lazaro to rectify the accounting. She'd give it a little time, maybe take the weekend to fully consider the risk she was taking. Paula pulled herself upright and raised her hands before her. They were trembling.

If only Gordon Hathaway had not backed away when she first showed him those discrepancies. She wanted his executive's take on the report and was disappointed with his reluctance to step into another department's affairs. He said that they would see it as interference. She didn't fully appreciate this 'separation of departments': Gordon's marketing from Lazaro's accounting. Weren't they all one company? Paula felt uncomfortable as the lone complainant and told him so, but she had done as he recommended and taken it step-by-step. At least he had told her that he wanted to be kept informed.

Paula was in earnest about maintaining a discrete, professional relationship with Gordon, despite their former involvement, however short it was. She directed her thoughts back to the confrontation with Lazaro. No doubt about it. This confirmed his guilt. As for going to Barkley, she'd wait for advice from Gordon. Paula consoled herself with the thought that once he heard how Lazaro ended up threatening her, he would stand by her.

She gazed at her face in the mirror. It was pale, but looked composed. A few pinches at her cheeks would restore color, at least temporarily. This is what Aunt Martha had taught her to do. What funny, old fashioned beautifying tips she used to recommend: brush hair 100 strokes a day to keep it glossy, shine finger nails with a special little buffer brush.

She pulled her suit jacket back, in order to tuck her blouse in, and then ran her fingers through the short, dark blonde hair that could use some highlights. It always turned a dusky color in the winter. This week-end she'd get it done. Now though, she'd walk back to her desk, print out another copy of that report and...then what? It was too early to go home. Oh yes, she could send out those letters she'd composed earlier.

Lazaro's Office

Michael sat at his desk ruminating. He wasn't concerned about her going to Barkley. They were in the same camp. Barkley would either put Paula in her place or boot her into obscurity. Still, there was the fear that she'd mouth off somewhere else. Didn't he hear her a couple weeks ago on the phone with Hathaway? He thought he overheard her asking if she could stop by his office. Were they fucking, or was she trying to enlist him for her goddamned crusade? He looked at his watch, 4:25. One thing was certain. She needed to be watched. He stepped across the carpet to his door, closed it, and returned to his desk. The mobile he used for calls home and to family was in his brief case. He pulled it out and punched in Mario's name. Two rings was all it took. "Hey Mario. How're you doing? It's Michael."

Mario was surprised to get a call from Michael. It had

been over a year since he'd seen his cousin. "Hey, nice to hear from ya'. What's the mattah? Nothin' happenin' in the corporate world?"

Michael pushed out a fake chuckle, "Too much, Mario. Too much. What I'm calling about is...uh, are you still out of a job?"

"Yeah." Jeezus, he thought. What's this about? He remembered that Michael had never paid off that bet they made...what was it, a year ago? But he held off to see what Michael was calling about.

"I was just wondering...how long were you at Hercules Salvage? It was office work, right? Not ..." Michael paused. He didn't want to say hauling. "Not working outdoors."

"Uh, yeah. I stepped up in the world, Michael. No more hauling shit. They brought me into the office."

"Doing what kind of work?"

"I was assistant to the Division Controller, doin' the scheduling but mostly key-punching budget and payroll shit. Oh, man. Not for me."

"So what happened? Did you get fired?"

"Nah. Three months of that was enough. I quit. Too much detail crap. Sittin' there all day long. I couldn't hack it anymore. Collecting unemployment's easier."

Michael felt a momentary ping of doubt, but then, who else would be available to do this job?

"What I can do, Mario, is offer you a couple days' work, under the table, ya' know? That way you can keep collecting your unemployment checks. It's a little data entering right here in the accounting department, similar to what you were doing at Hercules, but just for a few days. To bring us to the end of the month."

There was a pause at Mario's end. He could use the

extra money and this was family, but he wondered if Michael was good with the follow-through. "What kinda' pay are we talkin' about here?"

"We can go over that if you come in tomorrow, because I might want you to do a little extra weekend job for me too. Don't worry, I'll make it worth your while."

"Yeah, well Michael, you can convince me bettah if you start off by payin' me that IOU you still owe me, remember? That bet we made when we were all at Dominick's?"

"Oh, sorry about that. You're right. What was it, fifty dollars? Sorry, Mario, I completely forgot. I'll pay you back, plus interest if you come in tomorrow."

"I guess that's a plan. Where's your company at? It's Comp-somethin'."

"Comp-Coordinates, at 420 Lexington Avenue. I'll advise the security desk that you're coming. How's ten o'clock for you?"

"That should be okay." Mario looked down at his sweater and brushed off some cookie crumbs. With an address like that, he'd prahbly have to wear a friggin' suit and tie.

"Good Mario, you can call my cell number before you come up. I'll meet you on the 32nd floor, right outside the elevator." A sudden question came to mind. "You've got a cell phone, right?"

"Yeah, I got one 'a those new smart phones."

"Can you open attachments?"

There was a slight pause. "They tole' me it's the latest." Mario quickly threw in, because he couldn't resist, "And when you pay me back, I'll be able to pay off this month's bill."

Failing to acknowledge the quip, Michael gave Mario

his number, repeated the company's address, and flipped his phone shut.

26 Federal Plaza - 23rd Floor - Same Time

Agent Minicus had been working in the White-Collar Crime Division for over four years. He specialized in corporate fraud and was at his happiest when he succeeded in exposing the fat cats, those self-dealing, high power executives who robbed the public of as much cash as drug dealers sucked from addicts. The transfer from Atlanta to Manhattan two years prior boosted not only his ego, but his salary by fifteen grand. God knew, he needed it. Living in New York ate up a good part of the gain.

He gathered up some copies of news articles and several reports bound in plastic folders. Minicus was anxious to get this initial meeting in today so that his newly formed task force could begin work. It was too early to draw any conclusions, but the background fact-finding he'd done indicated that Comp-Coordinates was on its way to warrant a formal investigation. He checked his watch - 4:30. He headed down the hall for the conference room.

The four other Agents already sitting around the table looked up at Frank as he entered and took a seat. Two of them were fairly new to this form of white collar crime, so there would be some educating to do. He was pleased to see them alert and seemingly ready for a new assignment. "We think we have another corporate fraud case centering on options backdating, but in order to make firm allegations we have to prove that the top executives knowingly cherry-picked a low level to set the options price. But that's not all. We also have to prove that they registered improper disclosures with the SEC." Heads nodded in acknowledgment.

"Okay, first off..." Minicus picked up the bundle of clear plastic file folders and distributed them. "The SEC has asked us to join them in a parallel investigation. It'll be an informal probe. Remember, no allegations have yet been made. Here's what the SEC has given us going back several years. You need to be thoroughly acquainted with this information. It's a lot of reading and it won't have the appeal of a National Enquirer scoop, but it's important stuff. You've got to know that these guys are stealing from the public. These scam artists just keep on treating themselves to an unearned bonus, sometimes for years. Joe Average investor takes a risk when he buys shares in a company. In my mind, every shareholder should. That's including the biggies."

"Ever since the Wall Street Journal ran that big story a couple years ago... Here." He lifted them off the pile. "I have copies for you. Reading this article will give you an idea of how this whole game of timing CEO stock options caught on. Right now there are more than two hundred corporate fraud cases pending across the country, an enormous increase ever since this guy Eric Lie figured their scheme out and had his story published." He handed out the article. "Any of you familiar with Comp-Coordinates?"

One of the four said, "Yeah, don't they make audio and computer accessories?"

"That's right, along with a bunch of other electronic products. They're located on Lexington Avenue in the four hundred block. But we have a lot of homework to do before we can make any visits there."

Minicus directed his gaze to each of the four. "Are we on board?" They all uttered agreement. "Okay then.

By Monday I want you to be fully acquainted with this material. We'll be meeting with members of the SEC here at 10:30AM to go over assignments and strategies."

When he rose they did the same, extending hands across the table to shake with their new leader.

Friday, January the 26th

In the elevator lobby Lazaro leaned against a wall checking through his Blackberry but was soon interrupted by the ping of doors opening. Mario stepped out and strode over to give him a hearty hug of greeting with a couple pounds on the back. Lazaro's eyes quickly scanned the halls. No one there, thank God.

"Salve! Come va, and all that, Michael. It's been a while, hasn't it? So this is your place of work, huh. Pretty nice."

"Yes...well!" Michael cleared his throat and gestured a direction with his arm guiding Mario to the left. "This way. We'll be using a conference room up here where we can discuss this project in private. Remember this is off the books...under the table?"

"Yeah, shuah. Lead the way."

At least Mario had worn a business suit. It was one of those ridiculous double breasted jobs and looked about fifteen years old, but it would do. They walked into a small conference room furnished with a walnut, oval table surrounded by eight chairs. "Take a seat anywhere; I want to go over the plan with you. I don't have a lot of time, but I want to make sure that you understand what your job entails."

"First off, *I'm* hiring you, not the company. Nobody needs to know that you didn't go through Human

Resources. Got that? This is between you and me."
Mario nodded his head. "I have already announced to the department that you're a new data entry man we've hired and you're here on a temp job. Like I said on the phone - filling in till the end of the month. I'll introduce you to just a couple people, but mostly you'll be working on your own. Your desk is near my office and I'll be the one to give you work, nobody else. My executive assistant, Paula Metz sits close by. If she gets chatty or wants to know more about what you're doing, be polite but talk in generalities. Say that you're updating databases for clients. Any questions so far?"

"Uh, no. If it's like what I was doin' for Hercules, it'll come easy." Mario was wondering when they would come to the money part, but he stayed quiet.

"Good. Now we come to the bigger job. I'm concerned here about someone trying to make false accusations about me, but I don't have any real proof. Just say I have a strong suspicion. This executive secretary I mentioned, Paula Metz? She's the one. You'll be sitting to the side of her, near enough to overhear any phone conversations she makes."

"Yeah? Like to who?"

"One could be to the SEC." Mario frowned slightly. "That's the Securities and Exchange Commission. I have the name of that contact person written down here, the one she would most likely be trying to reach." Michael took a folded paper from his jacket pocket and spread it out on the table. He pointed to two highlighted names on a list. "There's Yardsley, from the SEC, but here's the one I'm most concerned about. He's our V.P. in charge of Marketing. That's his name, right there. Gordon Hathaway. I've included a few names of company officers

11

you'll probably hear mentioned around the office. For general use, it's good for you to become acquainted with them as well, but it's only those first two highlighted ones I want you to listen for. If Paula Metz makes a call to either one, I want you to let me know immediately, but...and this is important. Without causing suspicion. In other words, be alert and at the same time casual in your manner."

Mario's interest level was rising. This meant they were talking real money. "Shuah thing, Michael." He saw a quick shake of Michael's head. Mario corrected himself. "No, I mean Mr. Lazaro." He emphasized this with, "I got it. I got it."

"This is a professional company and I have a lot at stake here, Mario. No slip-ups."

"No, no." Mario held up his right hand, palm facing out. "I give you my word."

"Here's something else for you to reference, just in case. He pulled out his Blackberry. I'm going to send it as an attachment to an e-mail. What's your address?" He scrolled to his address book. "Go ahead."

"It's boccamario@blazenet.net. Want me to spell it for ya?"

"No, I think I have it." He keyed it in, tapped it into a new e-mail message, and typed PM as the subject. Then he attached two photos, hit 'Send', and looked up, waiting.

Mario came to, "Oh, right." and pulled out his cell phone. In a moment Mario heard his "O Sole Mio" ring tone. He pushed the green phone image.

"What's the PM mean?"

"That's for Paula Metz. You have two pictures of her there. One's a close-up and the other is a full profile.

"Yeah, but I can't see 'em. I mean, how do you open 'em?" Mario hesitated, feeling awkward and embarrassed that he didn't know how to work his new phone He held it out. "Heah. Could'ya take a look? I just got this super cell a coupla' weeks ago. They said it did almost everything."

With a few tap-ins Michael brought up the photos. "I want you to practice using your cell, Mario. You've got to be handy with these if you intend to make it in the modern world." He showed Mario the steps and handed it back.

Mario nodded his head. "Not bad lookin'. What was this, a Christmas pahty?"

"Right." Pleased with how he'd come fully prepared, Michael couldn't resist a self-satisfied smile. "We took a bunch and downloaded them for the whole department, so they could see themselves in a party mode."

"Yeah nice. But how come you want me to have these?"

"Just so you don't... shall we say, lose sight of her over the next two days." He was really thinking that Mario might not have a visual memory that lasted overnight.

"You mean this weekend?"

"That's exactly what I mean. You'll see Paula's name and address at the bottom of that list I gave you. I know she takes the subway down to Astor Place. She moved a short time ago, into a new apartment. I want you to keep an eye on her over the weekend. Follow her wherever she goes, starting right after work. But keep out of sight! If she gets on a train going out of the city, or walks into an office here in Manhattan carrying a brief case, I'll want to know right away. You'll call me and I'll direct you from there. You've got my cell number on that same paper as the names I gave you. Program it and my other e-mail address into your contacts.

"Jeez, this is a lot more than I first figured. What kinda' money are we talkin' about?"

"If you do the job exactly as I've outlined right up to the end of the month. I'll pay you four grand. That's six days' work including today. But! And this is a big but. There can't be any hitches." He saw a frown come onto Mario's face. Michael picked up the pace. "If I didn't think you could do this Mario, I wouldn't have called for your help. Now, she may not try any tricks at all. I doubt that she will." Mario's face relaxed. He reminded himself that this was his rich, successful cousin asking for his help and he could make a bundle.

Thorough as ever, Michael had covered the field the day before. Right after Paula left his office, he warned Dennis Barkley that she might come in to see him. He knew that Barkley was quite capable of pulling her off the stupid, righteous track she was on. Hiring Mario to monitor the weekend was the extra insurance he wanted. Yes, and the other possibility was that she'd get canned. In that case he could say good-bye to the both of them.

Michael continued, "Hey, you'll probably just be strolling around Manhattan watching a woman do her weekend thing. I'm not saying you can relax though. You have to be alert and ready to act. If she does try something... if she meets with Hathaway or tries to hand off a briefcase full of company records and you prevent that from happening, there'll be a big bonus."

Mario leaned back in his leather spindle office chair rocking back and forth, as if to consider the offer. Most of it was an act. He hadn't had any real action like this in a long time. Plus, Michael was family. "I'm thinkin' it ovah. It sounds decent enough. And if I do keep her from handin' somethin' off...I mean preventing what you were talking about...what kinda' bonus are we talking about?"

"Depends on the conditions." Michael sat back in his chair, allowing the weight of the job's variable risk factor to sink in. "You can understand that, can't you?" He paused again, confident of his negotiating skills. "It could be as much as five, six grand." He figured this might spur a little drive out of Mario, which was otherwise pretty dim. "I think that covers everything, but I want you to tell it all back to me, just to make sure we're both clear."

After fifteen minutes, with a few corrections and repetitions, Michael was satisfied. "All right. Now here's what I want you to do. Take this advance." He pulled a couple one hundreds out of his wallet and handed them to Mario. "Go to a coffee shop or someplace where you can sit down and practice using that cell phone. It's camera ready, so take a few pictures of our great city and send them to some friends. Tell them you need practice and have them send a few back to you, so you can get used to opening pictures on your phone. Documents work the same way. Memorize those names I gave you, and then come up to the 30th floor after lunch. Say, 1:30. I'll have you start with the office work then. Are we good?"

"Sure thing, Mr. Lazaro."

Later that Day

Paula leaned forward resting her forehead in her hand. She was tired and wanted to go home. The call she'd been waiting for, from Hathaway's office still hadn't come in. His assistant said he would be out of the office

15

all day and wasn't sure what time he'd be back. It was grueling, waiting in this limbo. Paula told herself that a meeting with Dennis Barkley was the necessary and forthright thing to do. But there were moments when it felt like she was entering the cold, dark recesses of a cave that had no exit.

At the very least, she wanted to get Gordon's reaction to yesterday's confrontation in Lazaro's office. No, she needed more. Was she ready to become a whistle-blower? Who would believe one executive assistant's word? She needed higher executive backing. Paula realized that nothing could or would happen without first getting Hathway's support. She gave her head a shake to drive out all the doubts and pushed back her chair. Enough. She'd try to reach Gordon later. Turning to say goodnight to those still there, she was surprised to see that Mario had left. What a strange character.

Outside, the night air was cold and clear. The walk to Grand Central before catching the subway downtown felt refreshing. There was nothing like the pace of New Yorkers exiting office buildings after a heavy week of work. She entered the flow, gradually picking up their stride. The damn thing was infectious. Occasionally Paula longed for the calm, friendly ease of her Midwestern background, but not too often. She was happy and proud to have made the move East on her own. Her salary now provided enough for an apartment closer to work, and she could select a business wardrobe more suitable for this corporate position. Trying to be optimistic she told herself that with the right help and American justice, she might get through this present situation.

Her subway ride downtown was as compressed as ever

with zoned out passengers. But it was a great improvement over the long one to Brooklyn. Walking up the stairs to her apartment, Paula decided she would concentrate on some domestic chores this weekend and also plan something fun to do, like a concert. The anonymity of city life and a commitment to long work hours left her pretty much to herself. If only she enjoyed the bar scene. Her last experiment with that put her off months ago. She was still unable to break through the shyness that froze her into a two dimensional mannequin in crowds. Was her fondness for solitude a negative trait? As an only child she grew up relying on herself to provide whatever resources would keep her interests going. Aunt Martha used to say, "You're the only child in this whole town who can keep herself entertained an entire day."

She'd have to start making more of an effort to develop social connections, maybe join a book club or even a single's group. Ugh. Ever since her three year love affair in college had broken off, she'd focused on getting her MBA and then her job. Aside from Gordon there'd been some dating but nothing that had held any deep meaning for her.

The apartment blinked into light, looking exactly as it had when she left. Not even a message on her answering machine. She walked into the kitchen and looked at the clock; it was going on 6:00. If Gordon returned to his office after hours, he might pick up the phone. She dialed the number feeling again that old quickening in her heart. Why! Why didn't this go away? Wasn't there anyone out there who was as good and as genuine as he was? But younger? At the fourth ring she hung up to avoid hearing the recorded greeting.

Paula recalled with some anguish how close she had

come to moving into a relationship with this man. All the sparks and body language were there. Whenever she entered the cafeteria she would scan the room for him When he *was* there he would look her way and smile. Sometimes he sat down with her to chat about work, how she liked living in New York. She had to admit to herself that most of this bond was ignited by her imagination, but there was that first time he invited her out for lunch. How thrilled she had been. She realized now that part of the thrill had been the implicit danger of unfamiliar territory with its secret phone calls and clandestine meetings. Just before the third date they'd planned he had called her desk. "What do you think about telling Lazaro you have a doctor's appointment at 2:00?" That's when she thought the relationship would take fire. And oh how it did. Paula could hardly keep herself from playing it through her mind, again and again.

Then after the next lunch date, as they were sipping coffee, Gordon practically stuttered some partial apology. He sat back looking at her and began again. In his very gentlemanly way he told her that although his attraction to her was real, he could not allow himself to get in-volved any further. At that stage in his marriage he could not take the risk of a love affair. It had taken months for her to feel anywhere near neutral toward him and to stop her imagination from creating love scenes.

Paula broke out of her reverie but stood looking at the counter top. First she'd change into her sweats, then go through the mail, check the refrigerator for something to eat. She turned to her right and opened the door. Not much there, but way back in the freezer, tucked behind a whole chicken she found one of those quickie bags of shrimp and linguini. That would do.

There was a note in the mail from an old college friend saying that she might be moving to the city by summer. That lightened Paula's mood. Feeling a little more connected, she reached for the bottle of Cabernet, and in her usual Friday night gesture poured herself a glassful. At last she plopped into an old stuffed chair she had bought at the Salvation Army. Her feet went up on the coffee table and she gazed off to the opposite wall. Oh the quiet; how good.

Paula awoke with a start. How long had she been asleep? She moved quickly to the kitchen and pulled out her personal phone book. It was a little past 7:00, not a bad time to reach him at home in Darien, something she would normally never do, but she had to get her mind set for Monday - whether to go ahead with this or to continue working and pretending that nothing had happened. A whole weekend of anxiety and indecision was unthinkable. Good thing she'd been able to find his number. It rang twice. Thank God he picked up, not his wife.

"Hello Gordon, I'm so sorry to bother you at home, but this just can't wait till Monday. It's Paula. I had a bad run-in with Michael yesterday after finding more transaction errors in October's accounts. This makes three separate instances." She went on to describe the entire office scene with Lazaro and then waited for his response.

"That must have been rough, Paula." He paused briefly, taking it all in. "I can't believe he acted in such an unprofessional manner. He told you he'd approved the report and then he took it from you?"

"Yes. I told him at first that I didn't want to go to Mr. Barkley - to, you know, give him a chance to change his mind, but that's when he told me I could be out of a job by the end of the month."

"If it's true that you have documented proof, it's not insubordination to go to Barkley. You have every right to seek guidance from our Chief Financial Officer, Dana. He cannot allow those accounts to stand."

This was comforting to hear. "I was thinking of going in on Monday, but it's a scary step for me. Can I count on your support if, for some reason, Dennis Barkley puts me off or even defends Lazaro?" Paula waited for his response, her heart thumping in her chest.

He said with a shade of hesitance, "Well you know that I've been reluctant to interfere in another department's affairs." She waited again. "I'd like to see that account- ing report for myself, along with the other two you al- ready showed me."

This was disappointing. "But you've seen those others already. Listen Gordon, I can't sit in that office working under these conditions. It's tense... Michael pretends I'm not there." She took a deep breath in. "I'll show them to you first thing Monday morning, before I set up an appointment with Barkley."

"Oh, dammit. That won't work. I have to fly out Sunday night for a conference in Chicago. I'll be back though Wednesday evening. How about waiting until Thursday?"

"I just can't wait that long. Wednesday is the 31st, the end of the month." She held on, hoping he would have faith in her to handle this ordeal in a professional manner.

"All right, Paula. I'll stand behind you. I'm sure Barkley will want to investigate, but in a worst case scenario, I will give you my full support. I want you to call me after you meet with Dennis. Here's my cell phone number. I'll want to know how that meeting goes."

Paula grabbed up a pencil and wrote down his number. Then her whole body slumped with relief. "Oh Gordon, thank you. I'll call you Monday."

Urban Tracking

Saturday Night - **East Village**

Already it was 9:30. It had been a long day and nothing was happening. He didn't think she'd be going anywhere now. Mario was tired and bored, plus it was getting too cold to stand around. He sat down on the steps leading to a basement apartment and pulled out his cell phone. In three rings Lazaro picked up.

"It's Mario. Nothing to worry about, I'm just reportin' in."

Lazaro was a little irritated that Mario would interrupt a weekend for no specific reason, but he decided to let him talk. "So is she at her place now?

"Yeah. Ya' know, last night I did the smart thing. I left when she looked like she was ready to pack it in. I waited outside your building and followed from a distance. Got the same subway, numba' 6. She didn't go out at all last night. Then I was here by 8:30 this morning. No action till about 10:00. She did the normal

Saturday stuff: picked up dry cleaning, stopped in a book store, went to the grocery."

"Yeah, okay, Mario." He was getting impatient.

"Then back home, but went out again this afternoon to a beauty parlor. Prahbly got her hair colored. I don't know. It took long enough."

"Michael!" It was Clio from the den shouting over *America's Most Wanted.* " They're on his tail; you're missing it!"

"Good, Mario, I gotta go."

"Yeah, well she was home again around 5:00. Nothin' since then. I coulda' been somewheres else watchin' a game."

"Okay, so then she never carried a brief case any-where."

"Right. And I don't think she'll be goin' anywhere's else tonight, so I thought I could go home now. Okay with you?"

Lazaro was thinking that at least it sounded like Mario was handling the job. "I guess that's enough for today."

Another shout from the living room, "Michael, c'mon!" He gave his arm a wide sweep downward as though he could shut her up with a gesture.

"Listen, Mario, you don't have to report in every day if nothing's happening. Just if she attempts a hand-off."

"I'll e-mail you at the office Monday. We'll do some reconnoitering then. I'll let you know where and when." The phone clicked off.

<u>Sunday - January, the 28th</u> - Paula's Apartment

So far the weekend had gone along in its rather lack-luster fashion, but time seemed to be crawling. Paula had decided to get herself out and try something different. Not since her childhood had she attended church, but it would represent a new effort to seek a social connection of some kind. She found an Episcopal church down on Madison Street, a pretty long walk, but it would get her outside and provide a different experience.

Different it was, but attending St. Augustine's had actually made her feel even lonelier. Most of these people were downright elderly. And they made her aware that she wasn't amongst those familiar church faces from back home in Wisconsin. She'd make another effort later on, at a more commercial venue. There was a new place in the Village called *Grounds for Coffee*. Maybe their open mic afternoon session would be good for distraction. Hey, it might even be entertaining. The sun was out and the air felt clean, so she walked the twelve blocks home.

There weren't many people inside *Grounds* yet, but the place looked cozy enough. Several small round wooden tables were set in a cluster. A couple upholstered sofas dotted with colorful pillows faced each other from opposite wood-paneled walls. She liked the jazzy, Picasso-like paintings that traveled in a line across the back, firebrick wall.

While a guitarist picked out the melody line of a familiar classical theme, Paula removed her coat and placed it with her gloves on one of the stuffed leather chairs. Then she walked up to the counter and ordered a "Depth Recharger". She wouldn't ask about its ingredients. That wouldn't be following today's plan - to experience something radical. It was probably just another espresso, but what the hell.

For nearly two hours she listened to semi-talented

musicians and poetry readers perform their various acts. Some of the poetry was laughably bad, but Paula always joined the others in polite applause. One guy at a table near her had nodded and spoken to her briefly, "Nice day, huh. You from around here?" She told him not too far. He smiled and stood to signal for another order at the coffee bar. And that was the end of it. Everyone else seemed to be there to hang and just listen. Oh well, she paid up and pulled on her coat. Although January was beginning to hold its daylight longer, by 5:30 the sky was black, and the city's streets were brightened only by shop windows, street lamps, and the sweep of headlights.

She walked back the same way she had come, glancing into store displays and checking out the few pedestrians heading...who knew where. Most of them kept their heads down against the cold. Within a few blocks of home she became conscious of footsteps from behind that seemed to echo her own. She made an early turn up Avenue B and slowed her pace to listen for the footsteps again. Still there, but slower now too. Paula wasn't sure whether to turn around or just pick up her pace and get home. At the next brightly lit shop she turned, looked in the window and then back down the street. Yes. A man with hands in his coat pockets was coming toward her. He quickly turned to face the street, looking up and down as though deciding whether to cross. She could see only a dark profile, no hat, a long coat. She waited to see what he'd do next. Why would he wait? There was no traffic coming. With only half a block to 12th Street she decided to go for it. As soon as she saw him looking her way again, she broke into a half run for the rest of the way home.

Once in the apartment Paula leaned her back against the

door, panting. Her brain was in a scramble. What should she do next? 911? No. First, fix the locks and door chain. Don't turn on any lights; he might be right out there, waiting and watching. She wanted to call someone. No. Aunt Martha would just worry and Gordon was probably on some plane to Chicago. There was no one at work she felt close enough to. What would she say, what *could* she say to anyone? Her breath having come back to normal, she stepped slowly to the window and peered down the street. No one. After a few minutes standing in the quiet, she dropped into a chair still wearing her coat. Was she getting paranoid?

Monday - January, 29th

Mario was at his desk by 8:50 pulling some more lists out of a folder. These were names and addresses of clients to update. Ugh, more boring punch-ins. But at least the other piece of his job was keeping him interested. It had been chancy last night. She'd almost caught him there on Avenue B. Good thing she hadn't gotten a look at him up close. He was pleased with himself. Holding off at 12th Street had been pretty smart, he thought. The only place she was going at that point was home. So he backtracked to Astor Place and then home on the subway. Still, he wasn't going to mention it to Lazaro.

It was funny how he felt now toward Paula Metz. Following her through a whole weekend somehow had brought him closer to her as a person. So this was how a woman in her early 30's spent her Saturdays and Sundays. It seemed kind of lonely, kind of like his own life. He was wondering about this different feeling when she walked in and started hanging up her coat. He quickly looked down at his computer and started typing.

"Good morning...it's Mario, isn't it?"

"Uh, yeah."

"Are you finding everything you need?"

"Oh yeah. Mr. Lazaro gave me enough here for a coupla' days." He wished she'd get to her own job. He looked back at his screen and placed his hands on the keyboard, thinking that she looked a little...not dumpy, but washed out this morning. He told himself to keep his mind on the job and his ear alert to her phone conversations.

The morning was moving at turtle pace. Two god awful hours of keyboard entries. Paula Metz hadn't made any calls that he would say were of any interest. He was beginning to think that nothing at all would ever happen and maybe this job was for shit, when his new smart phone vibrated an incoming e-mail.

It was from Lazaro. "Meet me upstairs, 32nd floor in the same conference room we used Friday, come at 12:30. That's when she usually goes to lunch." Good thing because by then, he knew he'd be dying to get out of this office.

Mario took the stairs up to give his 42 year old frame some exercise. He wasn't used to sitting for hours on end. It wasn't that he was getting pudgy. All those years of doing physical work with Hercules had kept him looking fit. Smiling to himself, he took the stairs two at a time. The conference room was empty of course, because he'd beaten the clock. He took the same swiveler chair as before, for good luck. It wasn't a long wait. Lazaro walked briskly in and took a seat. "How'd it go yesterday, Mario?"

"It went fine, fine. She just went to church in the morning, St. Augustine's Episcopal. Jeez, I haven't been in one since I can remembah. It was y'know, almost like the Catholic church. Well, not really." He saw Lazaro's head nodding impatiently. "Yeah, well then it was back to her apartment. I hung around there for a while. Later in the aftahnoon she walked all the way over to Broadway. And Michael, I stayed outside and looked in every once in a while at these people standing up reading out loud. Good thing there was a deli next door so I could go in and get warm, get a cup a' coffee." Lazaro's head was nodding up and down again. "She nevah carried anything but her pocketbook. After that she just went home. Around like 6:00 and nuthin' after that."

"Okay, that sounds good, Mario See? I told you it might just be a weekend of strolling around the city. So listen. Keep watch today. If she leaves empty handed, just see that she goes home. He already knew that Barkley had put the meeting with Paula off till tomorrow at 3:00. "Just stick with this another couple days. I'm sure by Thursday you can anticipate a pay day."

The Next Day - January 30th

Mario's cell phone vibrated in his pocket. He read another message from Michael to meet him upstairs. Again? Thank God it was almost the end of the month.

Lazaro started off. "This afternoon she'll be meeting with one of the senior officers. That'll be at three o'clock. You don't have to follow or anything. In fact you can take a short break, say twenty minutes or so. Go out if you want, for some air. Just keep a casual eye on the building, in case she should decide to leave suddenly.

I can call you if necessary. You've still got your cell, don't you?

"Oh yeah." He slapped his breast pocket.

"Okay, fine. When you get back to your desk, continue working on that assignment I gave you. Is that going all right?" Mario was about to say how it was pretty boring work, but instead lifted his head in acknowledgment.

Lazaro continued, "I want you to pay attention around quitting time. I'm talking about if she calls anyone on the phone. Watch for if she puts any papers in her bag or if she picks up a brief case." He looked off across the room for a moment, placing his fingers tips together. "Anyway," his gaze came back, "I'm not too worried about that. Hathaway's at a conference in Chicago, but you never know." He was thinking that by the end of today's meeting, Barkley would have set her straight.

"Yeah, so in that case, you want me just to follow her like I did Friday, right?"

"Yes," Lazaro thought a second. "But if she's not carrying anything, I think you can go on home yourself."

Mario pulled his right hand up in a half salute "Got it, Mr. Lazaro," and pushed himself out of his chair.

"Good. Now go get yourself some lunch."

Three o'clock

She was waiting outside his office while Dennis Barkley's secretary busied herself typing at her computer. In all the time she had worked for Lazaro, Paula had never come to this floor for any business purpose. Unlike the other top executives, Barkley was regarded as uncommunicative; some even said cagey. Soon her wait would end. That morning she had decided to come empty-handed so as not to appear too aggressive. She would simply state her case and allow him to ask for the documentation. Was that the best way to handle this? Looking down at her lap, she realized how nervous she was. Both sets of fingers were tapping against either side of her thighs. She quickly folded her hands together. It would be important to present her case calmly, professionally. She reminded herself that Comp's Chief Financial Officer would want to hear of any wrong-doing in the accounting department.

"He'll see you now, Miss Metz." This startled Paula. There had been no ring nor sound of a phone being picked up. She walked across the carpet to the paneled door and turned the knob. He was sitting behind an impressive walnut desk and beyond that was a stunning view overlooking Manhattan's skyline that shone in the afternoon sunlight. Off to her left a settee upholstered in herringbone blue suede faced two chairs in a similarly matched style. They wouldn't be sitting there. "Have a seat Miss Metz." He motioned to a chair across from his desk.

She sat down as he said, "I'm concerned about this private matter you wish to speak to me about. You say it has to do with recent accounts?"

"Yes, but first I want you to know that I would not come to you if I had not pursued all other means of resolving what I believe to be a serious problem." His face looked implacable. Paula pulled in a deep breath and began with the first discrepancy dating back to July '05. There was no response to this, so she gave a thorough account of the next two, including the alerts she had provided Michael Lazaro.

"But are you sure, Miss Metz? Perhaps you misread those dates." She gave a quick shake of her head. He continued, "Of course I'll take a look at them, but I know that Michael would never have approved them if they had not been correct."

"But sir, I checked them all just this week. They still have not been changed. I will show them to you. I can get them right now." He gave her a short condescending smile. "I am seriously worried, sir..."

"I said I would take a look at them." His face turned to stone.

In an anxious tone she blurted, "Altering company records to conceal fraud is**...**"

Suddenly standing up, Barkley cut her off. He walked around one side of his desk and with a deadly calm tone of voice said, "I need to warn you Miss Metz that you are committing what I would call unprofessional behavior toward a co-worker. " He paused for effect, "Which, can be determined as grounds for termination." Paula sat, stunned. "Of course we want to avoid such an action if we can." Touching the back of her shoulder he ushered her out of her chair and across the office to the door. "I urge you to reconsider your position. Perhaps a transfer out of company headquarters would be the most appropriate option. Think it over."

Before going through the door Paula turned and looked him in the eye. "I will." The door closed softly behind her, and she took the same route back, her spirits clogged with defeat.

That Evening

Paula threw a catalogue down on the coffee table. God! She couldn't even concentrate on pictures. How was she ever going to get through this? The desire to escape, to run somewhere was strong. A transfer, even though it

31

would be a step down, would get her out of this mess. She thought again. What it amounted to really, was a demotion. In money, in status. She needed to hear what Gordon had to say about it. When was he ever going to return her call?"

Those last hours at work had been creepy. She was sure Lazaro must have heard from Barkley. How was Lazaro going to respond to her? He had hardly even looked her way on the two occasions he came out of his office. He had said absolutely nothing. Well, tomorrow might be different. Paula came out of her chair with a sudden urge to do something physical.

She brought out two 5 pound dumbbells from the bedroom and began by raising one knee to her chest and then the other while lifting the weights overhead. She'd left a message for Gordon to call as soon as he could. She saw by the clock on the side table that it was close to eight. A re-run of "24" would be coming on, one of her favorite shows. She put the dumbbells down on the chair, clicked on the TV, picked them up again and began pumping.

The phone rang. At last! She almost dropped one of them grabbing for the remote to hit MUTE. "Hello, Gordon?" she asked into the phone.

"Hi. How'd it go Paula? Sorry I couldn't get back to you sooner. I just got back here."

"Oh! It was horrible, Gordon. Horrible."

"What! How?"

She felt herself welling up with tears as she described her confrontation with Barkley. Gordon interrupted her toward the end. "Wait a minute. He said he would take a look at the accounts, but then he backed up Lazaro?"

"Yes. But Gordon, his whole attitude was one... of dismissing me. And then calling my encounters with

Lazaro...he called it unprofessional behavior toward a co-worker."

"This is outrageous! It infuriates me." A moment of silence was broken with, "Is that how it ended? With a threat of termination?"

"No. He came around his desk and told me - this was when he was walking me to his door. He said that maybe a transfer would be a possible option for me to consider."

"And that's all? What about Lazaro? Did he say anything else to you before you left?"

"No. But Gordon, I don't know how to go through another day in that office. It's awful sitting there wondering what he's going to do next." He started to speak but Paula broke in. "Do you think I should take the transfer?"

"Listen Paula. I want you to hold tight. Please. Go in tomorrow as usual and pretend that everything's normal. You can do that for one day, can't you?"

"Oh, I don't think I can manage having him eyeballing me all day, gloating over his victory. Last weekend I was walking back from a coffee house and I swear, some man was following me. It's all been too..." Gordon broke in.

"Paula, listen to me. I told you that I would give you my support and I will; I promise. If need be you can tell them you're not taking it any further; you're thinking things over. I should be back home by 6:00, 6:30 at the latest. I'm booked on an afternoon flight. You can come out to Darien on the train; it's the Metro North Line. If I'm remembering right, there's a 6:20 out of Grand Central. I'll pick you up at the Darien station and drive you to a hotel nearby."

"You mean just to see those papers? We could do that here, Gordon, in New York early Wednesday morning."

"No, I'm talking about planning for us to meet with Peter Tompkins. Any CEO would have to know about this. And soon, so bring all the documentation you've uncovered. I can arrange for a place for you to stay near town."

Paula was taken aback. "I…I don't know what to say. Are you sure Mr. Tompkins is someone we can trust? What if he sides with Barkley?"

"I've known Peter a number of years, and I believe him to be a man of integrity." Privately he was hoping that this would bear out, given the possible damage an exposure like this could be to the company. "Now would you like me to get you a room? There's the Hyatt, just a ten minute drive from the train station. Or the Doubletree right in Norwalk. That's even closer."

She knew there was no time to think this over. They would be taking an enormous step, but she could sense Gordon's sincerity. She also felt it was the right thing to do. "Well, I guess I can get through another day. If you're sure about this."

"I'm sure. So we're set? Give me your cell number. I'm not sure I still have it…in case of any train or plane hitches."

This done, Paula said goodbye and zombie-walked over to her chair. She plopped down, gazing blankly at the screen. There was Jack Bauer in a crouch, leaning against a brick wall and making one of his urgent cell phone calls to CTU. She continued to stare at him wondering if her life was approaching his in terms of drama.

*

<u>Wednesday - January, the 31st</u> - Heading North

The signals were all there. First she kept looking up at the clock. And she seemed fidgety, opening and closing file drawers, desk drawers. It was after five, past quitting time. Why hadn't she gone home yet? It was when she pulled out what looked like an overnight bag from under her desk that he'd really come to the alert. How'd he miss that when she came in? It must have been when he was looking for those expenditure lists from the file cabinets. He'd sit it out a couple minutes to see what she was up to, even though others were leaving the office. Not for long though. Pretty soon he'd go outside and wait like he'd done last Friday. Mario glanced her way. He didn't have the best angle of view, because she was leaning over the other side of her desk, but from the looks of it she was riffling through some pages. For sure, if she carried that bag out of the office, he'd have to follow. Rats!

All day long he had hung on, telling himself that there was only one more day to go. Tomorrow he would collect his pay and go home. He sat there gloomily telling himself to look at this as an opportunity. He could collect a lot more by preventing a hand-off. If she carried the bag outside, he would follow, and hopefully she would go back to her neighborhood. Now that he was familiar with it, he could imagine grabbing the bag off her shoulder on one of those darker back streets. A lot depended on where she went with it. He remembered Lazaro telling him to call for instructions. But now was not the time. He had to get outside and wait for her to come out.

He stood up and muttered a "G'night, g'night," as he strode over to the coat rack. Soon he was standing outside, in that cut of the building, the one he'd used before, to keep out of sight, also to keep out of the wind. Man, was it ever cold tonight. And he could hear tiny pellets of ice beginning to ping on the sidewalk.

He didn't have to wait long. Within five minutes he spotted her coming through the lighted entranceway and sure enough, there was the bag hanging from her shoulder. Should he call Lazaro now? No. Too soon. He'd see where she was headed first. Maybe it was only for an overnight at one of her friends. Hey, maybe a guy friend. But he'd have to watch himself, so's she wouldn't catch him following her again.

She was taking the usual route to Grand Central through that marble archway they called the Graybar Passage. He expected her to turn down the left corridor toward the subways, but she kept on going to the main concourse. Wait a minute. Did Michael say something about how she might take a train out of the city? Mario stood there tracking her through the crowd till she stopped and stood still, looking up at the Metro North train schedule. Shit! This was not what he wanted.

Mario walked a wide circle around back of her to see what trains were up there. New Haven, Danbury, Stamford, all with stops in between and a zillion different tracks and departure times. How the fuck would he know where she was going looking at this? Next she pivoted slowly in a circle, scanning the crowd. He ducked behind the information booth quick enough for her not to see him. But this told him to keep his distance. Good thing there were so many people running all over the place. On the move again, she walked up to the ticket counter and pulled out her wallet. He couldn't hear anything from where he was standing, which meant he'd have to follow her to whatever the fuck track it left from. Shit! The more he thought about this the more he wanted to ditch the whole thing.

She was glancing up at the clock - it was closing in on 5:40. Then she threaded her way through the crowd to the stairs, her head turning, all the time checking around her, and finally down to the food court. Paula baby sure was being careful. When she stood at the cafe counter looking at selections, Mario decided this could be his chance to make his call. Lazaro would want to know what was going on. He stood to the side of the stairs watching her pick up a sandwich and soda, wondering how the hell he was going to say this. No way was he goin' outa' the city to some unknown place. As soon as she sat down he took a seat on one of the benches out of her line of sight and punched in Michael's number.

"Listen, Michael. It's Mario. I followed her here to Grand Central. She's down in the Food Court now eatin' a sandwich."

Michael's voice sounded anxious already. "Yeah? Where's she headed?"

"I don't know, somewheres north. Stamford, maybe New Haven. I couldn't tell. She was lookin' up at this big time table thing."

Michael broke in, "Fuck! She must be going to Darien. That means only one thing. Was she carrying a brief case?"

"No. But she has one a' those overnight type bags."

"You've got to get it."

"Well, I can't! Not here. There's all these lights. Security everywhere. Listen Michael, the job never included this. I'm not gettin' on some train to God knows where."

"Your job is to get that bag, Mario." His voice was rising. "You said you'd do this! Now listen to me. You can nick it when she heads down the track. Before she gets on the train."

"Oh, I dunno."

"Listen, you prick. I'll have your head if you don't get that bag!" Then he changed his tone. "It's worth five grand." Mario was trying to think of what else to say, but he didn't like how he was feeling. Michael added, "And if it goes without a hitch I'll up it five hundred."

"Wait a minute. Last week I remember you saying that it could be worth five or six grand."

"All right. All right. Six grand, but it's got to be a clean job. No mess-ups."

Mario hesitated then took a deep breath. "Okay, I'll give it a try when she heads down the track."

"Just get it, Mario! Do whatever it takes, but don't let her get away with that bag! And call me as soon as it's done. I'm counting on you."

Counting on me, he thought, and shook his head. He pocketed the phone and looked across the room to the table she was sitting at. Still eating and now she was reading some magazine. That bag was right next to her. With a crummy, sinking feeling, Mario brooded over how he was going to get out of this. If only she'd just keel over...with food poisoning. Nothing so easy had ever saved his life. She was still into that magazine. Must be the train wasn't leaving right away. Okay, he'd follow her down the track, but if there were too many people, or if the lights were too bright he wasn't gonna' attempt any lift.

Minutes were crawling by and Mario could feel his stomach rumbling with hunger. Should he take a chance and get in line for something? Smelling all that food cooking, watching those people chewing and swallowing was annoying as hell. Just as he joined a line, she stood up and started gathering her stuff. What fuckin' luck.

To keep out of sight he walked back around to the side of the marble stairs bordering the food counters; she might be going to one of those 100 tracks right on this level. That's exactly where she headed. He kept back about twenty feet and to the side. All the commuters streaming toward the gates gave him good coverage. He watched her turn left and go down the ramp for track 107. A sign at the gate posted the stops. Yeah, there it was Darien, then South Norwalk, on up to New Haven. Departure time 6:20. Ten, no twelve minutes to go. He started down the ramp but walked slowly; he wanted to case the layout. Well it certainly wasn't very dark. He wouldn't have an advantage that way. There weren't too many people now; it might be possible, but she could step into one of these cars at any minute. There'd be no chance then.

Paula had passed two cars, and then at the third she stopped and turned around. She was looking back, toward him. He jumped into the bar car. Christ! Did she recognize him? This was a dead deal, for sure. He stood in the small vestibule trying to think. What? What? Jeezus, would Lazaro ever be pissed. It occurred to Mario that he might not want to pay him at all. This idea sent him scrambling, frantically trying to think who he could call for help.

Wait a minute. Ritzy! *He* might do this. It's right up his line, and he lives up there, in Stamford. Maybe he's home now. Mario yanked the phone out of his pocket remembering that Ritzy's number was one of the first he'd put in his contact list. He had to be quick though. He punched it. *No Service* came up on his screen. Oh, for fuck's sake. He forgot about this being a friggin' tunnel. He raced out of the car and up the ramp. Please! Please! At the top he tried again, staring at his cell screen. Yeah!

In two rings Ritzy's voice came through, "Hey Mario! How ya' doin'?"

Mario, was an old favorite. Ritzy smiled at the sound of an old familiar voice. Mario had been the one who'd tagged him Ritzy on account of his high class taste in clothes and watches.

"Oh man, am I glad you're there. I gotta' ask you a huge favor. It'll be worth a bundle to ya' though."

"Yeah?" Mario could hear a slight chuckle. And then. "Well, I could use a bit of cash. Did you hear what happened to **B**ig **T**?"

"Uh yeah, but I can't talk now. Here's what I need." Mario spattered it out fast. "There's this lady on the train, right here at Grand Central. I'm supposed to lift the bag she's carrying. It's impossible. I can't do it here. Not with these lights and the security creeps. The job's worth four grand, maybe even more. I'll split it with you if you can just get it away from her. Will you do it?"

"How? I'm not on the train, you nut."

"No, listen. She's gonna' get off at Darien. Just go to the train station and give it a try, will ya'? Come on, *please*" There was no response. "Tell ya' what. I'll raise the stake if it goes off decent."

"Now wait a minute. Who's paying you this money?"

"Michael Lazaro. You remember him from the old neighborhood. He's good for it, Ritzy. There's these papers she's carryin' that he wants. And listen, I've got pictures of her, right here on my cell. I can send 'em to ya' so's you'll know what she looks like and everything. Will you do this?"

Ritzy was shaking his head in disbelief. Christ, who but Mario. The only "paisano" who'd never moved out of the neighborhood, always kept to the city. Then he thought about it again. Mario was talking money. It had been another empty day, and he didn't have any plans for tonight. Maybe he should play along for now, maybe bargain a better deal, depending.

"What time's the train get to Darien?"

"Oh shit. Wait a minute." He turned to face the entrance and intercepted a man in a business suit coming down the ramp. "Can you tell me what time the train gets into Darien?"

"Uh, I get into Noroton about ten after 7:00 so figure five, ten minutes after that."

Mario took a moment to compute this, then turned back around. "It'll get in to Darien about 7:10, 7:15, but try to get there earlier." Commuters were moving past him and faster now down to the track. "Are you in on this?"

"I don't know, Mario. It sounds like a long a shot. Do you know which car she's in on the train?"

"I think the third from the end, but maybe she moved up a ways." Mario was getting tense. "The train's gonna' leave soon."

"Well, get back on! Call back after you locate her. And send those pictures."

"I can't get phone service on the train!"

"Yes you can, dummy. Soon as it leaves the tunnel. Then you can get off at 125th."

"So you'll do it?" Mario could hardly contain his excitement.

41

"It's crazy Mario, but I'll give it a try. And send those pictures."

"Great! I'll call ya' back!" Mario clicked his call over to photos and sent the pictures. This was much better. Now he'd have some time. He was back on the bar car waiting in the vestibule collecting himself. The conductor was announcing the stops and sure enough, the first was 125th. She wouldn't be in the next one, but he'd case it first, before walking through. Mario pulled open the first door and then the one into the next car. It was pretty full. Just then the train jerked forward. He took it row by row moving forward slowly. Some of the seats in these damn cars faced backwards. He'd have to check those heads first before moving through any car.

She wasn't in this one, just like he thought. Or the next. Or the next. The train was just coming out of the tunnel when he entered the fifth car from the end. He checked his phone for service. Great, good to go, but he was getting nervous that they'd get to 125th before he spotted her. Row by row he eliminated them, until there, facing right his way! Luckily she was reading and her head was down. He moved fast back to the vestibule and faced into a corner to make his call.

Mario kept his voice low. "Yeah, I see her. She's in the fifth car from the end. Did ya' get the pictures?"

"Yeah, but Mario. She's got a red dress on. These were taken indoors. Where'd you get these?"

"Oh, right. Well, now she's wearin' a tan coat, and I think a black scarf, no hat. She's got short, blondish hair, no hat."

"You know, you're asking me to do the impossible?"

"No, I promise, Ritzy. C'mon, I'd do it for you. This is family."

"There *is* no family. Not up here, anyway. I want two grand, maybe more, or no deal."

"Okay, okay!" Mario's voice was getting desperate. Lazaro would do a real piece of work on him if he didn't get that bag.

"What's the bag look like. Is it leather?"

"No. It's a light canvas bag, with a wide shoulder strap." Mario was looking down at the floor, praying.

"I'm makin' no promises, ya' hear? Talk to me later. Around 9:00."

"I love ya'!" Mario let out a deep sigh and leaned heavily against the wall to wait for 125th. Should be comin' up soon. It occurred to him that he hadn't even paid for the ticket yet. Maybe he'd just treat himself to a cab home.

Metro-North

Wednesday - January 31, 2007 – **Darien Train Station**

The storm had come on rapidly with pelting slush gathering on Dana's windshield. She watched the woman rising up on her tip-toes, looking for lights advancing through the station's entrance. A line of cars was exiting, but nothing was coming in. The 7:08 had come and gone, depositing scores of hurrying passengers. The platform was empty, except for this one, lone woman huddling in her tan polo coat. She was rather tall with short blonde hair. A dark scarf blew about in the wind as she stood scanning the sea of parked cars. In the pale glow of a fluorescent lamp, all the color was washed from her skin. Dana thought she could make out a look of exasperation on her face.

At least she was something for Dana to watch. She had been sitting in her car since 6:50 waiting for Carson.

Why the delay and why hadn't he called if there was a change in his schedule? Did his service go out or what? Dana was getting worried. He had missed two trains. She thought about driving home and coming back later but flicked on the radio instead to check the time – 7:15, another twenty minutes until the next train. No, she'd wait.

As Dana glanced up from the dials, she watched the woman striding rapidly toward the stairs. She suddenly stopped, and then with drooping shoulders, turned away. Dana raised her head to see what the woman had been looking at. The beams of a car swept over the fence nearby; it was a white Land Rover. Dana turned to look over her shoulder as it backed into an empty slot behind and to her left The lights went out and the driver slunk down in his seat to rest his head on the back.

Well, now she wasn't the only one waiting in the dark. Her car was warm and she had music to listen to. That poor woman was out there on a cold platform with nothing to warm her up but her anger. Dana's too was beginning to heat up. These train pick-ups were becoming a nuisance. She could never plan on a regular stretch of time, one that was quiet for getting her work done. If only he could catch the same train every night. An old station car would be such a help...when they got the money. They'd have to talk that one over.

With only one car, making arrangements had become a daily chore. Their move was better for her what with the short drive to Darien High, but it meant a fifty minute commute for Carson, making it plenty expensive, living here in affluent suburbia. Darien was sandwiched between two small cities but provided the feel of life in the country. For them, it promised a great future.

For the second time the radio announcer broke in to update the weather watch that had turned into a winter storm warning. High gale winds accompanied by freezing rain and snow, continuing through the night. A possible 6-8 inches expected. God! Who would make someone wait out there on a cold night like this? It must be two inches deep already. The woman's coat blew open, and she hunched down into it seeking protection behind a billboard. Dana wanted to help. Maybe she should go up there and ask if....

Out of the night came a loud crack. Dana looked up, shocked by the blast. Was that a crack of thunder? But how could there be a lightning storm in January? She scanned the sky for lightning anyway and then at the station. The woman was down on her knees pulling what looked like an overnight bag around to her front, and then fell face down on top of it to the platform. Dana's eyes darted back and forth and then to the stairs exiting to the street. No one.

She started to push down on the handle, but then stopped. What if that was a gunshot? A shudder went through her whole body. She looked over at the man in the Land Rover. He was sitting straight up looking left and right. They looked at each other, each waiting to see what the other would do. Silence. Dana felt helpless. They just sat there gawking at each other. She could hear Carson's warning in her head. "Don't even think of it Dana. You're always jumping into other people's predicaments." Yeah, she thought. Like last Saturday after the hockey game. That could have turned out really bad.

It seemed wrong though to let her lie out there. She hadn't moved at all. What if she were hurt? In the next few moments of silence Dana gained a little confidence. The only sound now was the wind picking up. Ice had turned to quiet, falling snow. She slowly pushed down on the handle and placed one foot into the winter mash, but a sudden gust yanked the door out of her hand. God it was cold! And now, outside the car, exposed, she felt another clutch of fear. Dana wound the great length of her school scarf over her head and twice around her neck. Hunched over, she skimmed along the sides of parked cars until she was about twenty yards from the platform stairway. Should she run across that open space? She'd be a moving target. Dana gasped for breath and looked back, heart pounding, to see if the man had gotten out of his Rover. No, the coward.

She turned back around and shouted toward the woman, "Hey! Are you OK?" Nothing. Dana rose up a little, straining to see if she was moving at all...a finger, anything. The wind whooshed overhead. She rose a little more and darted forward.

A fierce warning carried from the figure on the platform. "Stay back! Keep quiet and don't move!"

Jeezus, what had she gotten herself into? She dodged to her left and crouched down behind a different car. Snow splattered her glasses, blurring her vision. The wind pushed her into the fender she was crouching against. Trapped. The two of them, in a waiting game, in this storm. Somebody would have to move sooner or later. The 7:35 should come in about ten minutes. Dana began to wonder how she looked, a 30 year old woman hiding behind a car in a public parking lot. She glanced up again. The woman lay out there as though dead. Pretty smart if she's just wounded. She might outlast the gunner. Where was he now? If she knows him, which was Dana's guess, she would have a better hunch about his next strategy. It seemed to Dana that if he believed he'd hit her, he'd take off before passengers heading for New Haven started gathering.

Dana's legs were locked with cramps and her toes were aching from the cold. She wanted to sit down, to stretch out, but the pavement was wet. She'd inched her way to the back of this car. Maybe she could make the run to her own car and call 911. There was a moment's quiet with no sign of anyone moving.

Just as Dana was thinking it might be safe to skim back along this row, a deep voice came from behind, "Hey, what are ya' doin' down there?"

Shocked witless, she whirled around, checking his hands. No gun. But his voice was gruff, and who was she to trust at this point? "I was watching out for...uh," Her mind raced. "Did you hear a loud bang a few minutes ago?"

"No, but I just got here. Is somethin' wrong?"

"I guess not. Maybe it was a tree limb that snapped off. This wind is strong." Dana was still crouching, her muscles tight with fear. His voice sounded familiar; it spooked her.

"Yeah, and it's cold. The car is prahbly' a better place ta' wait, ya' know?"

It was said in a sarcastic tone she didn't like. He frowned at her, pulled a woolen cap down over one eye and then looked up. His eyes darted back and forth, searching. She heard a sharp intake of breath, "Shit!" And he began to run toward the platform. Dana watched him and then, rising up, saw...she was gone! This was her chance. Quick! She raced to her car, leaped in, slammed the door shut, and grabbed for her cell. C'mon,

c'mon. A muffled rapping on her left made her heart
leap. God! She forgot to lock the door. The phone
slipped out of her hand as she groped for the all-doors
lock.

"No, no lady. I just want to know if you're OK!"

Dana stared at him, afraid to move. He raised his
gloved hands, turning them back and forth to show her he
meant no harm. Not the same one.

He yelled through the window, "I saw that guy running! You were out there and…I was waiting in my car
when I heard what sounded like a shot. You okay?"

This was "the coward" sitting in his Land Rover. Dana
changed her mind and rolled the window down a little. "I
was just trying to call 911."

"But that woman on the platform…the one who fell
down. There's no one there anymore."

"Doesn't matter. Did you see that man running? I'm
scared, aren't you? That was a gun shot."

"Yeah, I wondered about that."

"If he's the one who fired the gun, he could still be
around. And he knows I got a look at him."

"Yeah," he paused. "I kind of see what you mean." He
just stood there hugging himself against the cold, "But if
she got away, no harm has been done. Anyway..." He
peered at his watch. "The train will be in soon." Another
pause. "And people are starting to drive in."

Dana looked at him, absorbing his temptation to do
nothing. Then she glanced toward the station's entrance
way. Yes, cars were beginning to pull in for pick-ups,
along with some passengers who would be traveling on to
New Haven. Several were already heading for the stairs
to the platform.

"But what if that lady's wounded or hiding? Shouldn't

something be reported?"

"Well, go ahead if you want. You know better what she looks like. I need to meet my sister and get home."

"I should probably call the police." Her phone was somewhere on the floor where she'd dropped it. Dana groped the mat under her feet till her hand found it. "What time is it now?"

"Um, it's after 7:40. Okay, I'll head over...or should I wait for you?"

Dana could tell he was worried about being seen with her now. He had satisfied his curiosity knocking at her window, even exercised his manly duty by checking on her welfare. Now, he just wanted to be safely rid of the whole thing.

"That's up to you, mister." She started to punch in 911 as he backed away from the car. "No, wait!" She pushed open the door. "I'll walk with you." She wanted the company, and it occurred to her that walking with a man would make her less identifiable. She pressed 911. "Yes! Hello. I think someone might be in trouble...Huh?" Another fear took hold. What was she getting herself into? "Ann Black. Uh, I'm not sure." She pressed End and then the off switch and flipped her cell closed.

They were scuffling quickly through the parking lot, ice crystals grinding underfoot as they reached the stairs. Several people had collected, but except for the whipping sound of the wind, it was quiet. "What did the operator say?" he asked as they stepped onto the platform. "Will they send someone?"

"I don't know. She asked me if it was an emergency. I...uh, I think we got cut-off."

"Yeah. The service here is lousy with the storm and all. I got cut off while I was talking in the car." They clam-

50

bered up the stairs. "You know, it's just as well. There's really nothing you can do. We don't know if anything bad happened, anyway."

"Keep your eyes out for a man in a black cap." He looked down at her, and gave his head a nod. Dana didn't feel his confidence and was busy scanning each person, searching for a man in a black woolen cap. "It was right about here," Dana pointed a finger, "at this billboard that she went down. Could she have rolled over and then down to the tracks to hide?" She stepped over to the edge and scanned down the track, but the lighting was too poor to see well.

"Hey, step back!" he called. "The train's coming."

God! Finally. Dana just wanted Carson to take her home, to be close and safe. But then another shot rang out from the north parking lot. "Jeezus! Was that a gun shot?" someone nearby gasped. Dana said nothing. Again, she felt her whole body key up for another emergency run, but she didn't move. Christ! Was she murdered? Dana felt sick inside. The train was pulling in and slowing.

"Well, so long. I've got to go. Good luck." And Rover man quickly headed down the platform. Dana's whole body was shivering. Passengers stepped off the train hunched against the cold and strode swiftly toward the stairs. She searched eagerly for Carson. There! That looked like him coming. Dana ran to Carson and pulled him into a clinch. "Oh God, I thought you'd never get here. Please, just take me home."

"I'm sorry Dana. I couldn't reach you. There were train delays and then my cell kept saying 'no service'. It must be this storm. Come on. Let's get to the car." He put his arm around her and they descended the stairs. At the bottom he paused looking down at her. "You're all right, aren't you?"

"Honey, something horrible's happened. I think a lady got shot. Not by the first one. That's when I saw her fall to the platform. I ran through the parking lot to see if she needed help."

"You what?"

"I couldn't just leave her there."

"Start over again. Are you saying you got out of the car after hearing a gun shot?"

"Yes, but I crouched down and ran between the cars. I called out to her, to find out if she was hurt. That's when she warned me to be quiet. And not to move." A freezing gust of wind ripped through the lot. They picked up their pace. "I hid behind a car the longest time, too scared to move. Then this man came up from behind, and in a really sarcastic tone of voice asked me what I was doing down there. He had this Brooklyn accent."

Carson shook his head. "Dana, I don't know why you do these things."

Dana was still in her mind, "Bronx, Brooklyn. I don't know. He told me the car would be a better place to wait. I saw him look up and then run when he saw she wasn't there lying on the platform anymore." Dana pointed to her right. "Here's our car, over here."

"So you got back to the car all right?" Carson extended his hand for the keys, splitting away from Dana as she dropped them into his glove. He walked to the driver's side and then stopped to look across the roof of the car at Dana as she was opening the door. "Wait. Did you call the police?"

"Carson, I was so scared. What if he sees me again? I tried but..." A feeling of guilt swept through her. How could she tell him she lied about her name? She ducked her head to get into the car and pulled the door shut. Tomorrow, she thought, making a decision. And the next day they'd check the papers. If the police needed more information, she'd call in. This seemed a reasonable solution.

Thursday February 1, 2007

THE DARIEN DISPATCH

Body of Woman Found in North Parking Lot of Darien Train Station

A woman's body was discovered by commuters heading home in last night's snow storm. The 32 year old victim was identified by police as Paula Metz, a Manhattan resident. She died of a gunshot wound to her chest. The exact time of her death is yet to be determined, police say. There appear to have been no witnesses to the shooting, and no gun has been uncovered in the immediate area.

"I practically fell over her body," said Jeremy Proctor, who called in his discovery around 7:50 PM. "I was rushing to my car. It was freezing cold and very dark. When I nudged her, there was no response, so I yelled for help." Two other commuters joined Proctor and waited with him in his car. Busy with several car accidents due to the storm, it took another ten minutes for the police to arrive .

Saturday - February 3rd

The first sound entering her conscious state was the scrape of a snow shovel. She lay there luxuriating in an extended dream state, her arm reaching over to Carson's side of the bed. Not there. She opened her eyes but shut them against the glare of brilliant sunlight pouring into their bedroom.

53

Dana lay there, grateful that it was Saturday and she could lounge in bed. It had been hard these last two days focusing on school. Her mind cut back to that night at the train station. She kept wondering why Paula Metz was shot. She felt sure that the murderer was the same man who saw her.

Carson was supportive after it happened, but then he turned into his Eagle Scout mode. He kept urging Dana to call the police and tell them what she'd seen. The whole notion of getting more involved frightened her. She couldn't help it. To be that close to the victim of a murder ... God! She could have been killed too. If that man sees her again, who knows what he might do?

At other times, she was haunted with the idea that she could have helped prevent it. They kept checking the papers for news about Paula Metz. And yet nothing much seemed to be happening. What were the police doing? There'd been such an outcry from townspeople about not feeling safe living here anymore. Even the kids at school were talking about how most people were taking the train only in the daytime now.

Dana had to smile remembering how confident they were making the move out of Manhattan and into their new, live-in relationship. The house was finally beginning to look decent. It came as a surprise though, that his commute cut into time together even more than when they lived in separate apartments. It was actually ironic, moving out of a siren screaming city to "crime-free" Darien, and in only a few months hitting it head-on.

Dana lay still listening to the quiet. Must be the heavy snow fall; it muffled every sound. It felt so good just to lie there all warm, postponing the day. This first year teaching had been exhausting. Add to that, all the work it took to make their move to Darien.

At least they weren't too far from making their big decision. Finally! How long had it been... was it before Christmas? Yeah, two months ago they started talking about a winter get-away. Sun and sea. Right now that sounded a lot better than buying a station car. Maybe they could go ahead and book tickets to Ft. Myers, or even Key West.

Dana threw off the covers, bracing herself for hitting the floor in bare feet. The house felt cold by comparison to nesting under their down comforter. She looked out the bedroom window at the back yard, squinting at the brightness of the snow. It was so beautiful up here in the country with the boughs all heavy and icicles sparkling in the sun. She grabbed her robe and headed for the shower.

The bathroom mirror showed a pale face, stringy hair, and circles under her eyes. As she stepped into the shower she smiled anyway. Oh well. No school, no schedule, just their papers to correct. She wouldn't put that off to the end of the weekend again.

An Apartment in Downtown Stamford - Same Time

He was gripping his cell phone in one hand and holding a cup of coffee in the other. Saturday - all day. His shoes were plopped on an old, scruffy blanket chest. Ritzy stared over them at the gray TV screen. Every newscast was saying there didn't seem to be any witnesses. Three days now and the cops had zilch. His luck was running: at least so far.

If only **B**ig **T** hadn't tried to rig that bid. Christ! With the plea and all, it could mean he'd spend five/six years in prison. And then the friggin' FBI making **T**ony shut down all his transfer stations. Okay, so they slammed **T**

55

with a few other charges: some payroll kick- backs, tampering with a witness. So was that reason for killing all those jobs? Close to 80% of the carting business down the tubes, and now no job for him to go to.

In time, if this Metz case goes nowhere, he'd have to check around, make some connections. Not in the city though. He'd made that move and didn't want to go back there, even if it was a job with The Family. He was getting itchy, even though he'd been only two weeks without work. Ritzy would have to take it easy on his credit card - not eat out so much. Drink beer maybe instead of scotch.

And now Mario tells him this other pay-off will have to wait, maybe five days more. What a friggin' fuck-up. It pissed him off, but he wouldn't stick his face into that deal or make any chancy phone calls. This waiting around was getting stupid. He'd have to think up some-thing to do. If only there was another hockey game in town tonight. One was scheduled way up in Bridge-port somewhere, but he didn't feel like finding that rink at night. Scampi said there'd be a home game next Friday. He'd catch that one.

Something was connecting in his mind. It was the scarf. That ridiculous striped scarf she was wearing that must've been ten feet long and had all those fringe things hanging from it. It was what those "Blue Wave" freaks wore at all the games Darien played against the Vikings. So she was a friggin' Dairy-Land fan. He couldn't stop thinking that she might still go to the police. What with looking up at him from that stupid crouch and the plat-form lights being on, she might've gotten a clear look at his face, better than he could get of hers. If she does go to the cops, will they show her mug shots? He gave his head a little shake. The ones they took of him were from way back and not even taken in Connecticut. But that didn't stop him from worrying a little. If there was another game against Darien, she might show up. Naw, forget it. He hated all this back and forth shit. It was squeezing his brain. He'd just keep his head down and stay out of sight, and out of Darien for sure.

Back in Darien - Midmorning

"I checked the paper," Dana said. There's nothing as far as witnesses go." No answer. "And the police haven't called here either." Anyway, she thought, comforting herself. Tracking that number would only take them to her old Manhattan address. She looked back at him. He must be trying to think of some seven letter word.

"Carson, that must mean they didn't get my number." Still no reply. "So we can relax."

"Uh, huh."

Well, She'd just sit down here on the sofa and wait for him to look up. God. He looked so intent. How can people spend hours fitting words into boxes? Funny, how when she looked at his profile...the dignity of it spread through her. They should put it on a coin. It was the first thing she had noticed about Carson. That and a kind of regal bearing to his manner. His pencil stopped moving.

"Getting on that plane is going to make me so happy." *Now* she had his attention.

"I think you're deluding yourself, Dana. Even if the media finds something else to focus on. Will a week in the sun wipe out any sense of guilt you might be holding?"

He was right, in a way. But oh, how she needed this

break from school. Teachers don't get to choose their vacation times. "Dammit Carson, if you hadn't missed that train, I wouldn't have been put in this predicament. I was terrified. Twenty minutes of darkness and confusion, a gunman lurking around the parking lot? Maybe that guy is looking for me now! I don't want to get my face out there!"

"That won't happen if you ask for police protection. What's going on Dana? You're the one who runs through gunshot to help some woman." He put down his puzzle. "And remember how you stood up to your Dad when he called his own son a fuckin' fag?" He gazed at her. "Look, we've gone over this. You can still call the police and give them a description of that man." He waited, looking for her reaction. "Let *them* determine if your information is useful or not. It's not too late."

"But we agreed! You promised to take me on this vacation. What you're asking me to do might ruin all of that. Please, Carson! The guy who knocked on my window didn't go to the cops. If he heard me say my name was Ann Black and mentioned that to the police, it would be in the papers by now."

"That's a laugh. There is no Ann Black in Darien. This morning I looked it up on the internet. Just think if they had tracked down a real Ann Black...some poor lady who wasn't even near the station Wednesday night - who never dialed 911, and is now trying to convince the police that she's not lying! How would you feel then?"

The air went out of the room on that one. He was right. She'd never thought of a real Ann Black. Dana's face flushed with heat. "You know I wouldn't make someone play the heavy for me, Carson. I'm not that kind of person. It was such a strange, undefined...I don't know.

The man who came to my car seemed so careful about not jumping to conclusions. And I even wondered if Paula Metz was bluffing at first... after that first shot went off, when she was down on the platform."

"I know. You already told me."

Now what? He just sat there waiting, looking at her. Dana's reflection in the bathroom mirror came back, showing a tired, pale face with wet, droopy hair. She hadn't had a whole night's worth since it happened, and she looked it – a ghoul with a hang-dog cast to her face. Her heart went down. He was probably wondering where the woman who could defy the world in the name of fairness had gone. Now she wasn't even close to that person.

Sitting, staring down at a speck on the rug, she noticed again how these new glasses enhanced her vision. They sharpened the clarity of distant objects, and Carson had complimented her choice on the red frames. She'd been leery at first, but went ahead and bought them. He said they emphasized her dark eyes and hair.

"Listen to me, Dana. There was more happening here. Your experience was not the same as that guy sitting in the Rover. And you were worried about Paula Metz. Isn't that real? Don't your own feelings carry more weight than some stranger's doubt?"

"My feelings?" Dana pulled her glasses off and wiped one hand across her eyes. She was trying to clear her mind and to summon a convincing tone. "To who? The police? A court of law?" But her voice sounded tired.

"You just don't get it."

"Yes I do! The world out there functions on facts, Carson, not emotions. I care about what they care about – evidence. They have a body, no gun, no witnesses. No one saw anything in the north parking lot either. You and I both know that wimp in the Rover wanted no part of any of this. And he won't be going to the police. So okay, I didn't check the phone book. I'm sorry about that. But even if the dispatch lady heard the name I gave her, there's been no mention of it in the paper."

"They don't give the press *all* their information." She listened as he slapped his newspaper down on the side table. Next his pencil. He stood up.

"I'm going to take a shower." He strode out of the living room.

Well? For once he didn't finish his puzzle. Dana started picking at a scab on her wrist wondering why they couldn't come to an agreement on this issue. She felt a wave of sadness flow through her. They had always shared the same values, no matter what the subject. Could one jolting experience just wipe that out?

He was right about using that false name. It bothered her too. But it was thinking about Paula Metz that plagued her even more. When she was first standing alone on the platform…it really seemed as though she was nervous and looking for someone. Who could that have been? Maybe she had a boy friend or a girl friend, someone who was late picking her up. Where is *that* person? She wasn't the only one involved here.

One bullet through her chest and no trail of blood to the north parking lot. That meant she wasn't hit on the first shot. The papers said she was single, only 32 years old, and no family to speak of, just an aunt from Wisconsin. The police interviewed people she worked with in Manhattan. Paula had recently moved into an apartment on the lower East Side. Her neighbors didn't know much about her, except that she worked long hours.

And here was Dana Redman, a complete stranger. What could she say to the police about her? Nothing more than the way she seemed to behave. Dana believed that Paula knew someone was after her, but what good was that as far as evidence goes? Trouble is, there's this link between us. She couldn't shake it. Paula Metz had tried to warn her when she was down, even though it put her in danger.

Do other people who witness crimes go through all this mental torment? From what she'd read, most of them wished they'd never gotten involved. Worst of it is, the killer's still free and watching the papers. Oh, the hell with this. She'd go shovel the walk.

Metro-Line to Murder

Dana's Move

Later, that Afternoon

"Dana, I thought you said there was nothing in the paper."

"Oh?" She plopped down again on the sofa. "Well? What's it say?"

He pointed his finger at a page. "Some lady here, a resident of Darien, is making an appeal for anyone who has information to come forward. She doesn't understand why people sitting in cars waiting to pick up riders didn't see or hear anything."

"Maybe because they thought it was something other than a gun shot. And why would others necessarily be staring at some lady on the platform? It wasn't even the scene of the crime. Don't you remember? She died in the north parking lot."

Dana looked up at him. Carson's eyes met hers. She recognized his look of disapproval. She turned her head,

62

thinking how his face still reminded her of Colin Firth when he was younger: that square jaw and dark brows that accentuated his eyes. Their color would change from shades of green to hazel, depending on...she didn't know what. He was tall, fit, and always appeared clean, with a preppy look. At first it was Carson's manner, his quiet self-confidence that appealed to her so much. This was the man she hoped to marry.

Why didn't he see that she wanted to get some distance from this nightmare? She jumped to something different to get off the subject. "So how did your football game go?"

He tossed the paper on the chair. "Is that all you can do? Think up ways to avoid doing the right thing?"

This jolted and angered her. "If you don't stop it Carson... with your righteous...! She didn't finish the last part. In a quieter tone she explained, "If and when I feel like reporting my version...of really, not much of anything, I'll do it in my own time."

She wondered what Nancy would do in the same situation. Would she have gone to the police? She was such a straight forward, good person, and it showed with her teaching. Kids felt that she was honest and true. But what help would it be to report what she'd seen in the parking lot? It was mostly just a bunch of impressions. She wondered if the Darien police should even be working on a murder case. When was the last time a homicide had occurred in this town?

She watched Carson walk over to the window and look out. "Okay, okay," he said. "It's just that there doesn't seem to be any motion on this case. I don't understand what the police are doing. It seems like nothing."

"There goes the phone. Would you get it, Carson? I'm

going out." She put on her coat and boots, grabbed her gloves and hurried through the door.

Outside the air was clear and dry. She wanted to walk, run, punch something, but she stood there in the drive-way, at an impasse, studying the neighborhood. It was probably the only spot in Darien that still had an old, slightly run-down look to it. At least it was fairly close to the station, and - more importantly, the cheapest rental they could find.

Snow piled high in mounds at the ends of each drive-way. Walks and cars were cleared, but where was everyone? Amazing for this block to be so quiet. Usual-ly kids were outside, yelling and laughing. A couple of snowmen, like sentinels, stood silent watch over the street. Maybe families were running errands or just hibernating with TV and video games. Dana turned to check if Carson was at a window watching her. Not there.

With their move out, she no longer had to drive up I-95 before dawn, through the dark of winter. Okay, so it was one of those all white, wealthy suburbs. Darien High was a terrific school, and she was beginning to feel more confident dealing with the teaching load and managing her classes.

Their little white Cape, all clean and covered in snow, with the Christmas wreath still hanging on their red door looked like something out of a fairy tale. A foot of snow was so heavily piled on top of the front hedges, they toppled forward. It was a lovely picture, but she still felt at odds with herself. Should she go for a walk?

Instead, she found herself getting into the car. For a while she just sat staring through the windshield at the garage door. Here she was, practically a "suburban wife" but worrying now about Carson. This compulsion of his, his persistent need to keep after her, whenever they disagreed. In all other areas she admired him for being persevering. It was probably what made him such a success in business. All that diligent work. Carson had told her once that he wanted to be head of finance by the time he reached 40.

She leaned back against the head rest, thinking. We've been here almost three months now sharing the rent, the yard work, even a little of the cooking. Carson seemed to have taken to domestic life. His job demands were big …and then there was his commute. Dana had a mere fifteen minute drive to the high school. Maybe she was being unfair, letting a difference of opinion over one ghastly experience cause her to question their relationship.

She inserted the key in the ignition. As the engine chugged to a hum, she asked herself where she was going. Some instinct seemed to be at work. It was similar to the feeling she'd had last Tuesday night, the moment Paula went down, and she opened her car door. Dana backed out of their driveway and headed for the police station.

*

Behind a large tinted glass window, a young officer looked through his drawer and pulled out a form. "Yes Ma'm, we would be happy to hear your account. There were a few calls to station that night, but what with the storm, we weren't able to hear what was being said." This was a relief to hear. Now there was no need to mention that one of them was hers.

He rose from his chair with the form, "I'll see if Detective Hansen is still here. He's assigned to this case. Just take a seat."

It was her first time inside the station. She scanned the waiting area. A glass case displaying photographs and plaques citing Darien's police heroes dated back to 1946. A row of empty plastic seats was attached to one wall. There was no one coming in or out. It looked barren and official. The officer set down the receiver. "Nope, he stepped out. One of our other detectives will take your statement." He stood up and directed her through a door.

The gun in his holster, the sound of his keys jingling as she followed him down the hallway – all of it built up the tension again. "Do I have to put this in writing? I'm not even sure it makes the grade as evidence."

"Ma'm, it's just a signed statement of what you witnessed. You want to try to remember everything as accurately as you can." He led her then to a small room equipped with two chairs and a table and took down her name and address.

Dana wondered if this was the room they used to question criminals. "You know, Officer. I'm not even sure I'll be in town the next couple of weeks. Is that important? I mean, in case you find a suspect." He turned around and motioned for her to have a seat. "Do you have any leads on the killer?"

"We're working on it. The New York police are on the track too. You'll be seeing Lt. Frampton. He'll be right here to take your statement." He turned back toward the door. "Oh, here he is now."

The detective, looking casual in gray cords and a maroon sweater, swung into a chair opposite the table.

His face was worn and wrinkled, probably in his early 50's. But he sported a trim mustache. "Hello, I understand you were at the train station Tuesday night."

"That's right. My name is Dana Redman."

"Yes, I'll just be jotting down your information. Go ahead with your story."

"Well, I was waiting at the station to pick up the man I live with. This woman was standing alone on the platform waiting, and she kept looking out for someone."

"This lady you're talking about. Why do you think she was the victim?"

"Oh. Umm. Well, I assumed she was. From the way she behaved. She just seemed nervous. She kept looking for someone, I think, to pick her up."

"What was she wearing?"

"A long winter coat, maybe tan. No hat. A dark scarf."

"Was she carrying anything...like a suitcase?"

"No, but I remember seeing what looked like an overnight bag." Then Dana recounted the sound of a gunshot, watching her fall, and getting out of her car to see –

"Wait a minute. Where were you?"

"I was running from my car toward the platform. To see if she was all right. I was too scared to run into open space, so I called out to her. That's when she warned me to keep quiet." Then she told him about the guy with the dark wool cap and what he said to her before looking up. And how he yelled out 'Shit' and started running toward the platform. "That's when I went back to my car.

"Did you get a look at his face? I mean, did he have any distinctive features? Was he white, Latin – ?"

"I think so. White. No distinctive features. It happened so fast."

"What was he wearing?"

"Oh, let me think. A dark jacket...nothing that stands out." He kept looking at her face, waiting. "That's all I can think of. It was dark."

"Did anyone else hear the shot or see anything that you know of?"

"Well, there was this man in a Land Rover who looked over at me right after that first shot went off and I got out of the car. When I got back to my car, he came over to see if I was all right. He must have seen the man running off and then me running back to my car. When the train came in, he walked with me up to the platform. That's all I really can tell you. I couldn't tell you his name. And then, of course, we heard a second shot just as the train was coming in."

"Ms. Redman, why didn't you come in sooner? It's been three days since the murder."

Dana felt her jaw tightening. She sat there thrashing between shame and anger. Of course this was the very question she'd put to herself. But she didn't like him making her feel embarrassed. Pulling her thoughts together, she said, "First of all, I didn't really think I had firm enough grounds to come in. And I was scared." The detective simply sat there looking at her face. "I was scared...that the man would somehow come looking for me. I don't know. I was hoping that you - the police, had more evidence and would catch the guy. We followed the story in the paper, but there wasn't much that seemed to be developing."

"Do you think you could identify this man with the black cap if you saw his picture?"

"I don't feel very confident...it was dark. Snow

falling…and that encounter lasted only seconds."

He sucked in a mouthful of air and let it out with a sigh. "Okay, Ms. Redman. I'll need your telephone number in case we have to get in touch with you again. Did I hear you say you were going out of town?"

"Yes, by the end of this week. But you see, I don't understand how what I told you can help. It all seems so vague." To be truthful, Dana was more worried about having to come back. "Does this mean I might be called to testify?"

"Most of the time Ma'm, these cases don't even get to court. It's only if the accused pleads not guilty. And that's not bound to happen if there's enough solid evidence to prosecute. In this case we have a bullet, and they're working on what could be a real good motive right now."

"Did I hear right…that the New York police have something?"

"You keep watching the papers, and we'll call you if we need to question you any further. Your phone number at home? Detective Hansen may have a few follow-up questions." With a twinge of reluctance, she gave it to him.

"Cell?" She shook her head and explained about not being available at school, during classes, avoiding also another means of contacting her. He pushed himself up from his chair and opened the door. "OK, then. This way out."

On the drive back, Dana kept wondering why she didn't feel better. There was no satisfaction, no relief. It was all so cut and dry. Had it served any purpose, going in there? The only positive was that New York police were working on something. She couldn't figure out why she was feeling defensive. They: Carson and the system had won, but what? When she pulled into the driveway, she gazed at their small Cape again. "Our new home..." she whispered.

He must have heard the car door slamming, because he was opening the door, greeting her and looking excited. "Honey, where'd you go? I was worried. Listen to this. I got a phone call from my mother. She's all stirred up about the Paula Metz murder. It turns out she knows one of Paula's co-workers at Comp-Coordinates."

"What? I don't get it. Is that where Paula Metz worked or your mother's friend?"

"Both of them. So listen." Carson looked jacked up himself. She hadn't even taken her parka off. "Paula Metz was an executive assistant for one of the VPs there. Mother's friend said the place was swarming with detectives, even the FBI. They were doing all these interviews. And one of the big guns was escorted out of his office and driven off in an unmarked car. This'll be all over the front page tomorrow."

"When did this happen, yesterday?"

"Yeah, late in the afternoon. This friend of Mother's, her name is Wendy Hall, I think.
Anyway, she called Mother to tell her about it this morning. I love it, love it. Comp-Coordinates is one of our strongest competitors. You've probably heard me mention them. Honey, this means big trouble for them. I just know it. But what I really want to know is the suspect's name." He looked off behind her, lost in thought. "There's the CFO, the CEO of course, and three V.P.s... if it's Gordon Hathaway, that's even weirder. He lives right here in Darien."

Dana stared at him, dumbfounded. He was actually

happy. She slowly unwound her scarf, barely conscious of a world beyond the room.

He glanced back. "Why are you looking at me like that?"

"Well…I'm just surprised at this sudden news. I mean – do you know Gordon Hathaway? Do you think he's capable of such a thing?"

"Hell, Dana. Anything's possible. If he's got something to hide – or if the management has been screwing up with the accounting. Could be anything. But if the FBI is involved, you know that Comp-Coordinates is under scrutiny."

He looked at his watch and then toward the kitchen. "Okay with you if I grab something quick to eat? I talked to Jay; we're going to meet at his place – just to make some inquiries."

"Yeah, fine." She was thinking that she'd just save her story for later, when he was less occupied with his big news.

"We don't have any special plans for today, do we? Maybe I'll go to the Y."

Actually this was good. He could go on his investigation; it would give her a few hours to herself. She suddenly thought of Carson's mother. She was such a busybody, and Dana sensed her disapproval of their "live-in" situation. She couldn't help remembering her not so subtle warning about trying to have babies after the age of 35. Dana stopped Carson going down the hall. "Wait a minute. What about your mother? Did you tell her anything about me and Wednesday night?"

"No, I just let it be. She'd rather be excited about Wendy Hall's news than worried about us being implicated."

"Good. Let's just stay quiet on that front till we see what the newspapers say tomorrow. It's all so premature at this point. Maybe this stuff at Comp-Coordinates is just circumstantial."

"Oh I doubt it. I doubt it."

Sunday, February 4, 2007

THE DARIEN DISPATCH

Darien Executive Questioned Regarding Corporate Fraud

In an apparent surprise visit late Friday afternoon, a team of federal agents entered the corporate offices of Comp-Coordinates where Paula Metz, the murder victim, worked as an executive assistant. According to several employees, who wish to remain unnamed, high level officers were questioned behind closed doors and ordered to release files of accounting and governance issues. A longtime resident of Darien and employee of this major electronics company, Gordon Hathaway, has served as Vice-president, Marketing for the past three years. FBI Agents were seen hours later carrying more than a dozen boxes out of corporate headquarters. It was reported that one executive, who is yet to be identified, was escorted from the building.

Police are making no comment concerning its criminal investigation, but speculation is running high in the corporate setting. Coming on the heels of the murder Thursday night at the Darien Train Station, many believe that there is a connection.

In the past six months three other major companies have been charged with the fraudulent practice of backdating stock options, where high level executives are offered...

*

He was right; the story is in four different newspapers, and it looks like the picture of "quiet wealth" here is blowing apart. Dana couldn't believe how this whole thing was taking over their lives. The weekend was only half over, but she was almost eager to be back in school. At least the kids kept her mind occupied with other things. Yeah, very funny - like discipline and varied sentence beginnings. This yanked her back to reality. She'd better get started on grading their essays; they'd be asking for them tomorrow. And Carson wouldn't mind if she worked this afternoon. He'd been so intent on getting the latest breaking news that they'd been existing in two separate places. She hadn't even felt like telling him that she'd done her civic duty. Most of all Dana worried that he hadn't brought up making plane or hotel reservations. With all those phone calls back and forth to Jay, she saw where his real interest lay.

Well, at least the focus was no longer on Dana. It was on Gordon Hathaway and his fellow stock option manipulators. What an education she'd had on that bit of chicanery. Carson seemed to be up on all these high power transactions. Dana wasn't sure if she understood any of it yet. "Back-dating", "spring-loading", "bullet dodging". And some of it's not even illegal as long as the company reports it. She'd rather occupy herself with comfortable terms like character analysis, tone of voice. At least you think of human beings, not financial documents.

He had her wondering though. If an investigation finds those executives guilty of fraud, then maybe there *was* a connection to Paula Metz. In today's papers they were exploring possible motives. Carson thinks that because

73

Paula Metz came up on the train, she knew what was going on, that she was on some whistle-blowing mission and got snuffed. Dana couldn't imagine though, how a man of that caliber and community standing could resort to killing a woman in cold - The phone rang. She yelled, "I've got it, Carson!"

"Dana, I've been trying to reach you. Your phone's been busy for an hour."

"Oh, hi Nancy. Yeah, I'm sorry. Carson's been talking to all his buddies at MediaTech about the trouble at Comp-Coordinates. You must have read about it. Anyway, they're revved up over this latest scam."

"Yeah! I wanted to get your read on it. Boy, is Darien ever in the news now. Does Carson know Gordon Hathaway? I mean, Media Tech and this Comp company both do electronics, don't they?"

"Yes, but they're in different departments. He probably sees him on the train now and then. Carson doesn't know him personally, just by his business reputation." Dana gave a short laugh. "He's already convinced himself that Hathaway is guilty of fraud, if not murder."

"Really? Oh, that's terrible. Remember Tara Sampson from the middle school?"

"Uh, kind of."

"She called this morning to talk about the report in *The Dispatch*. You know she taught both Hathaway boys when they went through eighth grade. They're attending private school now, but a lot of kids still hang out with them when they come home. I'm curious. What's your take on this?"

"Oh Nancy, I don't know. This whole thing creeps me out." The temptation to spill, to talk to a friend was strong. They were of similar age and had both started teaching at Darien High that year. "You know I was picking up Carson at the station that night. It all seems so close.

"Yeah, I'll bet. But wasn't this later? The papers said her time of death was between 7:30 and 8:00. Doesn't he come home earlier than that?"

"Yes." She caught herself; better to stop here. Nancy loved any newsworthy items, and Dana didn't want to risk a big spread around school. Carson still didn't know that she went to the police station. She gave an audible sigh, "Actually, I'm trying not to get too wrapped up in all this. I've got forty some essays to grade this afternoon. What are we going to tell the kids tomorrow about this latest development?"

"Beats me. Well, I've got it easier, teaching Spanish. You already know they're barely coherent in English. For them to have to talk about stock manipulation in a foreign language is beyond their scope. But you, you'll probably have to take half the class discussing what this corporate stock stuff means."

"Ugh. Do you think there'll be another teachers' meeting, like Thursday's, to give us some guidance?"

"Could be. Maybe we'll get a call tonight. Of course, that would mean going in a half hour earlier again."

"Yeah, you're right. Where did a simple life go, huh Nance? I guess there's not much else that matters to people in Darien these days. They're still trying to absorb the first murder in twenty years. I hope the police find some hard evidence and crack this case. Otherwise, we may be reading about a fiscal investigation that drags on for months."

"BOR-ING! Well, I'll let you get back to your work. I don't envy you one bit. We'll catch up tomorrow sometime."

"Bye, Nancy. Thanks for calling."

Now she wished she'd never gone to the police. The thought of being drawn into public scrutiny made her cringe. At least she had the presence of mind not to mention it to Carson. It might just go away. She could hear his footsteps coming down the hall.

"Who was that?"

"Just Nancy. We have to figure out how we're going to treat this latest news in class. Even though the Hathaway boys go away to private school, a lot of kids grew up with them and will be asking questions."

"Oh, right." Carson looked down at the pile of essays on her desk. "Honey, since you're grading papers, I'll go out for a run – see how the town looks in the glare of scandal. Do you need anything?"

"No, Babe. I'll be a good three hours with these. Do whatever."

She pulled one of the essays from the middle of the pile covering the name so she could try to guess whose writing style it was before the end of the first page. The title, "Take the Money and Spend" provided the first clue - female. She read down the page absorbing all the tips on the most tantalizing products and where to find them at the Stamford Mall. Also places to meet, eat, and greet. Dana had the writer figured out at the bottom of the first page. Oh please, two pages more of excess? Press on, girl.

She read the next five. Four students out of the six so far had improved with arguments that truly supported a good thesis. They would get read aloud in class tomorrow. It was so encouraging to see progress being made. The next six essays set her back a little. There was only one month of preparation left before CAPT testing. Dana worried so thinking about how many of her kids would be able to gain competency. Keeping her job might depend upon it.

Five more days till winter break. God, she needed a change of scene. Hold on! That's it! She'd just go ahead on her own and book flights and a hotel. Carson wouldn't be able to use any of his moral leverage when she told him about her visit to the station. The phone again! Jeezus, she'd never get these done. "Hello?"

"Yes, this is Detective Hansen calling from Darien Police Headquarters. Is this Ms. Redman?"

"Um, yes." Oh shit, shit.

"I have here a statement that Detective Frampton took from you yesterday... concerning the Paula Metz case. I'm sorry to disturb your Sunday afternoon, but I was wondering if you could come into headquarters and answer a few more questions for us."

"You mean today?"

"Yes. We would just like to get a couple things straight. It won't take too long."

"Um, well I'm in the middle of something at the moment." Stall, stall. Think, think. No, go now and get back quick before Carson gets home. "Actually, it's all right. I can break away. I'll be down in ten minutes."

"Thanks very much. I'll be right here waiting for you."

Same Time - The Lazaro's House in North Stamford

"Michael, find something to do. I'm about ready to sign up for charity work."

"Cut it, will you? Do you think I like being watched round the clock? Every time I look out the window that same Chevy Suburban is out there. "Jeezus! Get real!"

Clio slid her black eyes down Michael's slight, hunkered form, shaking her head back and forth. She was used to spending her days under her own power, free of Michael's presence. She stood 5'9'' and with hands on hips could inflict a mental spanking. "It's been two whole days now we've been holed up here. All you do is sit there and sulk. No job, no hobbies..."

"I've got a job! This is just a leave of absence until they finish their investigation. For God's sake! Do you think this is fun for me? Those fucking agents battered me for five hours, one friggin' question after another. Christ! What was it, eleven o'clock when I finally got home Friday night?" Michael glared at her and then suddenly sat forward, "Is this the kind of wifely support I deserve?"

"You must be joking! So what about me? I'm married to a possible crook whose assistant's been murdered. The FBI's ready to pounce on the place, and you're acting like I'm a dumb head." She slumped onto the sofa, "Well duh, I guess I must be." They sat there staring at each other. "You should be grateful that I haven't taken an underground train somewhere." She kicked out one leg adorned with thigh-high opaque, black stockings and crossed it over the other, at the same time flouncing the skirt of her chiffon, animal print dress. Clio wasn't used to spending a whole weekend trapped in the house. She had dressed up, hoping to go out for dinner at a nice restaurant. Ever since she'd married Michael she could count on choosing from Italian designers like Cavalli and Taviani. "Think a minute, Michael. A devoted wife sticks by her husband. Have I left the house even to carry out the garbage?"

Michael squeezed his eyes into slits and bit down on his

lower lip. It was his favorite 'menacing pose', the one that intimidated any newcomers at work, but it was completely wasted on Clio. "What are you talking about? You haven't taken the garbage out since 2000...and three. I've kept you in cleaning services and clover ever since I picked you up at the Zebra Club, so don't get all uppity."

"You don't even have *that* right. It was 2004 we got married."

He hauled himself out of his chair and strode over to a front window. "Still there."

"At least tell me why you think this Metz woman was coming out to Darien. Was it to see Hathaway?"

"I don't know, I tell you! It could've been for anything."

"Well, was she happy, unhappy? Christ, you work with her all day long. Did you ever exchange conversation? I mean on a personal level? I've a *right* to know, goddammit. I'm your wife!" Now she was back on her feet with her fists clenched.

"Listen to me Clio." He whirled away from the window. "You are going to clamp your mouth shut and leave me alone. I've got enough to worry about without you interrogating me half the day. Do you think I like this? If it hadn't been for Hathaway meddling in areas that don't belong to him, this wouldn't have happened."

"Wrong again, Michael. I've been a meek and silent shut-in until just now. So continue – tell me what Hathaway did."

He yanked a straight, warning finger up to his mouth. "Will you keep quiet? This place could be bugged for all we know."

"Oh, now you're getting too dramatic. We're not under house arrest, you know. They can't put a wire tap on you if you haven't committed a crime."

"Oh, yeah? I wouldn't put anything past the FBI when they heat up. Was anybody else from Comp taken out of the building by the FBI and slapped with an 'investigative detention'? Huh?" He shook his head. "Almost five hours on the grill. How would you like it?"

"Not much. But you're not under suspicion for the murder. They already know you were right here with me Tuesday night. And if it weren't for me backing you up and those phone company records for proof, you wouldn't have an airtight alibi." She sank back into the sofa cushions with a confident 'hmph'. "So there."

Lazaro sat staring across the room, his gray eyes lifeless. He brushed a hand over the top of his head, through thinning wisps of hair, "It's not that simple. Fraud's a crime too."

"Fraud-Maud. I'd just like to understand if…excuse me… *when* you'll be working again. When can life, for God's sake, ever be *normal* again?"

Making Headway

As Dana was parking her car in back of headquarters, a tall, lanky man approached, leaned over, and peered through the glass. "Are you Dana Redman?"

She nodded and started to open the door, wondering what was coming next.

"Good. Lt. Hansen here." He pulled up his badge and gave her a friendly smile. "Tell you what. I thought we could save a few minutes if we just zipped over to the train station. That way you can show me firsthand what you saw Tuesday night."

"Oh. Well...all right." She opened the door farther, hesitating. "Are we going in your car?"

"Yeah. You might prefer my Toyota over a squad car." He grinned. "I don't want you to feel like you've been arrested."

81

Getting into his car she was thinking what a weird Sunday experience this was and imagining telling her students about it someday. This Lt. Hansen could have starred in "Law and Order". He had a rugged outdoorsy look, but with a high forehead. Green eyes that snapped around quickly, taking everything in. His brown hair was cut short in the current mussed "bed head" style. It made him look boyish, but Dana figured he must be in his mid-to-late 30's. Attractive.

"So do you work here in town, Ms. Redman?"

"Yes, at the high school. I teach English."

"Well, what about that. We're both public servants," he said, smiling. He seemed so much more relaxed than that other detective, less formal.

"You don't have to call me Ms. Redman. Dana is fine. Did you grow up here in town?"

"No, but pretty close by. I went to Norwalk schools."

"Yeah, I've been to a couple sporting events on their fields." As they continued with the small chatter during the short distance to the station, Dana began to ease down. His manner was casual and yet personal, some-how. Soon they were pulling up the drive to the parking lot. Even though it was practically empty the sight of the station brought it all back. She didn't like the idea of reenacting the crime scene. Flashes erupted in her head: the crack of the gun, that man's voice, and his scowling face peering down at her. She tightened up like a cat.

There was no getting out of it now though. They parked and got out at the approximate parking space of her car. "Dana, it's best if you keep what you're going to tell me confidential. We can't afford any leaks. You okay with that?"

She nodded, wondering if that meant Carson too. They walked the same path Dana took as she ran toward the platform. He stood with his feet planted apart and a clipboard in his hand drawing a diagram of her position in relation to the train platform. "Show me again where you were standing." He looked down at the statement.

"Now - I'm reading here - You say you were 'crouching' when she warned you?"

"Yes, behind a car about over here. It doesn't look the same in the daytime... and with cars parked in different spots. I remember looking up at her form, lying on the platform. But you see how far it is to the steps. I was afraid to run through that open area." Dana wished he would hurry up. How would she explain this if anyone she knew came along?

"And you say that you heard footsteps coming from behind. This man wanted to know what you were doing out in the cold. Let's see here. What were his words? 'The car is probably a better place to wait.' Right"? Dana nodded. "That was all he said?"

"Let me think." She played the scene through her head, from the man's point of view. "Um, first he asked if I needed something, and I said there was a loud bang...I was going to add that it was like a gun shot, but I checked that and said that the wind must have broken a tree limb off, did he hear it. He said no and then the stuff about the car being a better place to wait."

"And that's all. Nothing more?"

Dana shook her head. "No, because that's when he looked up toward the platform."

"Do you think you would recognize him or his voice if you heard it again?'

"Maybe. I'm not positive. I don't think he was from

83

around here. It sounded like a Brooklyn accent. He didn't really say that much, and I was terrified." She wondered why he was asking about recognizing his voice. She felt wary of the direction this was going. "Look. I've come over here with you, answered your questions. I think I have a right to know whether or not I'm in any danger. Can you tell me if you even have a suspect?"

"We appreciate your help, Dana. As for putting a watch on your place? I don't know. It's not likely the perpetrator would be looking for you. He has about as much to go on as you do for him." Hansen stood there gazing into the distance, thinking. He looked a little tired, but confident, at ease with himself. "We think we've got the gun."

"Oh, that's great! Where did you find it?"

He turned and strode over to his car. "I guess I can tell you. The reporters are all over us, as it is. It was buried under snow and ice. Apparently it had skidded under that dumpster in the north parking lot. We have to do some forensic work yet." He pocketed his notebook. "I'll take you back to headquarters now." He opened the passenger door for her to get in. She was glad to be leaving.

Coming here, seeing the station in the light of day must have given her some vague hope of ridding the vision of Paula Metz lying on that platform. It hadn't worked. How long was this going to hang with her? Dana told herself to hope that they'd get the guy soon and then regular life could begin again. Driving back down the Post Road, she decided to try her luck finding out how the New York police were doing. "I've been under the impression – maybe from what I've read - that local police departments are competitive when it comes to solving big cases. Is that true?"

"No, not really. Not with the computer communication that's available to everyone. We're mainly interested in making an arrest, so we take advantage of all the cooperation we can get."

"But what about when the victim lives in another city, another state?" They were getting near the turn-off for the police station. "When I came in yesterday, were you in New York investigating that end?"

"Yes, we've gone over the details together. Even though they have more experience with homicide, the murder occurred here. We handle our town investigations. That is, with the help of our state troopers. Working on homicides in The City doesn't compare to ones in the suburbs. They can move a lot quicker down there, because they know the neighborhoods and the right people to talk to. Those guys have a whole other mess now though, with this corporate fraud stuff. You know... that the FBI is involved with?...well, I'm just as glad not to get drawn into that."

They pulled into the driveway and around back to a line of parked squad cars. "Okay. Thanks again for coming over. Keep those kids of yours in their seats, Teach." He got out of the car and looked across the roof at her, smiling and thinking - here's a good-looking woman. He nodded his head. "We know where to find you if we need you."

"Yes, but you understand that I'm on vacation starting Saturday, and our tickets are already booked." A lie, but it would be the first thing she did when she got home. He nodded and started heading for the entrance, "Yeah, well, we'll hope to have him by then."

Dana felt much better driving home this time. They're

close to nabbing him! If there are finger prints on the gun...or if it's registered... that could do the trick. And maybe she had done the right thing, after all. Now Carson will be proud of her. She turned on the radio to get the news, but they were delivering traffic and weather reports.

He'll be so amazed when she tells him what she's learned. And if they don't need her to help with identifying him, she'd be home free. Now she was as excited as Carson was yesterday. She wondered how she'd ever get back into those essays this afternoon. Her focus was gone.

Music suddenly cut into the weather forecast with an urgent beat...

Breaking news has just come in on the Paula Metz murder case. We go now to our reporter in Darien, Connecticut. Ralph? Yes, Paul, we have just been told that a possible murder weapon has been found. A .45 semi-automatic pistol was discovered under layers of ice and snow in the north parking lot of the train station. Apparently it had slid under a dumpster. This may be an important break in a vicious crime that has rocked this quiet, affluent community. As soon as we get any additional information, we will /

She turned it off. Detective Hansen was right. The media is all over this. Turning onto their street, she noticed by the clock that it was already 4:30. Maybe she should have left Carson a note.

Sunday, Late Afternoon - Back Home

Dana was surprised to see a sporty red Porsche parked in the driveway. Who owns one of these? Before going in, she decided to hold her story, shifting her big news to a back compartment.

"Carson? Where are you?"

"We're back here, Dana, in the kitchen."

She walked down the hall pulling off her gloves and parka. They were sitting at the kitchen table drinking beer. Newspapers were spread around.

"Hi."

"I want you to meet Bill Westerly. He's General Counsel for Media Tech."

They did the conventional pleasantries while Dana considered his title, deciding not to mention the snazzy car in their driveway. Instead, she pointed to the discarded newspapers on the floor. "I bet I can guess what you've been going over."

Bill rose from his chair, hiking up his pants by the belt. "Yeah. Quite a story. Could be real trouble ahead for Comp-Coordinates." He grabbed his jacket from the back of the kitchen chair. "Well, I'll be off, Carson. Marge is probably wondering where I am."

Carson jumped up, "Let me walk you to the door." As they headed out, Carson looked back at Dana with a commanding stare. She took it as a signal to stay where she was. Still holding her parka, she stood there, in the kitchen trying to hear their conversation. Bits of it carried down the hall - about keeping in touch by phone, not e-mail, and then something about "reaffirming next week's schedule". When the door closed, she walked to the hall closet and gave Carson an inquiring look.

"What," he said flatly.

What do you mean 'what'? You never had anyone come here on business before. It's Sunday. And you've already been with Jay half the weekend. What's happening?" He leaned over to pick up a glove she had dropped and handed it to her.

"I didn't *plan* this, Dana. Bill called from his cell wondering if I was home."

She watched his face. "So I'm interested. What is it you're all talking about?"

"Oh, it's all so complicated. It's this backdating stuff. If Comp executives have altered company records to conceal fraud, some major changes will take place at their executive level – maybe an administrative leave - a lot of shifting and moving."

"Isn't that what got you so excited yesterday when you went over to Jay's?"

"Uh, not really. We just ...I don't know." He looked distracted.

"Carson, I'm totally confused. MediaTech isn't under investigation. What's their lawyer seeing you about?"

"The whole picture is ...I don't know... spreading like a plague. We're supposed to keep our mouths shut...on Comp, on everything. I just don't feel like talking about it right now." He stepped around her and moved toward the living room. "Anyway, I thought you were going to work on essays this afternoon. You keep disappearing."

Whatever was going on here with them – the stilted talk, the separateness - was bothering her, and she wanted to break through it. "I'm sorry. I forgot to write a note." He walked toward the door saying nothing. "Carson, let's *talk*." She could see the back of his head give a slight shake.

"Please, at least explain to me in simple terms what

backdating means. I've read about it in the papers, but it still isn't clear to me how there's a pay-off."

Carson stood there staring out the window. "It's when companies award stock options. And they're sometimes offered to senior executives at artificially lower prices. When some of these guys manipulate the date of purchase to an earlier date...so that over time the shares are worth more, it's called backdating. It amounts to ripping off the common shareholder by short-changing the company treasury."

"What rats," Dana muttered. Aren't their six figure salaries big enough?" She decided to try lifting his mood. "You'll never guess where I've been this afternoon. First, police headquarters and then the train station to show them exactly where I was when I saw Paula Metz...and that creep with the black cap."

He turned abruptly. "You what? You went to the police?" The frown combined with a look of astonishment gave her pause.

"I thought you *wanted* me to go." He stood still a second, looking blank.

"But that was when nothing was happening. They weren't getting anywhere with the investigation. Now there's all this stuff where she worked going on. I mean, they're onto it now– the FBI, the cops, even the media – they're all over this."

"Yes, I know!" Her excitement took over. "Carson, listen! I found out that a gun's been found. It was buried under ice in the north parking lot. It might just be the murder weapon. Isn't that great?"

"How'd you find that out?"

"I was telling this detective that I was nervous about, maybe being in danger –stuff like that. And then I asked if they had a suspect - or anything to go on - so he told me about the gun. Hey! It was even on the radio. You know - 'Breaking News'."

"Good Lord!" he said, staring past her ear. He turned and walked over to his chair. "Tell me more about what's going on with this...the detective. Did you give them a statement? *Why* did you go?"

She glared at him.

"I mean. I know you wanted to do the right thing, and all." He stalled. "I'm just a little worried now about being involved with...you know, the exposure and all. And this could lead to a long, drawn out deal. Subpoenas, court appearances, a trial."

"Not necessarily. And not right away. I told Lt.Hansen we were going out of town this weekend."

"You said what?" Again the astonished look and then an angry retort, "You didn't tell me!"

Carson's reaction set Dana back, but she held to her plan, the same that she had mentioned to Hansen - that their vacation was a fait accompli. "I was going to tell you, as soon as you came home from your run. I just got sick of all that postponing we were doing, so I went ahead and booked tickets to Fort Myers."

He clenched his fists and stared hard at her. "You have a lot of nerve, Dana. Did you even ask me about going this weekend?"

"We can always cancel them! It's not as though we haven't talked about it..." Her voice grew louder, "which hotels looked good, that resort you pointed out!" The more she said the madder she got. "Don't tell me you don't remember! You *know* my winter break starts next weekend. I can't go any other time. Just what do I have to do to make everything perfect for you, Carson?" This time she didn't storm out of the house; she sat down and stared back at him, waiting for an answer.

He lowered his head and studied the floor for a while. "It's just not a good time now. Bill Westerly wants me to be available for future compliance checks the SEC might require."

"Huh? Why does MediaTech figure into this? I thought all the attention was on Comp-Coordinates."

"This is completely separate from Comp. Ever since the backdating scandal was exposed, the SEC has been conducting probes. They've been filing civil fraud charges right and left; we could be next. Bill thinks we should perform an internal investigation."

Either she wasn't following this, or he was trying to push her into some other direction. "You're not the chief accounting officer. Why is he coming here on a Sunday?"

"You have to understand that I'm heavily tied in with accounting and responsible for the quarterly statements we send out to shareholders." He looked at her quizzically, as though she was discounting the importance of his job. "It will mean longer work hours." Then his brow furrowed as he looked sideways. She waited. "Lots of companies are going to be doing this...it's in their best interest." They sat looking at each other. "Dana, what's going on? You act as though I'm doing this on purpose. I'm not. It's just that the timing is all wrong." Another silence. "I know you're disappointed, but you can't take things into your own hands like you do...booking plane tickets, driving off - without my knowing what you're doing."

She could see that they were going nowhere but downhill. She stood up and walked down the hall. "You don't have to worry about your ticket. I'll ask Nancy if she'd like to go.

"No. Listen. I'll pay for it!" he called out.

She felt like crying, but she was too mad. How could he not see what this was doing? Dana walked over to her desk and riffled through the pile of essays. Only twelve had been graded, but she was too upset to attempt the rest. The clock read 5:35. Where had this day gone? Her mind kept spinning from one convulsive event to the next. She thought about calling Nancy, but somehow it seemed premature. Maybe she should just go away on her own – think things out. The separation might do them some good. In the end, she decided she couldn't make a sensible decision, so she picked up the next paper from the pile and forced her attention to "Pumping for Sports: Right or Wrong" by Terry Wozniak.

When the phone rang, they both picked up before the second ring. Two "Hellos" bounced onto the line. "Hi, you two. It's Jay. How's your weekend going? Busy?" he chuckled. Carson replied with a, "Yeah, pretty much. What's up?"

Dana wanted to stay on the line, but courtesy took over. She hung up and sat back in her chair. A big lung full of air whooshed out. God, what a horrible day. If Carson hadn't behaved so awkwardly with Westerly, if he'd supported her meeting with the police, they wouldn't be this twisted out with each other. The trouble is, every-thing's happening too fast. Now Jay is back on the scene. And in his present mood, if she asked him why Jay was calling, he'd probably think she was interfering.

In a moment of personal scrutiny, she began to wonder if curiosity was going to over-ride her normal sense of ethics. It did. She got up and tip-toed down the hall toward the kitchen, trying to make out the words on Carson's end.

"Yeah, that's what I told him, but we know those stocks have plummeted. Any company with the FBI in their files takes a hit. Comp's stocks will do the same. Bill wants to head that off. He says an internal investigation will keep us on the straight and moving ahead of the game." There was a slight pause. Dana shook her head, thinking how it always comes down to money. He continued, "I'm just afraid of what might turn up. Westerly insists on keeping a low, clean profile, but now…I don't know Jay; he makes me uncomfortable."

That must be it, she thought. Carson's afraid she'll draw the wrong kind of attention to his precious company. She stood there in a daze of hurt and confusion.

Then she heard Carson break in, "Hey buddy, you're in marketing. At least you won't have to put in late nights and weekends. Dana's all bent out of shape because her vacation plans are fucked up." Jay must have asked more about this, but Carson quickly said, "I don't want to talk about it. Everything's a ripping mess. But get back to me if you hear anything about Hathaway."

Dana stood there thinking that he seemed to be more at ease talking with his buddy than they were with each other. He's completely embroiled in this company crap, but he doesn't want to talk about their own situation. This was the first time...Dana couldn't remember another...she didn't know how to think about this.

It was closing in on 6:00 and she was getting hungry, but she headed back down the hall. There were only four more essays to go. "C" period would at least be done. She'd finish them and then see about some dinner.

It was slow going, but she finished the job. Pushing

back the chair and away from her "teacher homework" she checked her watch. Almost two hours had gone by. She headed down the hall for the living room half hoping that she had misread his comment about not "exposing" MediaTech to any tainted news. He was sitting in the big wing back with his fist in a Cheez-It's box staring at his cross-word puzzle. "Don't you at least want some soup with those?"

"Not really…what time is it? Did you finish grading your papers?"

"I can't believe it's going on 7:30 already. And no, I have all of "F" period left, but I'm not going to attempt those tonight. I'm too wiped."

"Yeah, it's been a long day. Did you call Nancy?"

"No. I decided to wait and see how things go. Who knows?" She said brightly. "Maybe there'll be a break somewhere – something that'll take this pressure off. You hungry?" He shook his head and picked up a beer from the far side of the chair. Several empties were scattered on the floor. This was unusual. "If you've been drinking beer all afternoon, I can see why you're not very hungry."

"Don't get on me, Dana. I'm sorry we can't go to Fort Myers together, but nothing is going to change what I have to do." He continued in a defensive tone of voice, "I don't like it any more than you do," and turned back to his puzzle.

That was it as far as she was concerned. Let him hide in his puzzle, get drunk, commit his future to MediaTech. Screw it. She headed into the kitchen and then to their bedroom for an old movie on TCM.

All Aboard

Monday, February 5, 2007

THE DARIEN DISPATCH

Darien Police Recover Possible Murder Weapon
Hathaway in Seclusion

A .45 semi-automatic revolver, buried under layers of ice and snow, is now being matched for tracings with the bullet extracted from Paula Metz's chest. Forensic analysis will determine whether this is the actual murder weapon. At the same time, police are tracing the gun's serial number to its registered owner. In an interview last evening, one of Darien's chief investigators, Detective Stephen Hansen, expressed guarded optimism. "If this connecting evidence does what I hope it will, we have a better chance at apprehending the assailant."

95

In the meantime, teams of reporters surrounding the gateway entrance to Gordon Hathaway's mansion wait for news related to charges of fraud in the FBI investigation of Comp-Coordinates. Hathaway, V.P. of Marketing, has not been seen in public since interviews were conducted at corporate headquarters last Friday. Darien Police maintain that he is at home and will be working from there most of this week. They have been unwilling to state why a crew of officers has been posted on round-the-clock guard.

Another senior executive, identified as Michael Lazaro, chief accounting officer, was escorted from company headquarters last Friday night. Comp-Coordinates announced this morning that Lazaro is now on administrative leave of absence. Paula Metz worked as Lazaro's executive assistant for two years, which gives rise to many questions: what was her relationship to her boss, why was she traveling out to Darien, and how does Gordon Hathaway fit in to what appears to be.. ...

January 6th - Tuesday - Darien High School

"Hey, it's late girl. What're you doing still here? The buses left two hours ago."

"Oh, hi Nancy. I could ask the same of you." Most of Darien's high school teachers were out of the building by 3:00. For some reason they preferred to prep and correct at home. Dana wondered how they could do it, with children to tend to, plus so many other distractions and temptations. For her, the quiet that descended in the classrooms and hallways after dismissal was soothing. She guessed it was for Nancy too.

They were still pretty nervous about measuring up to the standards of such a high caliber school. Thank God the faculty was friendly and helpful. Dana felt honored to be a part of them. Maybe she and Nancy could ease up a little this semester and enjoy the rest of the school year. Well, once the CAPT testing was over with.

Nancy was leaning with one elbow up against the door frame, hand on hip, looking spiffy, as usual. She wore trim, brown wool slacks with a butterscotch lamb's wool sweater and a small paisley silk scarf at the neck. "I went to the teachers' union meeting; not much came out of it. I just thought I'd check in on you. Are you still working on those essays?"

"No, that's off my back. I finished them last night. Right now I'm trying to figure out a way to get these kids to use the past participle."

"Good luck to that! 'He shoulda' came', 'She coulda' went.' They understand its existence only in Spanish. Well, maybe French too."

"Yeah. And how about this one I heard today, 'If we'd a only drank half of it, we'd a never got caught.' I don't know, Nancy. Am I fighting a losing battle?"

"Keep her chugging, Teach." A sudden feeling of familiarity flashed in Dana's head. Oh yeah, the detective called her that too. "So are you and Carson going anywhere warm next week?"

Dana sat back in her chair and let out a long sigh. "He can't go. Frankly, I'm trying not to hate him. The lawyer for MediaTech has this idea for a do-it-yourself investigation to keep their company looking good - you know - through all this corporate scandal stuff. Carson says he can't get out of it. I don't know, Nancy. I'd go myself, but everything's so strange."

"Gee, that's too bad. Here, I think of you two having the perfect life together while I trudge from one stupid singles event to the next." She sent Dana a sympathetic look and smiled. "I guess nobody gets permanent happiness no matter what the combination. So, where is it you were going?"

"Oh, just down to Fort Myers, maybe a couple days there or someplace nearby. Are you free, m'dear?" It was an impulsive, light gesture that suddenly made her worry that she might regret it later.

"Oh Dana I'd love to. Believe me, but I need to finally paint my apartment. I've invested in four gallons of paint. And the other thing - I promised myself I'd clear my credit card debt by June. Thanks anyway. Hey! Let's break outa' here and go get shit-faced. That's a kind of vacation, right?"

Relieved, Dana picked right up on it. "Let's do it! I'll meet you at 5:30. How does Maxwell's sound, good? Carson won't be home till late, anyway."

Maxwell's

They were on their third glass of chardonnay and trashing the math department when Dana switched over to *the subject*. "You know this whole mess with Gordon Hathaway and Comp-Coordinates?" Nancy nodded, looking up from her glass. "It's been so much on my mind. What do *you* think? Was Paula Metz coming up here to see Hathaway?"

"Hell, I don't know. This case gets juicier and more complicated every day."

Dana watched Nancy's eyes brighten as she launched into soap-opera fantasy. "Maybe they were carrying on an affair. I can just see it. He's about to go out *again*, but his wife stops him and says, 'If you go out that door, we're through.'" Nancy smiled and shook her head. "Who knows where this thing is going. Actually, the one I wonder about is her boss Lazaro. He's the guy they arrested. And then I read that he was put on executive leave of absence." She frowned and asked, " Is that what they call it?"

"Something like that, but I think the paper said he was just 'detained' by the FBI - for questioning. We haven't heard any news on that yet. No, what I meant – do you think Paula Metz was looking to Hathaway to help her out of a bad situation at work?" A vision of the train platform suddenly came back, taking Dana by surprise. It was of Paula on tip-toes scanning anxiously for car lights. Then the weight of it all descended. "Oh, I might as well tell you. I was there, at the station, when she was shot."

"No! You were there? Then? "

"Yes, I had to wait for a whole hour in that storm, because Carson was late. Oh Nancy, It was such an awful night. I even went to the police on Sunday, to tell them what I saw."

"Jeezus, Dana. Tell me everything."

She grabbed Nancy's forearm and said imploringly, "Only if you swear to keep it just between us. I can't have the whole school talking about it. I'm not kidding Nancy, do you promise?"

She promised and Dana began her story, just as she had recounted it to the two Darien detectives. By the time she got through with the part of Hansen and her returning from the train station, Dana felt like she'd taken off a thirty pound jacket.

Nancy was shaking her head in wonderment, "You know what? I think you should feel proud. I don't know if I'd have had the civic-whatevers to have gone in." Dana deliberated telling her about her original reluctance, but Nancy cut in. "Are you worried that they'll call you in again?"

"I told the police we were going away this weekend." Feeling a little guilty, Dana checked for her reaction, but Nancy just kept looking at her expectantly. "Now that Carson's going to be working non-stop, there's no reason for me to hang around. I might just get my own ticket and play the rest by ear." Dana thought, well - there's a decision, of sorts. It felt peculiar, the idea of going by herself, but she could also think of it as an adventure in self-exploration. At the moment, she was beginning to feel that heavy, relaxed, who-gives-a-shit feeling of being drunk, but not ready to go home yet.

Just then Nancy said, "Do you think we should get something to eat? I'm getting trashed." She squinted, trying to read a chalkboard menu set on an easel near the bar.

What a great dame. They should probably be married. Dana looked around for a waiter. Walking toward them was the silhouette of a man obscured by backlighting. "Hey, is that you, Dana? It's me... Jay. I thought that was you when I came in."

"Oh, hi. Well if this isn't the week for Media-Tech visitation. Jay, I want you to meet my friend Nancy Blanchard. She's the best Spanish teacher in the whole Darien school system." Her ready smile greeted him. Dana wondered why Nancy didn't date more often. She wasn't striking looking, but certainly not unattractive. Hell, a natural blonde, without the dumb part. Just what Dana always wanted to be.

They exchanged pleasantries, and Nancy, sparking to his good looks, invited him to sit down and have some-thing to eat with them. Dana turned aside to flag a waiter while listening to their intros. It wasn't long before the evening's mood changed for her. The warmth of their bond faded as she watched those two perform the single life, bar routine. Carson had told her that Jay and Sally were having trouble, but weren't they still married? Dana just kept smiling and staying appropriately quiet through dinner.

They decided to skip dessert and were asking for the check when Jay turned to her, "Hey, I'm sorry Carson is caught up in this heavy work load. I hear you won't be going to Florida."

"Yeah, that's the awful truth, but more for Carson than me, I guess. I might go for some time in the sun, just to get away from Darien and all its woes. Every day there's more speculation in the papers on Comp's people. What's your take on Hathaway, Jay? You both are in marketing."

"I've run into him several times at conferences. He's always seemed to be a pretty decent guy. I'll tell you both, though. Our office is buzzing with angles on all those big guys at Comp, particularly Lazaro. People in his department say he's a real hard-ass. And you can bet he's not on administrative leave for nothing."

Nancy flipped in, "I knew it! That's just what I was saying before."

"You know he lives in North Stamford? Word is out that the cops were up there today." Eyes narrowing Jay gave them a little nod of 'yeah, I'm in the know'.

"Looks like the plot is thickening by the moment," Dana offered, picturing Detective Hansen pushing a search warrant in Lazaro's face. "Wait. Did you say it was the cops or do you think it was the FBI? Because they're involved with the white collar part."

"Good point. I don't know for sure," Jay hesitated, then shrugged, "Whoever it was. The heat is on."

They split the check and Dana got up to go. Jay and Nancy sat there looking hesitant.

"Night-cap anyone?" Jay offered.

"Not for me," Dana said, giving Nancy a wink. She turned, and gathered up her coat. "I need to do some future conditional planning,"

Apartment in Stamford - That Same Evening

Ritzy was just coming through the door with an evening paper in his hand. He wanted to see what else had broken in the Metz case, especially with Lazaro. Christ! He was that broad's boss! He gave that bit of news some thought. She must've had the goods on him. Now they had the gun. Was this whole thing gonna' turn into a royal cock-up?

It seemed like they were coming one after the other. Only weeks ago the FBI puts the squeeze on **B**ig **T**; then they make him forfeit his carting and hauling operations. No job to go to anymore, and then comes this.

On the front page, one of Darien's prize detectives was saying that there were no new developments. Okay, that was good. The police had decided to make no further statements on the case in order to facilitate progress with the investigation. Even still, it made him a little uneasy when they clammed up like that.

Yesterday's news was what kept his mind going; they'd found the gun. Not great, but they'd never be able to track it to him. In the first place, it wasn't registered in his name. Plus, he'd scratched off the serial number. It was what? Almost a year ago that Sal loaned him the gun for that job. And then not a month goes by and the poor "babbo" screws up on the Danbury hit. Now he has two years to go in the slammer. Ritzy wondered if anyone else owned the gun before Sal. Not to worry; the Metz bag with all her overnight shit was taken care of. He'd torched it, except for the folder. Those papers were what was important.

But what was this new stuff about Lazaro? It must be close to twenty years now. At least that long since he'd seen the likes of that geek. He was the only guy who broke out of the Bronx big time. Christ, he used to be the school's math wizard, and at 40 something he's a big corporate success. Ritzy pushed out a short "Phuh" Now his ass is in a sling. Still, those big executives made a shit load of money. He understood now why Mario said that doing the job held a guaranteed pay-off. Ritzy shook his head. It's crazy how old high school people can get back into each other's lives. Of course Mario and Lazaro were cousins, but even still.

Ritzy shrugged out of his coat and threw it on a chair. While he poured himself a drink, his brain caught onto another angle. Maybe those papers Lazaro wanted so bad could be used in a "persuasive manner". There was a thought. He'd been smart hanging onto them. All Ritzy knew was if he didn't get his half someone was going to pay, big time.

He'd have to hold on till he heard from Mario. Ritzy wondered if they were being fools waiting for Lazaro to wire the damn money. Screw him. He wasn't in the mood to care how much heat was on that chiseler. It was the word "wire" that bugged him. One of the charges brought against **T** had been for wire fraud. Maybe Lazaro was into that stuff too. Or maybe he was just stalling. Jeez, here they were, the both of them, living right here in Stamford, and he hadn't even known it.

Ritzy considered a couple other pieces to this story.

One was the FBI. They were investigating all those Comp people. Maybe that was good, having the legal focus on Lazaro. Also on the plus side were the Darien cops. They knew for shit about murder cases.

This waiting around though was not his style, and he was getting antzy about the money. Those papers were right in the desk drawer there. They could be put to use. He'd send a message to Mario. Convince him to force a pay-up. Yeah, why should they wait for when that prick was ready?

Back Home

It seemed strange coming into an empty house. Dana wondered how late Carson would be. Before shedding her coat, She headed to the kitchen. A yellow **3** blinked from the message panel on the wall phone. Funny how that small signal canceled the sense of loneliness she felt a moment ago.

The first message was from Carson's mother, just wanting to catch up with the latest on "that poor woman." Then came a jolt.

"Hello, this is Lt. Hansen calling for Dana Redman. When you get in, would you please give me a call at 662-5330, ext. 4? Thanks very much." She looked at her watch – 8:20, and then pressed "play" to listen again. The recording registered 4:35 as the time of the call. Dana's first reaction was a flash of relief. Thank you Nancy, for keeping us out on a school night. Then that familiar sense of unease seeped in. This meant exposure. Maybe he wanted her to look at a line-up. What had she gotten herself into? Dana pulled open the refrigerator door and reached for a bottle of water. Think, think, chug, think. It could be that he just wants to recheck something from her statement. But that would be sheer luck. She walked back to the phone and pressed "play" for the last message.

It was Carson. "Hi Honey, it's about 6:30. I still have so much to do here. If I don't make some headway I'll be going into next weekend with this." He paused and Dana listened to him give a sigh. "So I think I'll camp out here tonight, or maybe use Rick's place to bunk down again. Haven't decided yet. Anyway, don't wait up for me. Call me on my cell if you need me. Night." He sounded so tired. Dana chugged some more water and sat down to figure out her next step. If she bothered him with this latest, it would just add to his burden.

But this could affect both of them. Trouble is…she wasn't sure what form it would take. With this tension in their relationship and the vacation... Oh hell, that was a mess anyway. Carson talked about subpoenas and court appearances, but that other detective said most of these criminals cave under the pressure of evidence and accept a plea bargain. Did she have anything or anyone to be afraid of? She remembered Hansen saying there wasn't much chance of that, but Dana couldn't help feeling like she was tied up in some kind of cage.

As she sat there weighing the bad and not so bad, something began to settle in. She decided that it amounted to one thing only – a general hassle. She wouldn't bother Carson with this tonight, and she'd wait till morning to call Hansen - after her first two classes. That would make it close to nine; he should be at the station by then. That's good. Then she'd find out what he needed. Hey, there's a chance that some other incriminating stuff would come up that had nothing to do with her. Maybe he'd even change his mind.

Dana finally took off her coat and flung herself on the sofa, tired but resolved. It was 8:45 when she remembered the other message. Heaving herself up again, she dialed Carson's mother. At least she knew how to handle the news with her: let her do the talking.

<u>Wednesday - the 7th</u> - Calling from School

"Detective Hansen here."

"Hi, this is Dana Redman returning your call."

"Oh yes, thanks. There's something I want to ask you about your encounter at the train station last week."

"Oh, sure." Dana felt immediate relief.

"I was wondering if you would be willing to listen to some recorded statements. You might be able to identify the voice that you heard the night of the shooting." Dana paused, thinking she had already told him that she wasn't confident enough to recognize his voice. He waited and then said, "It could help us, and it won't take long." Dana said nothing. "All you have to do is give it a try."

"Well, but I'm calling from school and teaching all day. This is just my free period." He waited again probably seeing that she was stalling. Feeling her resistance weaken, she continued, "Uhm...I suppose I could come in later this afternoon."

"That's terrific. I'll be in and out today, so here's my cell number. Do you have a pencil?" She took it down. "Call anytime you can get away. I'll be right here in town or at the station. We'll coordinate."

"OK"

"Thanks, Teach."

The building was quiet as she walked down the corridor toward her classroom. Twenty-five minutes left in "C" period. Dana wondered how she would be able to concentrate through the rest of the day. With a big intake of breath, she thought, I might as well let the cards fall as they may - and blew the breath out. Maybe it was the only way to treat life.

Another good thing about being with kids is that they don't allow you to think about yourself. She just had to go through lunch and the next four periods… and not run into Nancy. She would want to cover anything new that had come up. Dana wasn't ready for that. She called him after lunch to say that 4:30 at the police station would work.

*

Dana was back again peering through the darkened glass, asking for Detective Hansen. "Oh yes ma'am. He's expecting you. Just come through the door to your left." A sharp click informed her the door had unlocked. She entered, feeling her heart speed up. You'd think she was going on stage or something. Directly ahead was Hansen, walking toward her. He smiled and motioned with his arm to follow him, then pivoted and entered a small office on his right.

"Sit right down here, Ms. - is it all right if I call you Dana?"

"Yes, that's fine." He looked brighter, less tired. She began to wonder what kind of hours a detective put in, but quickly slipped back to the present. "I'm just kind of surprised that you would need me again. Didn't you track the gun or find some fingerprints?"

He cracked another smile, cocking his head. "Were you wearing gloves that night, Dana? It was pretty cold out." Then in earnest he said, "Actually we can do a lot more by tracing the registration number of the gun. We can find out the distributor, the date of sale, the dealer and who they sold it to. Today forensic people know how to read serial numbers, even if they've been scratched out."

"And?" She was excited to hear who they'd found, but instead he placed both hands face down on his desk and said, "OK. This is where I need your help. First, I need to know who you've told about coming here – even the first time, because it's important that we maintain a tight circle of information."

Dana wasn't sure exactly what that last phrase meant, but she liked the sound of it. "I've told Carson, the man I live with." She paused, feeling a little sheepish that she'd not kept her word. "And one other person, a friend. But I made Nancy swear to complete silence – we're at the high school and she knows I don't want anything to get out. And no one knows I'm here now."

"All right." He looked off a moment. "Now, what about Carson? Will he be talking about you coming here?"

Dana wondered herself how he was regarding her "cooperation", or, and more likely, if he was even thinking about it. "Carson is working non-stop for his company right now in the city. He spent last night there. I don't think he loves the idea of my being... 'implicated' was the term he used. It's pretty doubtful that he's mentioned it to anyone, but I shouldn't make any guarantees."

Hansen settled back in his chair and folded his arms across his chest, looking thoughtful. Then he looked directly at her. "Okay, we'll go on that. If the subject comes up between you two, make little of it. Take a mental note if he or Nancy has told anyone else, but say no more. And needless to say... but I'm supposed to - don't talk to the media about anything. Is that good with you?"

"I don't know. I mean, unless I can understand this better, I'm not sure I want to continue here."

"Right. Right. Here's where we are. We have a suspect; he's the registered owner of the gun, but he claims that he hasn't seen the gun in over two years. This is what they all say. Or that they lost it." He shook his head. "Right now we're lobbying to get a bill passed in Connecticut. It'll require anyone who owns a gun to submit a report of its being stolen or sold within 72 hours. If that's not done, the owner will automatically be charged with any crime committed with the gun. Unfortunately, our state legislative body moves slowly."

"So you couldn't hold him?"

"We had him long enough to learn a few things during interrogation, but there's nothing that ties him directly to the murder."

"I heard last night at 'Maxwell's' that the police were up in North Stamford at the home of one of Comp-Coordinates' V.P.s. I think Lazaro is his name. Is he the one?"

"No, no. That's a separate issue – we think. These damn reporters are all over the place. I wonder if I should get myself a disguise." Another rueful shake of the head. "Police are making no statements to the press on that front. The FBI has ordered a media black-out on the Comp investigation for now. So! Are you ready to hear how the 'recording session' goes?"

"I guess so. It sounds less threatening than a police line-up."

"Oh you don't have to worry about that. We haven't done those in years."

"Really?"

"Yeah. It's not like what you see on TV. What we do

instead is a photo array…six to eight of them on a table top, much easier on everyone." His hand strayed to a phone on his desk. "Shall we proceed?"

<u>Going on 5:00</u> - The Lazaro House

Clio had just come downstairs and through the foyer to the living room. She stood a moment with her hands on her hips looking at her husband. "This is nuts, Michael. We can't just hole up here forever. Four whole days now you've done nothing but look out that fucking window. Or sit in a chair reading a newspaper, or one of those stupid investment magazines." He continued with his reading, never looking up. "Excuse me," she added in a sarcastic tone, "I forgot to include your precious time on the computer." She walked over to his chair and stood directly in front of him. "Look at me, Michael." He did. Clio was leaning over to match him eye-to-eye. She was dressed up again in her favorite sexy outfit, the animal print chiffon.

"Well? What is it now?" he asked.

"I want us to go somewhere nice. *Any*where, just as long as there are some human beings to talk to. The only people I've seen are customers at CVS or in the grocery store ...well, except for Gemma." This was her sister who lived at the bottom of Stamford.

"It's like I said before." Lazaro pulled himself up from his chair with an arm gesturing for her to step aside. He walked over to the wet bar and poured himself a scotch. "We've got to wait for the investigation to end."

"Christ! What does that amount to, a month, a year? All this high finance stuff makes my brain spin."

"It's a complicated, crappy situation, Clio. And it's not just us. A lot of companies are going through it now.

The SEC is on a big-time witch hunt. They've got our accounting files and are going through them looking for anything and everything.

"Like what, for instance?"

"Executive stock options that are back-dated, slush fund schemes, security fraud."

Clio looked up at him with a blank stare and shook her head once. "Huh?"

"But with this Metz murder there's a much harsher focus on Comp." He took a large swallow and headed for the window again, then changed his mind. Almost snarling, he said, "And if Hathaway hadn't gone whining to Peter Tompkins, I'd still be taking the train into work."

She regarded her husband with new eyes. His height of a mere 5'8 seemed to have shrunk further. He was dressed in brown corduroy slacks and that old zippered fleece that she was sick of looking at every weekend. "Aren't you starting on the booze kind of early? It's not even 5:00 yet. And I know I should remember this, but is Tompkins the CFO or the CEO. I keep getting them mixed up."

"How many times do I have to tell you? He's the CEO, Chief Executive Officer, the head honcho." He plunked back down into his chair. "Tompkins! Jesus, what a ninny! He lets himself fall prey to public opinion - leaves his own team, for Christ's sake!" Lazaro nodded his head. "Oh, I get his game, all right. He put me on executive leave in order to glow in the media."

"So you're their fall-guy?"

Clio swung around and walked to the bar. "Thanks a lot for pouring me one." She pulled out a bottle of Chianti and a wine glass. There was a thoughtful pause as she uncorked the bottle. "Yeah, but does that explain why the FBI is sitting outside? I think there's more to Paula Metz than you're saying. I mean, where's the sorrow? She worked for you for two years. Didn't you like her?"

"She was okay…efficient, but a grumbler. Always coming in with picayune comparisons." The phone rang. He shot out of his chair with a loud, "Uhn! It's the phone." He pushed his right arm straight out, holding Clio at bay. "Never mind," he warned, "I'll get it."

"Sweet Christ! Except for the press, the phone hasn't rung in days. Maybe it's my sister." She was shouting by the time Michael had reached the hall.

He quickly turned his back, blocking out the living room entry way while shielding the mouth piece with one hand. "Hello?" His hand pulled away. " Mario, I told you not to call here," he whispered fiercely "Are you crazy? I'm hanging up." But he held on listening a full minute. "You tell that crook if he tries anything like that, he's finished." Michael paused for effect. "And you disappear. I don't know you." He quietly hung up. He wondered who this Ritzy guy was that Mario mentioned. Lazaro stood in position, staring at the floor for a full minute before turning around. He wiped his face of expression and marched back to the living room and picked up his drink.

Clio looked up at his balding head. "So who was that?"

"Just some jerk wanting to sell me an insurance policy."

"So did you buy it? We might need some on your life if you don't get your job back."

"Very funny. You know, Clio? Your humor just grinds the old ax down to a brutal tool."

"Okay, okay, sorry. But I gotta' get out'a this house."

Swallowing the last of her Chianti, she brightened her tone. "How about we go to Silvio's later and have some pasta?" She sauntered toward his chair, hips swaying as she leaned over to give Michael a little pat on the cheek. "Huh, Baby?" He paused a moment staring into her cleavage, but shook his head. "I can't do that. The idea of that black Suburban trailing us just ruins an evening. You go. I'll stay here."

"FINE! Stay here for a month for all I care. I'm making my own plans from now on!" She strode out of the room and stomped up the stairs.

"Maybe that's a good plan," he muttered, watching her skirt disappear from sight.

<u>Same Day</u> - The Gordon Hathaway Estate

"Did you check the gatehouse too, Gordon? I don't want to see those media stalkers or another man in uniform - for at least a month." Marion was standing at one of the tall, living room windows peering into the darkening sky. She could still make out the silhouettes of trees that broke up the expanse of their hilltop estate. Until now it had been overrun with official cars, even a few brazen media people who had somehow leapt over the property's six foot wall.

"I checked. Just a few reporters out on the road. They accosted me at the gate with their microphones. I gave them the same old line 'No Comment' and headed back." Gordon walked over to turn her gently around. He put both hands on his wife's shoulders and gazed into her face. It was looking a bit drawn but still contained that sense of calm he had always found so appealing. "Are you sure this is the right decision? Are you going to feel safe enough with them gone?"

"Yes! Like I said honey, all I want is a little privacy and quiet." She gave Gordon a little smile and patted his arm as she started for the sofa-back table. Amongst a neatly arrayed group of magazines was the new issue of VANITY FAIR she hadn't had a chance to read. Midway she turned back around. "Oh! Jamie called while you were out, and then Collin grabbed his cell phone. They were both pleading to come home, again. I said No Way. You can't stop life because of one horrible act. They have papers due, and then mid-terms right before their break."

"You know they're just feeling protective, don't you?"

"Yes…but that's the small part. It's more likely that they're wishing they could be here, where the action is." Marion stepped back and crossed her hands over her chest, gripping both arms. "Jamie's got to do well this semester or he'll be back on probation." She thought a moment. "Anyway, why would we want the boys to be in the midst of this when they can be in Massachusetts on a safe campus?"

"You're probably right. They need to concentrate on their schoolwork." Do you think Jamie will stick to his word?"

"He said he would." Marion sighed. "These prep schools don't let them slide through. I mean they don't grant 'favors' to the children of alums anymore. I told him that and he promised."

"Good. We have enough to deal with right here." He let out a little chuckle. "I did wonder how the police department could afford this "round-the-clock" coverage. What's been happening all this time to the people com-mitting traffic violations?" He smiled and they both said, "Nothing!"

Grabbing up her magazine, Marion plopped into a stuffed chair and swept her feet onto a matching jacquard hassock. "Is it too soon for a martini?" I feel… half like celebrating and half like cocooning." She let out another big sigh, looking across the living room to the grand piano. "Would you put on some soft jazz? Diana Krall, maybe?"

"Honey, we've *been* cocooning for four days. Well, you have. Today I was given the royal escort to Manhattan." Gordon headed for the sound system. "I can't believe you're not stir-crazy yet."

"Getting there. It's a good thing Ellen's been around to get groceries and run errands. Having her company has been a help too. I'll tell her she can go back to her sister's. Don't you think we should give her an extra $300? I mean she's really been good to us, rescheduling her other jobs, giving up her weekend."

"Sure thing. Do you want me to make out a check or…?"

"No, no. I will. Just fix the drinks, will you?" She stared down at the cover. Demi Moore was staring back, looking gorgeous in a simple, white terry cloth robe. Did she want to read about the rich and famous now? She scanned the article titles: "WHY BRITAIN'S SEX SCANDALS ARE SO MUCH JUICIER THAN OURS", "WILL JOHN McCAIN'S TEMPER DERAIL HIM?", "HOW TYRA BANKS WALKED HER WAY FROM MANNEQUIN TO MOGUL" and flipped the magazine onto the carpet. Later, maybe. These past four days had placed a different emphasis on life.

Gordon returned holding two martinis. He set one of them on Marion's side table and then nudging her feet over, he plunked down on the hassock. Except for a

115

small but expanding belly, his 50 years had preserved an otherwise handsome, trim exterior. He was just shy of six feet and kept active with frequent hand ball and tennis games at the club. His light brown hair was thick and held a slight wave. Marion always regretted those regular haircuts that clipped the medium sweep of waves too short. What never changed were his blue eyes and those long, dark lashes. Ever since their first meeting, she had been bewitched by them. Still was. Lately his demeanor had come across as a little hesitant, so unlike the usual, buoyant, "extend the hearty hand shake" one that had bolstered all those sales. Given their situation though, that was understandable.

She noticed that his face had turned serious. "What is it? Are you still feeling guilty?"

"Yes, but not quite so much. I keep dreaming though, about her making phone calls to me – either from the office, or the train, even waiting on the platform. I can hear her voice, but she can't hear what I'm saying."

"I know what you mean. What is it about dreams? You're trying your best, but the other person can't hear you. Or you're running and you can't catch up to them."

He sat, staring at his drink. "If only I could have helped her...gotten to her sooner."

"Gordon, you can't keep tormenting yourself with this. The weather is God's department. A plane delay is the airport's department. I'm just glad you weren't at the station when the bullets were flying."

He was quietly thinking - or even if I'd provided more support that first time she came to my office with those files. He patted Marion's leg. "Anyway. I'm going to change the subject. He took a mouthful of his martini and swallowed slowly. "I'm afraid the pressure at

Comp is going to cause us even more trouble than we already have."

"Why? I thought putting Lazaro on leave of absence was the answer to that."

"Let me talk, all right?" She looked down at her drink and nodded her head once. "Dennis Barkley, you know Lazaro's boss, is pissed off that he got bumped out, and now Dennis is trying to stir the pot. He's putting out stories, trying to point a finger in other directions."

Marion blurted angrily, "I never liked that man. I can't understand why Peter made him CFO." She saw Gordon look up and frown. "I'm sorry. I'll be quiet."

"It's what he's saying that has me concerned." Gordon pulled in a deep breath and then locked his eyes onto Marion's. "Dennis told Peter that I was having an affair with Paula."

"WHAT?"

"Marion, honey. Please stop and listen to me." Gordon spoke the next words in even, slow measurement. "I was not having an affair with Paula Metz."

"Oh, Christ! We have to go through this...AGAIN?"

"I swore to you that it would never happen again and I *meant* it. Marion, I am resolved...believe me. I love you and want our marriage to last. If you can't trust me on this, I don't know what I'll do."

Marion swung her feet to the floor and strode to the console. She flicked the audio switch, snapping the room into silence. She stood for a moment in the quiet and then turned. "Tell me more. Why is it *you* that Barkley's after, and not somebody else?"

"Lazaro must have overheard Paula calling me. She was trying to arrange a time to meet - to talk to me about something she was worried about." He kept looking at

Marion's face for some kind of acknowledgment. It registered nothing. "There were these documents that bothered her."

"Well, did she? Did she meet with you?"

"Just once...in my office. I noticed some discrepancies in a few statements, but I wasn't sure they amounted to enough to push the issue. I asked her what Lazaro thought about them. She said that he just got angry and told her, in effect, to mind her own business...that he would take care of them. This was months ago." He took a long sip and continued, "There were two more times she called, asking me to corroborate what she was holding - proof that Lazaro had sent false accounting statements to the SEC."

"And?"

"I...I put her off. I didn't really want to get caught up in any interdepartmental friction."

"Why didn't she go to Dennis Barkley? The CFO is ultimately responsible for all the accounting."

"That's exactly what I told her she should do. But she must have made the mistake of telling Lazaro that that was her intention." Gordon paused, looking into Marion's eyes... "that she'd have to do go to Barkley if he continued to sit on them. This was last week, just as I was about to fly out to Chicago." It looked to Gordon like Marion was somewhere else thinking along another track. "Are you still with me?"

She shook her head sadly and walked out of the room.

On Track

With his hand resting on the phone, Hansen looked steadily into her eyes. Dana paused. Should she go ahead with this? She wondered whether being raised to respect authority... and portraying the ever-helpful teacher, was going to work against her. Something about this man though, inspired trust. She looked around his office, very clean and orderly. She nodded once.

"Okay, I'll have them pull the samples." He picked up the receiver and punched in a number. "Paul, get the WAV files ready on the Metz case, will you? Thanks." He turned back to her. "Here's how it goes, Dana. We'll go down the hall in a minute and set you up. You will hear six different audio recordings of voices saying pretty much the same couple of sentences."

"Oh? That's interesting." She thought it was pretty smart to keep the content simple and redundant. "But

119

what if I mix them up? I mean the sound of their voices, one after the other?"

"You can listen as many times as you wish, and we'll give you a pen and paper if you want to jot down any reactions." He sat there looking down at his desk. Then he raised his head and said, "Normally we don't call in witnesses for audio line-ups like this unless the suspect has made a verbal threat of some kind. That's not the case here." Dana nodded, crossing her legs. It felt like the room was getting smaller. "I hope you don't mind giving us an extra hand. We'd like to cover every angle so that we can nail this guy." He paused, thinking..."but I want to be square with you."

Dana wasn't sure what Hansen meant by this. She was back in the parking lot remembering that feeling of being threatened. It was the man's tone of voice, not what he said. She came back to Hansen, "Do you mean, did he say something like 'Get outa' here or I'll kill you"?

"What I mean is, certain types of evidence can stand up in court; others are more difficult. It goes back to individual rights, probable cause, a lot of legal stuff." Something flashed by his window. It was a blue jay, flying toward some distant trees. Dana felt a momentary longing for similar flight... but then she hurriedly caught up to what he was saying. "What you can do is give us a hand with pushing the suspect. It's a kind of police strategy. If he thinks we've got him identified, he might cave. It's worth a try."

She sat a moment, considering. "Well, okay, but I'm not sure I understand all this. He won't ever know who I am, will he? What if this case goes to court?"

Hansen slid his chair back from the desk. "Now, on your first question. Our first priority is to protect the witness. Live audio line-ups are not allowed, just like I described with those old fashioned police line-ups. You remember - the ones with the guys standing there looking into the dark. We do photo arrays instead, where you view just one photo at a time. And as for this case going to court? There's a possibility, but a small one. Anyway," Hansen rose out of his chair and walked toward the door, "the court would likely see your testimony as inadmissible."

Feeling a little muddled, she followed Detective Hansen down a hallway of grey concrete blocks. Truth be known, all she could think about was his name. If this detective could call her by her first name, why couldn't she do the same? Dana had noted the "Stephen" on his name plate back in his office and decided she'd drop it lightly at some point down the line.

He turned left and entered a small room jammed with a lot of complicated equipment. "This is our forensic lab. Small, I realize, but Darien is a small town. We coordinate with the State Troopers for Major Crime Activity on any high profile crimes. They have all the up-to-date technology for police investigations. Like the electronics that convert recorded video interviews to digital copies - MPEGs to WAV files." He must have seen the confused look on her face, "... to assist us with voice identification," he added. "What I mean is, you never see the person on the video who is speaking. You just hear a voice."

Swiveling a battered chair facing a computer, he motioned her over. "Have a seat here. I'll show you how to operate the samples, so that you're in charge. Take all the time you need. Repeat them if you like... and here's paper and pencil for note-taking." He looked at her questioningly, with a little smile. She nodded and sat down at the computer. He leaned over her shoulder and brought up a playlist of titles: Metz #1, #2, #3, and so on. "Do you download music at home, Dana?"

"Sometimes, not a lot. Most of my time is spent correcting papers, but I recognize the format. I should just click on the mouse for each sample, right Steve? Or is it Stephen?" She caught a quick recognition of a self she'd forgotten about. Was she flirting?

He laughed. "Okay. What's fair's, fair. Steve'll do fine. Now then, if you're sure you don't need help, I'll leave you to your own... expertise."

"Thanks, I think I'll be able to concentrate better if I'm alone." Dana was glad he didn't want to hang over her shoulder. It would make her feel self-conscious.

"Be down the hall if you need me," he said. The door shut quietly behind him.

She sat there a minute in the silence to calm herself and to get her senses ready. It might be better if she had a plan of approach here. She thought about closing her eyes and going quickly through the six to see if there was one that rang with any recognition. Or she could listen to each one, repeat it, and write down a description of that voice, sort of like doing character studies in Lit. class. Oh hell, this was getting too complicated. She clicked on #1, deciding to go with her gut.

A heavy voice came on, "Yeah? Well, it was cold out 'der. Whada'ya think? I'm gonna' wait all night? I wished I was at my own place, not waitin' in a stupid cah'. Shit. Who knew."

That wasn't it. The Brooklyn accent was too much, almost funny. She listened to the second one. They were the same words, but not as strongly accented, still from the Bronx or Brooklyn. This voice, was a baritone too, like the first...not it though, too smooth a tone. #3 sounded New Yorkish as well, a little gravely, but her memory recalled something less harsh. She wondered if they purposely recorded men from the city. They all sounded about the same age, too. After the fourth voice she stood up and swung her arms around to break the tension. No ringers yet. What if none of them sounded like him? She sat back down looking at the blank note pad. Should she be writing out her reactions? Dana held off with that, deciding to stick with the same M.O. on this first round. She clicked #5. "Yeah? Well, it was cold//" Her throat tightened. This one? She listened to it through and then through again. That same gruff, but smooth tone and the inflections felt right. Goose bumps rose up on her arms. Again she stood up and moved about the room, twisting her head back and forth, rubbing her arms for warmth. She waited a bit to calm down.

The 6th was a no. This last guy had a tightness to his voice, like he was making an effort to talk. She listened through two more rounds of all six to make sure she wasn't discounting a possibility. No. Number five felt like the right one; she was pretty sure of it.

Dana could hear "Steve" talking as she walked toward his office. "Yeah, well he's not supposed to be speaking to anyone; it could contaminate the case. I'm wondering why they even let him go back to work. Right, right. I'll get back to you in an hour or so." She paused at his door. He hung up and waved her in and then with a deft jab pitched his pencil into a cup. " I gotta' stop doing that," he said, "I keep breaking the point. Hey! Well? Any luck? Come in, come in."

Dana sat down and chucked it right out. "I'm almost sure it's # 5." He couldn't hide it. His face brightened and a tiny smile slipped sideways. "You're agreeing, aren't you," she said.

"What is it with you teachers...mothers too. Always reading way ahead. Okay, so how did you know for sure?"

"Honestly, I surprised myself. It was what... a week ago? I thought his voice would fade, or that none of the samples would register. But...as soon as I heard the first couple of words I was taken back to that..." Dana cut herself off, because she was curious. "How did you get them all to say the same stuff?"

"It's part of this WAV technology. We can excerpt sentences from the suspect's video-taped interrogation and then splice them onto an audio file. After that we just get guys around here who are about the same age to say the same words."

"Were they all from New York?"

"Well, let's say the Metropolitan area. We wouldn't mix a Southern accent in there, that's for sure." He leaned back in his chair, thought a moment, and then pushed himself up extending his hand. "We really appreciate your coming in, Dana. You've been very helpful "

"Oh." She stood up too. "But do I get to find out who it is?" Immediately she guessed that no, he wouldn't give her a name now. She shook her head - to acknowledge his position. They both smiled. "Okay, I can find my way out. You have to get back to work."

"I probably don't need to say this, but please avoid discussing with anyone what we've done here this afternoon. Remember. We're keeping a tight circle, right?" He winked. "You're my prize ear-witness, y'know."

On the way home Dana measured her reaction to this

visit against the previous ones she had made. She certainly felt better about herself, having made that identification. And whatever risk there was to her safety didn't seem significant enough to worry about. She was mistaken the last time, coming back from the train station. She thought they would make an arrest by tracking the gun back to its owner, or by using the fingerprints. Hunh. Dana smiled to herself. She was thinking of those WAVs or whatever they were called. Police work was like other professions. The more you know, the more you know you don't know. A feeling of satisfaction spread through her as the town's shops and restaurants flowed by. Her need to fly South didn't have the same urgency anymore. She glanced at the clock - 5:32, Happy Hour at Maxwell's. Maybe some of the regulars would be there. Should she?

Her cell phone rang. Nope, she wasn't going to answer it. This was a New Year's resolution: no more talking on her cell while driving. She continued another block and pulled into Maxwell's parking lot, then punched in her voice mail. "Hi honey, it's me. I'm calling from work, but maybe I can get out of here in time to catch the 7:42. Could you pick me up? Give me a ring."

Dana stared out the window into the dark feeling everything sink. What would she be able to say to him? They were in two different worlds.

Later That Night - Hathaway Estate

Gordon took down the rest of his martini, sickened by the mess of the past week. A woman murdered, his house under watch, their chief accounting officer put on leave ...then Barkley making that slimy accusation, which was a complete lie. What an astounding prick. Gordon was thinking that if he hadn't gone in to work, he might not have heard about it.

And now his wife was giving up on him. He shook his head, stood up a moment, and then sank back down on the hassock. What could he do or say to convince Marion he was telling the truth? He found himself looking through the foyer, wishing he would hear her footsteps coming down the stairs.

It would be two years this May...or was it June when Marion finally forgave him and he moved back in...it was just before the boys returned for summer vacation. Since then he had thought that their relationship had grown closer. Maybe he should have said it...not just think it. That's the trouble with life. You get used to going along when the road is smooth and your talk goes into an everyday catch-up mode. Especially since Comp had grown so fast in the past year. He had been putting in nine, sometimes ten hour days. And the traveling had increased.

Gordon wondered if he should go upstairs or leave Marion to be by herself for a while. What would Chandler advise? This was the therapist they had gone to as a condition of his coming back home. He had suggested that they make weekly check-ins with each other. Ask each other how things were doing, find out if there was anything bothering the other. It had felt a little stilted at first. To him anyway. But Marion seemed to get into it. Then these check-ins had gradually become less frequent. When had they stopped? He shook his head, searching through life's friggin' puzzles. It turns out that relationships are as hard to maintain as competitive marketing strategies.

That's another thing Chandler had said. Marriage is

work. Gordon remembered Chandler looking directly at him. "It's the same as running a company. I'm sure you have management meetings, for updates and reviews, don't you? What's working, what's not working?" And then he had emphasized applying this tactic to marriage as well.

Maybe they should go back again. Chandler had said that they could come back any time communication started breaking down. Right now though, Gordon felt jammed against a wall. Too much to deal with: the police, Barkley, the SEC, the FBI...and all the while keeping his managers upbeat despite this investigation. So much to think about. He didn't want to add another. His head felt like one of those blood separators, spinning with centrifugal force. If only life would calm down for a while. It occurred to him that through all this mess there had been one constant - Marion's support. Now that was gone. The obvious suddenly became clear. Communication. That was what he had to restore. Gordon stood up and headed for the stairs.

She was sitting on their bed with her back to the door. "Marion?" he asked gently, stepping part way into the room. There was no response. "Please. Can we talk? I have nothing more important to me right now than you." Still nothing. He walked round the bed and sat alongside her. "I've been thinking downstairs about us...how we have lost touch...I mean those regular touch-base talks we used to have. With work being so all-consuming, I'm afraid I've allowed it to take first priority."

Marion looked at him sideways and then back down at the floor.

"You still don't believe me, do you. I am telling the truth. I have not slept with or lusted after anyone since I

127

no *before* I moved back in." Again, no reaction. "Please say something, Marion. Anything. What are you thinking right now?"

"How I'm wanting this to be the truth, but knowing that you've lied to me before. Many times."

Gordon dropped his head. The near affair with Paula came to mind. They sat in silence. "I did. And I hate myself for causing so much damage." Another awkward silence. "Marion..." he took hold of her hand and turned his face to see into her eyes. "Try to forgive me. Please. If we can work through this together - even go back to Chandler, if you like, I believe we can build up your trust in me again. You have been selfless this past week. I haven't told you and I should have - how much I appreciate all the support you've given me. That's what I realized downstairs, and...oh, I don't know what more I can say."

She lifted her head, staring straight forward, with a look of grim resolution on her face. She waited. "You have to understand that this is no longer just between the two of us. I have far more at stake than another personal agony to contend with. The whole town of Darien - No, the whole metropolitan area will be lapping up the sordid details of our lives."

"Wait. It's important that you know exactly how this came out. We may still escape... I mean get through this without the public knowing about Barkley's accusation. So far, only Peter and the FBI - I don't know yet about the Darien investigators - but I have stressed confidentiality with them."

Marion shook her head and gave Gordon a look of disbelief. "You believe that? And that Barkley will keep his mouth shut? That man will do anything for his own gain."

"I agree with you, Marion. You have no argument from me, but we have Comp's Chief Executive Officer behind us. That's something. Just let me tell you how it all came about okay?"

She stared at the wall, sliding from anger into a well of sadness. And then she nodded her head. What difference did it make now? Everything was either horrid or it would end up being a total disaster.

Gordon started right in, afraid that she might charge out of the house if he paused for a second. "You know that I've been asking to get back into the office. And the FBI consented today, but only because Peter told them that Barkley had accused me of having an affair with Paula. They wanted to get the three of us together, in person, to put it all out on the table. We were all there, in Peter's office, when he looked straight at me and repeated what Barkley accused me of. I was livid."

Quickly turning toward her, he went on. "Anyway, I think Peter must have said something to the agents in my favor. I mean Peter must have stressed the importance of keeping this private."

"Wait." Marion cut in. "I'm not following this. When did Barkley break this open, yesterday or this morning?" And then she shook her head. "It couldn't have been this morning, because they called around 8:00 to say they'd pick you up. Barkley wouldn't have come in yet."

"Right. Barkley made it last evening after most of the office staff left. The Feds were still there going through accounting records from last year. Peter approached one of the Agents to tell him something had come up and to come into his office - while Barkley was still in there. So then this morning they heard my vehement denial. I told them they could track my every move for the past six months if they wanted to, but they'd find no clandestine meetings between Paula and me."

Marion turned to face him with a look of disbelief. "This morning, when they called. Didn't anyone mention the reason for your going back to the city?"

"No, they just said that I was being allowed to return to the office, but under escort. I didn't suspect anything was wrong. I just thought the heat was off me. The driver didn't know anything, as far as I...oh Christ, I can't say for sure. Nothing was said on the way in."

"But Gordon." Her voice registered exasperation. Marion stood up abruptly, "The heat off you? For days we've been surrounded by the media, Federal agents, the cops. It's been hour upon hour of questioning. They may call it 'investigative detention' but in my mind we've been held hostage in our own home for four days now. First it was the Feds and that Detective Hansen, then the media in full force."

"I know!" Then in a softer voice, "I know. It's been awful. Honey, I just..." he looked down at his upturned palms and shook his head. I just have some notion, that when you're innocent..." Gordon stopped. His head slumped, and he waved it back and forth. "Maybe it's preposterous, but you think that some form of justice will pull you through...that they'll see you're innocent." A heavy moment of silence filled the room. Gordon glanced up and held Marion's gaze.

The smallest of smiles started at one corner of her mouth. "What a naive optimist you are."

Night Crawling

Silvio's Restaurant - **That Night**

Clio was starting to roll having finished her fourth Chianti. "Listen Harry, I wanna' tell ya'. Life is not always that dandy in Fairfield County. You take any of these upscale towns - New Canaan, Wilton, Darien. They're not real. You drive down these country roads past one mansion after the other. You're driving along, and ya' start picturing these people in their designer outfits sipping cocktails, right? Whada' ya' think *really* goes on inside?" She squinted her eyes. "I'll tell you. Just about everything you can imagine that's going on in the Bronx - your standard robberies, wife beating, child abuse. Only these WASPS don't talk about it, b'cause they gottta' keep up the image. Am I right? I mean you should know. You got an ear, being in your line of work."

Harry stopped wiping the bar top and leaned toward her. He had recognized Clio from her younger, more available days when he filled in to tend bar at the Zebra Club. "Yeah, I get what you're saying Clio, but I'm doing the same thing. I'm keeping my mouth zipped. Playing their game too, ya' know? Because it's bad for business if I don't. In the restaurant business, once you start the class act you gotta' keep it up, so I don't repeat what I hear. Take this place, for example. The owners. They're talking now about hiding the bar around back. In a new addition."

"You're kiddin' me. Why would they do that?"

"Well, they don't want the big execs and their wives to walk into what looks like a local hang-out with a set of tables for eating." Harry shook his head. "I don't know. A couple of these towns still have one old neighborhood bar left, with a menu of food you can recognize and afford, but they're vanishing fast."

Clio looked around at the dark, wood paneled walls lined with 20 year old pictures. They were all spots of interest to townies: Bobby Valentine's old Sports Cafe, the Bulls Head Diner, a bird shot taken at Cove Island, and there was one of her favorite night spots, Jimmy's Seaside. She bet if she looked, she'd find one of the old Bloomingdale's somewhere. So okay, the furniture looked a little battered but Harry made up for that. He was the kind of bartender who could be personal but who did the job right. Plus, he had a Jackie Gleason - Joe the Bartender look to him without the huge fat. You could count on him to get your order up and get to know you.

When Clio swiveled her head back to Harry, it felt a little spinny, but then things righted themselves, "If this place stops servin' their rigatoni and veal scalloppine Harry? *I'm* leaving."

Harry gave her a smile and pulled away her empty

glass. "You got a ride home, Clio?"

She kind of hoped this was a come-on, but then he was eight years or so younger. Maybe it was a vague warning to stop drinking. "Sure, I got a ride home. I'm drivin' my new Beemer. How come you're askin'?" She looked down at her lap and swiped away a few invisible crumbs.

"Hey, no reason in particular. Did you want to order some pasta from the bar menu? They're still serving it, last I heard." He cocked his head and gave her a questioning smile, hoping she'd decide to eat something. Harry didn't want to alienate Clio by refusing her drinks.

"Oh hell, I guess I better before this place gets too classy to serve basic Italian. Yeah, okay, I'll have the baked rigatoni and another Chianti... when dinner comes," she added to play along.

"Sure thing Clio. It'll be right up." He strode down to a window at the end of the bar and slid an order slip through just as two men walked in from outside.

While Harry was making their drinks, Clio's thoughts traveled to the home front. If Michael continued with his paranoia she'd have to find some other place to go. Never had she imagined him sitting in the house day after day. Part of the unspoken bargain, at least in her mind, was his marriage to Comp Coordinates. Clio's and Michael's had been a marriage of convenience. He could spend all the time he wanted to at work with his wonder boys and accounting books. She could live in high style and the freedom to move about with cash in hand. They'd have their occasional home cooked dinners and then the boring sprawls in bed.

A burst of laughter from down the bar interrupted her thoughts. She looked their way vaguely wishing herself single again. When Harry caught her eye, she raised an imaginary glass to her lips, mouthing 'water.' "Sure thing, honey."

It came to her in a rush that this was a weird way to be spending her time - in limbo and on the prowl. On impulse she pulled out her cell phone and started to punch in her sister's number. Maybe Gemma could break free and they could do some carousing downtown. But a surprising pang of guilt stopped her hand. Her thoughts went backward. Michael had saved her from a life of topless writhing at the Zebra Club. They had bought the big house in North Stamford and gone to vacation spots she'd only dreamed of before. Her life of comfort and security was still pretty new. They'd been married only three years. She'd be a fool to break the tie now, particularly if his job worries were only temporary. Yeah, he's been a general prick since that lay-off thing, but why the hell doesn't he at least wanna' get out of the house? It would do him good. Better than sulking in a chair with a glass of booze.

Harry appeared before her with ice water and a place setting. "So Clio, I haven't seen you at the Zebra Club in years. Have you gone on to better things?"

Clio looked up quickly, having been brought back to the present. She had been in the midst of reprimanding herself for not calling Michael...to see if he'd eaten. It was already going on 9:00, and he would never cook anything on his own.

"No, wait a minute." Harry stopped himself, "What I mean is..." He gestured toward her, "You look great, even covered up for the snow and cold." He paused a moment, not sure where to go next. She wasn't wearing a wedding ring. "Um, I've seen you here a couple times with the same guy. I was just wondering if that's your main man."

She nodded and said, "Yeah, pretty much," remembering now that she'd pulled off her ring in a fit of anger before leaving the house. "Hey, it was a good idea to put that order in. I'm all of a sudden starved."

"Sure thing. I'll check on it." He turned away, wondering if he had misspoken.

Clio punched in her home phone number, but got their voice message. Here was Harry coming with her dinner anyway; she'd call after. The noise level was beginning to rise with after dinner drinkers filtering in. As Clio waited for her wine, she leaned over and breathed in the parmesan aromas of Silvio's famous baked rigatoni. How familiar the bar sounds were: guys hailing drinks, an occasional high girlie laugh, those same hip tunes for background music. Except now she was no longer a part of this scene. She wasn't working at the Zebra or on the make with her girl friends anymore. Harry set her glass down. "Eat hearty my girl," and he moved off to build and pour. She lifted her fork and dug in.

Part way through her meal she looked up and around, aware of her separateness. Clio never used to feel awkward at a bar if she was on her own, but for some reason - was it just the eating alone part? Or was being married and accustomed to Michael's company the reason. She started to ruminate over his job situation. He'd better be telling her the truth about it. She wasn't sure if this leave of absence was like what pregnant women took or just a fancy phrase for "you're outa' here". She didn't even know if he was still getting paid. And what if the FBI *was* onto something? Panic took hold. She swallowed the last of her pasta, took a huge gulp of wine, and pulled up her phone again.

135

It rang only once. "Hello." His voice sounded gruff, wary.

"Michael it's me. Did you eat anything?"

"Jesus, where are you calling from?"

"Silvio's." She waited a moment, but nothing followed. "So what're you doin' for dinner, anything?"

"Listen Clio, I got enough to worry about without you wanting to know my eating habits."

"Like, what are you worried about, the FBI?" She tried to keep her voice sweet, to stay away from the sarcastic tone. "I just was trying to touch home base, honey. I've been thinkin' about all you've gone through and everything. I know it hasn't been easy and all, what with the leave of..."

Michael broke in, "Yeah, well that might just change."

"Really? Whadaya' mean 'might change'?" She checked herself from asking if the leave was with pay.

"I didn't tell you about Barkley calling. Last night he told me the heat might shift to Hathaway. They called him in today for more questioning."

"I don't get it. Isn't he the one in Darien? He's been surrounded by all kinds of authorities for days. Am I right?"

"I'm not gonna' go into it on the phone, Clio. What're you doing to me? All the time with these questions. I thought you were going to make your own plans from now on. That's what you said...three hours ago."

Now she was mad, "The hell with you, Michael! I try to reach out a little. Then you go and ruin everything!" The sudden quiet at the bar brought her head up; to her left she caught the eyes of six people dart away. She lowered her voice. "We gotta' talk, Michael. We can't let this Comp mess get the best of us." She waited but he said nothing. "So do you want me to come home?" Again nothing. Clio punched the end call button.

Fuck him. She'd check in at the Hyatt. "Harry!" She called out. "Can you bring me the check please?"

On the way out a man in a leather jacket swung around on his stool and tapped her once on the shoulder. "Hiya' sweetheart, can I buy you a drink? You don't want to leave now; it's too early. And anyway, it's cold out there." Clio gave him a once over. He looked okay. She remembered what she'd been told a long time ago. There are two things men wear that girls should check out: the watch and the shoes. If both passed muster, go with it. "Well, maybe just one," she said and sat on the stool he pulled out.

Metro-North - The 8:07

This train was at least quiet. Carson leaned back with his eyes closed. Every cell in his body cried for rest. It would be so good to sleep a little before reaching Darien. As he sat there waiting for the train to pull out, he could feel his muscles gradually relaxing, a sense of drifting... but then the sound of Dana's voice broke into his glide downward. It wasn't what she had said when she returned his call so much as the tone of her voice. He'd been hearing it off and on ever since the night of the murder, but at least the police seemed to be moving on the case. He was hoping that by now they would be free of any more interference from the police.

Westerly's warning last Sunday on "appropriate legal procedures" still irked him. "We want to keep as much distance from Comp-Coordinates as we can get". He was being such a pain with that stupid "MediaTech keeps a low profile" bit. Westerly kept on repeating it over his shoulder as he checked the date Carson was working on. And then of course "We must be able to show spotless paper work." He'd been passing by Carson's desk all week muttering that other stupid line of having to account for each month's accounting. So far Carson had seen nothing that could be interpreted as fraudulent, but he was only two thirds of the way through '06. What stuck in his mind though was when Westerly had said, "If you can produce for the board a pure, white set of accounts for last year, I'll see to it that you'll get most of the credit." Maybe these endless work days would ultimately result in something good and they could afford to start looking for a house of their own.

Carson wondered if Dana was still mad about their canceled vacation. Probably. Or maybe it was because he had to take an even later train. But he'd been away for two nights now, and he was hoping she'd be glad to have him back home. He thought of calling again, once the train came out of the tunnel, but changed his mind. Dana might not want to be interrupted if she was correcting papers.

"Hey Carson, Baby!" With a jolt Carson sat up and looked back. It was Jay coming up the aisle. "Hi, buddy. I *thought* that was you. What are you doing out of the office? You're supposed to be working, aren't you? Okay if I sit here?" He took an empty seat opposite the aisle.

"Yeah well, I need a good night's sleep in my own bed. What are you doing on the 8:07?"

"Just heading back after a long and thirst-quenching Happy Hour. You know, they've added another new martini at The Union Bar? It's got pomegranate seeds in it, for God's sake. So you can get your antioxidants in with your natural, alcoholic high."

Carson smiled. "I'm so out of it. That's what long hours and suburban living does to you."

"True enough. So how's it going? With work, I mean."

"Other than Westerly looking over my shoulder all day, I'm making headway. I hope to God I never have to go through his style of internal investigation again. What is it with lawyers? Are they all picky-pricks like him?"

"Oh, I don't know. I'm just glad I'm at the marketing end of Media-Tech's focus right now. You poor guys with this SEC crap are suffering big-time. Of course, the big boys upstairs and on The Board are plenty nervous too."

"Yeah, the whole place is tense. What's the latest with Hathaway? Have you heard anything new?"

Jay shrugged his shoulders. "Haven't heard anything about him or anybody else at Comp-Coordinates in the last day or so. I think the Feds are staying hush-hush until they've got something real to say." He sat up suddenly, "Oh, by the way. I ran into Dana last night. Did she tell you?" The train jolted forward and then rolled slowly along the lighted platform.

"No, I haven't had time to do anything but leave messages on her phone. Where'd you see her, at Maxwell's?"

"Yeah. Sounds like she's decided to take a couple days in Florida on her own, huh? Says she's sick of Darien." A silent pause fell. It had never occurred to Carson that she might go off by herself. Sensing something awkward, Jay quickly added, "She was with her teacher friend Nancy, the one who teaches Spanish. We... I mean Nancy and I, stayed for a night cap. She seems pretty laid back. Not bad looking." He looked over at Carson, who returned an amused glance.

139

"You sure have a life there, Jay, what with the bars and new chicks. I'm so out of that scene. How do you like being on the prowl again?"

"It's kind of fun really. Well you know it beats the strife that Sally causes day in and out. Honestly Carson, I'd rather pay alimony than listen to her never-ending worries. Money, her boss, the dog getting loose...name it; she'd worry about it. And then the monthly thermometer sex." He paused as they continued up and out of the tunnel. "If rents weren't so high in Manhattan right now I'd quit this crazy commute."

"Your place is okay for now, isn't it? You said that Sally was going back to Jersey. She can worry about the dog in her Dad's house. Besides, I want you around to run with."

"Oh yeah, that's another big one she worries about - her Dad. Now she'll be there to watch his bad health up close."

"Well, she'll be out of your hair in a little while." A big yawn took Carson by surprise. "Sorry, I'm just so tired."

"Hey man, I'm sorry I interrupted your quiet time. You go ahead; take a nap. I've gotta' catch up on last week's sales reports, anyway."

They rode along in their own thoughts as the train pulled into 125th Street Station. Only a few passengers boarded, and they were soon on their way again. Carson wondered if Jay would ever be content in a permanent relationship. He seemed happiest when he was either running or running around. Carson couldn't remember a single time when he had called to go for a jog that Jay was unable to meet him. He never allowed any domestic plans of Sally's to take precedence. But then he too had seen Sally's preoccupation with silly worries. With a sigh he told himself that no one could judge the worth of someone else's marriage. His thoughts turned to Dana. Their relationship seemed solid enough. If they could get through this heavy work period and get back to normal, there'd be time for some relaxation, maybe a trip.

He gazed out the window into the night. Something about the rocking and clicking sound of the train had always filled him with a sense of calm and reassurance, ever since he'd been a kid. Carson gazed out the window for a while in a semi-hypnotic trance. A stark, black sky interrupted by occasional parallel rows of vertical lights indicated that they were near the outskirts of the city. Apartment buildings and large factories were giving way to uneven dots of lamp-lit houses and streaming bands of headlights. His eyes followed the cars alongside the track as they headed north on I-95. And then they fell shut.

Traveling North on the Merritt

Mario was getting madder the closer he got to the exit. If he had to break into Michael's house he'd do it. How dare the bastard... his own cousin. Mario pressed down on the accelerator with each reminder. First he hangs up on me and on top of that, I gottta' come out here to get the money he owes me. If he'da wired it last Friday like he said he was gonna', this other shit wouldn't have to go down. Ritzy's idea with the papers was good; it gave him some leverage. He just hoped he could get his check before the fake pass-over. Still, this sucks. I gotta' rent a stupid car to go after my earnings. What a way to treat family!

Well he wasn't going to do jail time on anyone's account; that's for sure. He'd get his money and bail out. Go somewhere like Mexico or Honduras, live on pesos.

That's it. On that northern coastline where the jungle comes right up to the beaches. With the rest of the money he could set up and live on the cheap for a while, then find some work. All he had to do was get out of this friggin' country...and some distance from Ritzy, till it all cooled down. Christ! How did he fuck things up so bad? Mario shook his head in dismay. If it hadn't been for him screwin'-up, none of this would've been necessary. It was just like it had always been in his miserable life. You couldn't count on anyone.

Mario scanned the road ahead. There was the sign for exit 34-Stamford, one mile ahead. Wait a minute. Was it 34 or 35. Shit! He slowed down trying to remember which one to take. This was Long Ridge. Or was it the other one? He knew they were close together. He'd go past this one and see. It had been a couple years since he'd been out here. It was when Michael got married to that looker. Yeah, Clio. You couldn't forget *her*. What a mouth she had. He told himself to pay attention. It was so friggin' dark up here in the country. You couldn't see anything.

Okay, there's the next sign...High Ridge! That's it. From here it would be okay. He'd take the ramp off and then go to the left. The only turn after that would be about two miles up on the right. All he had to do was look in the fuckin' dark for Pebble Run Road. What a piss-ass name. As far as Mario was concerned you could take the suburbs and ship 'em off the planet. The only good they did was provide the Guatemalans with a shit load of yard work.

Heading north away from Stamford, the night grew blacker. Mario had to slow down to 30 mph in order not to miss the occasional street signs. At last, he saw it. He turned onto Pebble Run scanning for the first house. These places were huge; they must be on a couple acres each. Way up ahead on the right, where Michael's would be, he spotted a car heading out of its long driveway. Mario slowed down, hesitant about his next best move. He squinted his eyes; it looked like a big Chevy SUV. Michael wouldn't be driving one of those. He was always bragging about his Volvos and BMWs. He accelerated and swept by the driveway. It'd be better if he went on up the road a bit, check the scene out. Better yet, he'd try calling once more. He didn't want to run into any fancy-dancy suburbanites. In the rear view mirror he saw the SUV turn left and head back toward Stamford. He pulled over and pressed in Lazaro's number. It rang twice.

"Hello." Good, it was Michael answering. Mario jumped right in. "Don't hang up on me, 'cuz I'm right outside your house and I'm comin' in."

"Jeezus Christ, Mario? Is that you?"

"Yeah, it's me. I'm almost in your driveway, so don't do anything smart."

"Are you fucking crazy? I got the FBI watching the house 24/7." His voice sounded near panic. Mario was almost smiling.

"Relax. They just left. Anybody else in there? Besides Clio?"

"No, but Jeezus, Mario. Don't do this! We'll *all* go down!"

"Not me." Mario did feel a small alarm go off, but he spoke right back. "Soon's I get the money you friggin' owe me I'm gone. I'm outa' heah."

Lazaro's mind was racing. He would have to pay the hush money. If only he could be guaranteed that the papers... "Listen Mario, I haven't been able to get out of the house all week. These pricks have been on my back since last Friday. You must have read about it. I was put on a leave of absence. Those papers..."

"Yeah? Well, whadda' ya' know. I'm so sorry for you. My part of this job's been done. So either open the door and come out of the house with five grand, or I'll come in there and get it. You know I won't mess around. Family or no family. You got five minutes." He hung up.

Darien Train Station - 8:53

She didn't know why she still got the creeps. Her head went down, hands covering her eyes to blot the images. She would have to get a grip on this somehow. It wasn't like this last Sunday. The daylight made such a difference...that and having Detective Hansen standing at her side. She remembered how nervous she'd been that someone in town might recognize her, that she'd have to explain what they were doing while he mapped out the positions.

Now all she could think about was that stupid theory of criminals returning to the scene of the crime. Oh Christ, this witness thing was a mistake. She turned her head to the right for distraction, watching Darien's night time traffic gliding up the Post Road.

Carson would tell her she was getting paranoid. But what were those two empty messages on their answering machine when she got home? And then this evening that pause after she answered and kept asking who was calling. Only breathing in the background...could it have been one of those porn calls? She shouldn't have deleted them. It wouldn't have been Carson calling and then hanging up. Dana shook her head. It was probably nothing, but they should get caller I.D. Maybe she'd call the phone company tomorrow.

The sudden ping of a stick blown against the car jolted her upright. She felt herself tightening up again. The clock read only a few more minutes before train time. She flicked on the radio for another distraction. Just a weather forecast and then...

Reports from Wall Street indicate that the SEC has begun yet another probe.
This time, into large trades with favored clients.
The Securities and Exchange Commission sent out letters in mid-January to investment
banks requesting information on all stock and option trading data for themselves and their customers through the last two weeks of September.
The commission's inquiry will be aimed at determining just how pervasive insider trading is. We'll be back after the hour for more details on this latest...

Dana pushed the power off, sick of hearing about more bad stock behavior. But then she thought - maybe there'll be a break in the Metz case. She leaned forward to push it back on but stopped, hearing the sound of the train churning into the station and grinding to a stop. Lights shone down on the suited parade pouring through the doors. They were all wearing dark suits and carrying brief cases. It was somehow comforting.

Dana saw him coming down the stairs. With...that looked like Jay. The two of them with their slightly disheveled executive aplomb. And then she laughed at herself. This was a vocabulary word from Monday's quiz for her sophomores. She got out of the car to wave Carson in the right direction and watched as Jay gave a nod of goodnight and headed off to the north parking lot.

"Hi Honey. Thanks for coming so late. I just didn't want another night crashing at Rick's." He leaned over and gave her a kiss. She felt detached, outside herself, awkwardly observing herself playing the role of a Darien housewife. Carson had been gone only a few days, but it seemed much longer. He walked around to the passenger's door. "So how've you been?"

"Uhm. Okay." She didn't know where to go from here, so she opened her door and settled into the warmth of the car. "The kids are always hyped the week before vacation. You know. They're restless and complain about getting homework...as though they should be able to start vacation now." She started the car and they drove out. "Have you made good headway with this internal investtigation thing you're doing?"

"Actually, yes. Well *I* think so. It's Westerly who's gotta' think so. Dana, you can't believe how exacting that man is, even with the most picayune figures. But the big guys tell us..."

Dana broke in. "Hey! In last week's *New Yorker* there was this cartoon. It was really funny. A bunch of guys in an office are standing around a waste basket feeding papers into a fire burning in it - in the waste basket. One of them is gagged and tied to an office chair. Anyway the head guy says to the others, 'First rule--what happens in accounting stays in accounting'." She started laughing, but Carson was quiet. She looked over at him.

"I suppose that's funny," he said. "I just can't appreciate the humor right now."

"Oh, sorry." It looked like they were not off to a good start. "But go ahead. You were saying something about the big guys?"

"Just that they want us to make sure everything on

record is legal and/or justifiable." He sighed. "Oh Dana, enough of that world. Tell me how your night with Nancy was. Jay mentioned on the train that he saw you there, at Maxwell's."

"Yeah. It was fun. I always have a good time with Nancy. And I was amazed that Jay was kind of coming on to her. Isn't he still married to Sally? Or couldn't he at least act that way in Darien? What's their story?"

"Jay's Jay. And Sally's going to move back to New Jersey. To live with her dad for a while. I think they've accepted the fact that it's a no-go. Anyway, Jay prefers life in the city."

"Whoa, that far gone, huh. And I thought everything was okay with them. You just never know." They were approaching Sherman Avenue so she slowed down for the turn, wondering now about their own feelings of separation, not sure of what she should or shouldn't say. Or even what she wanted to say. Dana took the first right onto Ledgewood and then turned into their driveway. Carson interrupted her thoughts.

"Jay said that you were thinking of going to Ft. Myers on your own. Can't Nancy go with you."

"No. She doesn't have the cash flow. And she needs to paint her apartment."

"So you're going by yourself?" A jab of annoyance took hold at the tone in his voice. It was a combination of annoyance and disbelief.

"That all depends on what Detective Hansen finds out."

"What?" he said in a louder voice. Carson resented her continuing tie with this cop.

She put the car into park, and turned to look at him in the dark.

x

Show-Down Time

<u>Lazaro's House</u> - North Stamford

Mario stood leaning against his car, tapping a crow bar against his leg, counting down the minutes. He wanted to be alert to any strange noises. Who knew what kindsa' animals lived out here. He had pulled the crow bar out of the trunk to be ready if Michael didn't open up by ten after 9:00 and he had to break in through the terrace doors. That would give him two minutes beyond the limit, which was better than what the bastard had done for him. In his other hand Mario gripped a folder with a bunch of meaningless data papers. He'd hold back on those till Michael handed over the check. If he somehow got wise to the contents, Mario would use the threat Ritzy made him memorize. "There's a hit man down the road ready to carry out this job if you don't come through with the five grand." Mario was feeling pretty anxious, but he was angry as well. In his mind Michael was getting off cheap.

His eyes were trained on the front door only five feet away. Just then the outside lights went out. Mario jumped. What's he doin'? Then he heard the door opening and his name called in a harsh whisper.

"Yeah? I'm right heah. Jesus, Michael, put the fuckin' lights on. I can't see a thing out heah."

"Just wait a second. Your eyes'll adjust. I have to get back inside fast, so come here."

"You better not be screwin' me."

"No, I've got your money; I wrote out a check. It's good, don't worry." Lazaro knew he had to placate Mario and get him out of the picture. He was sure to screw up sooner or later. "I don't know where those agents went, but they'll be back. So you've got the papers?"

Mario stepped forward carefully, listening to the gravel crunch under his feet. The folder was in his left hand. He had switched the crow bar to his right, holding it behind his leg. That way he'd be ready if Michael pulled anything. "What a total fuck-up this turned out to be," he said as he closed the gap. "You're not the only one with the heat on, y'know."

Michael cut him off. "Look! The less said, the better. Nobody ever told you to kill her! So give me the papers."

"It wasn't me! If you'da given me a chance on the phone!" He saw Michael's eyes dart left, then back again.

"Shit! A car's coming up the road! Hurry-up! Hand them over!" he commanded. Mario passed off the folder when he saw his check coming up. Michael quickly stepped back into the house and closed the door.

Mario whipped his head round, checked the road, and started running to his car parked near the end of the driveway. He watched as the headlights grew closer. It was too late to make a move out, so he stood, panting at the driver's door not wanting to trigger the interior light. He watched the headlights as the car approached and slid on by. "Hooh!" That was close. He'd get outa' this hell hole now and keep going till it was all finito, over-and-done-with.

He bounced behind the driver's seat. Okay, that was the heavy part. He didn't even have to use the threat. Great! It's done. With a sigh of relief he decided from now on everything he did would be according to the law. He buckled his seat belt, turned on the ignition, the bright lights, and slowly pulled out of the driveway. With no headlights coming toward him, he smiled his way down Pebble Run at the recommended speed limit. He'd cash the check tomorrow and book a flight. What a relief it would be to lie on a beach and drink some Bacardi.

Just before the left turn onto High Ridge, he caught the lights of a car in his rear view mirror coming out of some driveway. Then a blue light flashed from its roof as it sped up behind him. "Shit!"

He pulled over and sat still. No arm movements, he told himself trying to shove down the anger at Michael for putting him here. If he was being made the fall guy for Michael Lazaro, he'd take him down, even if it was from jail. Fuck. What's taking them so long to walk to his friggn' car? He sat waiting until a tap on his window and a hand making a rotating motion signaled the order to lower his window. "Yes, sir?"

"May I see your driver's license, please?"

"Uh, sure. Can I ask why I'm being stopped? I was

going the speed limit." Mario saw that this was no cop in uniform. Maybe Michael was right. He leaned forward and reached into his hip pocket for his wallet.

"We have an investigation going on here."

Mario took out his license and handed it over. What kinda' dumb-squat excuse was that? This was the FBI, for sure. "Somethin' happen here, on this block? I mean this road?"

"Yeah. Please get out of the car."

Now it was going too far. "Well, wait a minit'. I got my rights. You're not even wearin' a uniform. How do I know you're not some robber or somethin' - makin' out like you're the police?"

The Agent reached up and turned a lapel presenting his FBI badge.

"Okay, okay, but I ain't done nothin' and I'm supposed to be back in the city. I'm meeting someone."

"Just keep quiet and get out of the car." He flicked on a flashlight and trained it on the license "Mario...Bocca... negra? Is that *right*?"

Mario squeezed the door handle and pushed it open. "Please, no comments. I tell everyone it means speak no evil." He stood up and faced the agent. No smile. This guy must be a WASP.

"Just turn around and put your hands on the roof. We want to check your car."

"So you got probable cause? Or a warrant?" Mario was irritated now, but he caught himself. Everything according to the law. That's what he had decided, so he changed his tone. "It's just that I'm in a hurry, ya' know?"

"You ran out of the Lazaro house carrying something in your hand."

Oh, man. He put his hands on the roof. They must've been watching from somewhere close by that whole time. So Michael *was* right. He watched the Fed's partner come up the other side of the car and open the passenger door. The light blinked on as he leaned in, reached around the floor on the passenger's side and pulled out the crow bar.

"What's this for, Mario?"

"Nothin', I swear! I was just bein' careful. I get spooked comin' out here. It's all so dark..." Mario was scuffling his feet. He knew he sounded ridiculous.

The first Agent cut him off, "Stay still! You aren't going anywhere yet, so stand tight." He turned to his partner. "Go check him out, okay? I'll see if there's anything else here." He patted down Mario. In one jacket pocket his hand swept over something that felt like a cell phone. He pulled it out. "I'll just hang on to this for now." Then he instructed Mario to pull his pants pockets out. "What were you doing at the Lazaro house?'

All Mario could think about was the check and where he'd put it - in his jacket pocket, he thought, the right side. He reached under his jacket and put his hands into his pants. "I got some change in this one."

"Just hand it over to me. Mario scraped up the change and started to turn around. "No! Put your hands back on the roof. Answer my question."

Mario turned again and placed his left hand back onto the roof. With his right, he emptied the change into the Fed's extended black glove. "Uh, what?" He was stalling for time, worrying now, trying to decide who was going to give him the most trouble down the line - these Feds or Michael. A cold wind blew against his face making his eyes water. Then he remembered his vow,

'Everything according to the law'.

"You heard me. What were you doing at the Lazaro house?"

"He's my cousin. I came out here to get some money he owes me." Despite the cold he could feel sweat sprouting on his forehead and under his arms.

"Have you ever been arrested, Mario?"

"No..." And then he checked himself. "Well, maybe a driving offense. Nothing too..." He was shivering now and irritated. "Jesus. Do I have to stand out here to answer these questions? I didn't commit any kinda' crime here. I got my rights, ya' know."

The other Agent stepped out of the Suburban and called out, "Jack, I got it."

"Okay Mario, I'm gonna' let you sit in your car to get warm. But in the back seat. Just don't try anything cute." He opened the car door and Mario slid in, relieved to feel some heat. He sat there with his arms clutched over his chest, worrying about how he'd get this stupid rental back if they arrested him. What did they have on him though? Nothing. Anger switched to dread and back again. He stared out the front window at the sky looking for the moon, or at least a star. Nothing. It was as black out here as death row. He jumped at the sound of his door opening.

"C'mon out." Mario swung both legs around and pushed himself out and stood up. "First of all, you told us a lie. You were arrested only days ago on suspicion of murder.

"Wait!" Mario yelled, "That's not the way it was! I was just questioned about a gun I used to own. They let me go!" Mario's face was turning into a map of desperation.

"Now *listen* to us, Mario. You can do one of two things: you can do us a favor and answer some questions at the Darien station. They're going to let us use their building. One of us will drive your car down there. *Or*... we've got enough to arrest you for suspicious activity, which means we take you into the city ourselves. If that's what you choose, you'll be paying the tow charge back to the Bronx." He paused as Mario stared into his chest. "Which will it be?"

Parking lot at Silvio's Restaurant

"Honey, listen. I wanna' see you again. For sure. But I can't go with ya' t'night. See? It's 'cuz I got this..."

"Got this what? Are you taking me for a ride, Clio?" Nick swung his arm around Clio's waist and pulled her in close.

" Whoops." She lost her balance and stumbled over the gravel, pulling him sideways.

"Sorry," she giggled. "I musta' had a few too many. No, really. I promised my sister that I'd meet her at the Hyatt later t'night. Yeah, around..." Clio righted herself and for emphasis added, "That's who I was talkin' to earlier at the bar. Maybe you saw me."

"Baby, I just saw you take down that pasta like you were comin' off a fast. But you didn't look too happy with whoever it was you were talkin' to. What's the deal? You got a boy friend?"

Clio pushed her hands against his chest. "NO, silly. I just was mad about somethin' she said. Girl stuff." He let go of her and she fell forward.

He caught her at one elbow, "Hey, you better let me take you to the hotel. You're in no shape to drive."

She pulled herself up again and looked into his eyes,

"Ya' think so?"

"Yeah, I think so. C'mon. You can always get a cab back here tomorrow to get your car." Nick led her to his prized Chevy Camaro and guided her into the passenger seat. He had bought it in '02, their last year. They drove smoothly through back roads heading for I-95, with the sweet clarity of Chris Botti's jazz trumpet playing them along. Clio snuggled into the heated bucket of her seat and passed out. Nick looked over and chuckled to himself. He hoped she'd come to by the time they got there. It was only a twenty minute drive.

*

"Perk up, Chicken. We're here." Clio felt something shaking her shoulder and a strange deep voice urging her to "come on", more than once.

"Huh? Where are we?" She looked up at this man's face, trying to put together where she'd seen him.

"At the Hyatt. Isn't that where you said?" He took hold of her arm and eased her up. "We'll go in here and find you a room. Or do you already have a reservation?"

"Hunh-uh."

"I thought so. Come on sweetheart, the night is still young." They walked up the steps and into the lobby. The lights were too bright. Clio squinted her eyes against the glare of glass and marble. At the reservation desk Nick said, "This lady would like a room for the night."

"Yes, sir. And Ma'am will that be a single or a double?"

Clio struggled with this decision. She turned her gaze from the clerk to the man on her left and back. "Please, a signal. I mean a single." Both men smiled.

"He just wants your credit card, honey. Do you have it

155

with you?"

"Course." She fumbled through her bag for her card holder. "Here. See?" and handed it to the clerk. They progressed through the data collecting, and he handed the key card to Clio.

"Have a nice evening. The elevators are to your left and behind that wall there."

A thin blade of unease began to cut through the boozy blur as Clio turned in their direction, "Well, goodnight."

"I'll just see that you find your room all right, Clio." He was whispering in her ear with his arm around her shoulder. They started walking.

She knew that she had wanted to stay at a hotel. She remembered that, and she remembered an argument with Michael. Oh, and then this man. He was the one sitting at the end of the bar. Now she was with it. They reached the elevators and he pushed the up button. Then he turned and pulled her warmth tight against his body, planting a firm kiss on her mouth. His tongue slid its way in and probed below her own.

This was not unfamiliar territory for Clio; the action had just been absent for several years. Her mind was moving faster now. What was at stake here? Would Michael find out? More than that, did he even care? Nick pulled away as the elevator door slid open with a ding. He looked into her face. She liked what she saw.

On the fifth floor they walked down the corridor marked 500-540. Clio was walking with a wave-like motion but under her own power. "I guess I really tied one on tonight. Um, I know I should be remembering your name and all, but... Lemme' see if these things work right." She pushed the key card in. A green button flashed. "Hey!" She smiled up at him and pushed the door open.

He caught her up and swooped her past the closet and bathroom heading straight for the bed. "Whee! Baby!" she giggled. They fell with a whomp onto a plush, white comforter, and he grabbed her face to lay a deep one on her. "Hold on a minit'," she cried out. Then rolled to one side and started unfastening an earring. "Just wait a second, will ya'? I hate these big digger things. They get in the way. Whad'ya say your name is?" She sat up and pulled out one ear ring, then kicked off her heels.

"Nick," he told her. He reached up to her other ear. "Here. I'll help with the other one."

Clio pulled back, looking at him, amazed. "You do this kinda' thing?"

"Sweetheart, I'd like to help you with it all."

She smiled and bounced once on the bed like a ten year old. "Know what? If you can hum a sexy tune, I can undress for ya' real nice. All by myself. But first I gotta' get a drink 'a water. I'm too thirsty."

Nick shook his head again, smiling. What a crazy chick this one was. He pulled himself back to a sitting position against the pillows. Christ, there were more pillows to get rid of in these damn places. He threw three stiffies on the floor and settled back. He kicked off his shoes. A faucet was chugging in the bathroom and then he heard the toilet flush. Soon the door opened and there she was on tip-toe with raised glass in hand.

"Let's hear it, Nick!"

"Da-duh-duh, da-duh-duh. Da-duh-duh, da-du-duh - Dunh!"

"You gotta' be kiddin'. Is that all you know?"

He nodded. "Fraid so. I'm not much of a singer."

"That's all right. We'll both sing. Da-dah-dah, da-da-

157

dah," and he joined in, happily anticipating her first move. Clio set her water on the desk and smiled, singing,"Ba-bah-bah..."

She started with both hands on hips, rocking. Gradually her hands pressed forward across her stomach and upward, smoothing the puckered gathers across and over her breasts. Lifting her arms overhead, she waved them back and forth, like Nick had seen them do a dozen times on "American Idol". She crossed them and bowed forward, then down past her knees. Back and forth her hips swayed as she delicately caught the hem of her dress between her thumbs and index fingers and slowly raised it up past her waist and to her breasts. There, her dress caught for a moment.

Nick observed that she had left the black leg hose in the bathroom. On view was a pair of red silk bikini panties. Not the thong type, Nick noticed, but probably better for those generously sized hips still swaying to the rhythm. He felt a hot urge swelling in his groin. With an extra tug, she hoisted her dress over her breasts and up, over her head. She threw it to the side and placed one hand on her left hip and beckoned with her other. "This is where I could use your help, Nicky."

A slight pause of quiet surprised both of them, and they dove at each other.

Back Home on Ledgewood
They sat for a moment in an awkward stand-off, which was broken by a sudden stab of shame. She shouldn't have thrown Hansen's name out like that. Getting dramatic would only worsen their situation. "Carson, we need to talk. Let's go inside and straighten out where we are." He continued to sit there saying nothing; she could

feel him steaming. Then came the sound of his door opening and an "OK". Dana followed him into the house and shed her jacket. "Would you like anything to drink?"

He dropped onto the sofa and bowed his head. "I don't understand what's going on here, Dana. You keep disappearing and then acting on things as though you're the only one involved. I know you're upset about our vacation plans and all, but..." He looked up, appealing to her more reasonable self. "Please include me." There was a small pause as one hand came off his knee, palm facing up. "I've never seen you like this."

The concern on his face chipped into the protective wall she had been hiding behind. She could feel her throat tighten, making it difficult to speak. Then she sank down next to him and buried her face in his shoulder. His arm came around and he pulled her close. It felt like she was coming back. "Tell me all of it," he said, and then pushed Dana away to look into her face, "and don't bolt out the door tonight, all right?" He was smiling, so she did too.

She took a deep breath and let it out slowly. "So much has happened this week. I hardly know where to begin. And you've been so busy..."

"Let me ask first about this Detective Hansen and how you got so involved in this case. Why does he have any say over your plans for Florida?"

Dana described all three meetings: the first interview with Detective Frampton last Sunday, the second at the train station showing Hansen what she had seen the night of the murder, and then about the audio files he asked her to listen to. Carson paid quiet attention the whole way through and then he stood up, shaking his head a little. She waited.

"So much of this is difficult to take in. I mean these

audio files you listened to...Did you really think this was the man from the train station, or did his voice just sound similar?"

"It's interesting that you would ask, because I get less sure as time passes. There was just something very familiar and threatening about it." Her mind was shifting all over. "You see I was excited at the time...being able to help out, but... and this is important - Detective Hansen stressed confidentiality so strongly that I didn't even think I should tell you. Anyway, you seemed so preoc- cupied at the time. And then you haven't been home for the last three days."

The phone ringing startled both of them. "Who the hell could that be? It's going on ten o'clock." Carson started for the phone.

"Wait a minute! Don't pick up. I want to hear if there's a message." He turned toward her, a puzzled look on his face. "I'll tell you why in a minute; just wait." After two more rings her greeting came on and then dead air. They both held still, waiting. Then came the click of a hang- up. "Again! Carson, this is the third time that's hap- pened today. There were two blank messages when I got home and now this one - before going to the train tonight. When the phone rang I picked up and kept asking 'Hello, who is it?' but there was only the sound of breathing on the other end. It really creeps me out."

"Well honey, maybe it's one of your students...who's madly in love with you." He smiled a little and then offered an alternative. "Or maybe a different one trying to give you a hard time."

This was something that hadn't occurred to her. "I... I didn't think of that. I suppose that's one explanation." She pushed her glasses to the top of her head and brushed her hand over her eyes... so tired. "What keeps bothering me is that somehow the man in the wool cap, the killer, got our number and is trying...oh, I don't know. I'm so consumed with this whole thing." She sank back into the sofa, "One thing I know. We've got to get caller-ID."

Carson sat back down, next to her and took hold of her hand. "Okay. We'll do that tomorrow. But Dana, I'm more concerned that you're getting too wrought up over this."

This made her mad. "How can you say that! You're the one who wanted me to go to the police in the first place. Then you back off because of ...I guess because of orders from Westerly to keep clear of any mention of Comp-Coordinates...which in my view is just stupid."

Carson interrupted, "I know, I know. But you told me that the police found a gun, so it looked to me like they were going somewhere on the case and having you get involved wasn't as impor..."

She cut him off. "But now I'm in the midst of all these expectations - from you...and from Detective Hansen. On top of that I'm supposed to keep it all secret." Dana threw herself hard against the back of the sofa and her glasses flew off the top of her head, onto the floor.

"I'll get them, Dana. Sit still." He got up and went around behind her. "Here," he said handing them back, "You don't want to be an eye witness who can't see."

She smiled as she remembered. "Detective Hansen calls me his ear-witness."

Carson gave a short chuckle, "Well let's hope for your sake they clear this case soon and you don't have to use those ears in court." He sat back down and picked up her hand again. "Let's decide right now to call this whole past week a disaster of bad timing and start over. That okay with you?" She nodded. "Here's where I am on all of this. If the police make headway on their own, good. If you are called in again, or if the media gets a hold of your name somehow, I'll just have to tell Westerly you did what you needed to do. Media-Tech will have to stand on its own business merit. I've got a lot to do there yet; maybe I'll have to work some of this weekend, but I'll try to get home at night. I don't want you to be alone here. Boy, they better appreciate this."

All the accumulated tension in her body began to flow out. It felt like she was melting. "Thank you," she said and then said it again. They sat there in the quiet, sharing a moment of retrieved intimacy. "And if it's all right with you, I'd like to change the way we meet at the station, so that I don't sit there, waiting in the dark."

"Sure, babe. Whatever works. I can walk down to Starbuck's or wherever you like. Now one last question. You booked tickets, but for when, Saturday?"

Oh, God. She'd forgotten about that little masquerade. Now the great, bold Dana was going to show her scummy side. "I have a confession to make, Carson." He turned his head to face her, on the alert for something bad. "I didn't really book them; I just acted like I did so that the police wouldn't try to hold me in town."

Carson dropped his head into one hand and covered his eyes. She sat there waiting for the sermon to begin. But then his body started shaking in silent laughter. "You are one conniving woman."

"But I still want to go!" She practically yelled.

Carson leapt up, turned, and grabbed her by both arms. He said, pulling her to her feet, "Come here woman. I have some distracting intimacy I wish to express."

162

Later that Night - Darien Police Station

"Just sit tight, Buddy, we'll be putting you up for the night." Mario looked up at a young cop in uniform who grinned and said, "Nice of us, huh?"

What a fuckin' wise-ass this one was. Mario was so low at this point that he almost felt like crying. He was sitting in a crappy holding room, gnawing over another bust. What a royal screw-up this whole Lazaro job had been.

And who could've guessed that the FBI was communicating with local cops nowadays. He used to think it was a non-item, but apparently they'd started some kind of "get-along" policy, probably because of 9/11. So they checked his record from way out there on Pebble Ass Road. With computers! Even in their cars! Mario shook his head. And now they're back on the gun thing.

Shit! What else could he do to prove that the gun wasn't his anymore. They had nothing else on him. Was he the only putz around who wasn't a criminal? To be that close and then to have everything turn on him. Was every lousy fuck gonna' get off but him? He was asking himself now just how far protecting for family should go. He wondered if cops had somehow traced the gun back to Sal, who was not one of Mario's favorites. Sal was about as loyal as a tom cat. That summer night when they agreed on a price for the gun he remembered worrying about Sal's check for 300 bucks, whether it would be good. Turned out okay. Anyways, he's doing time now, and he doesn't know anything. Well, he wasn't going to take the rap for something he didn't do. But he didn't want Ritzy to get caught either. Not his longtime pal... ever since third grade.

He thought back on that night when they were still sophomores in high school. What a high that was. Ritzy hot-wired that Jag and they'd ripped it around the 'hood' for a joy ride. If Ritzy hadn't taken the wheel after the beer stop at 7/11 they'd never have lost those cops. Mario was still pretty new at driving. He'd never have had the confidence to go that fast.

But now. Jeezus, he better be lying low. How could he have screwed up so bad? For two whole days Mario had waited for Ritzy to get back to him. Nothing. And then he learns she's dead. From the radio, no less. Never an explanation. Next comes that stupid text message, "job done - pay time." Yeah, nice work, Ritzy. What, in Christ's name, went wrong at that train station? Mario thought again; maybe it was better not knowing. He'd kept that other message pretty short too, the one explaining how to handle Lazaro.

And he expects to get half the cut, even after screwing up. This bothered Mario a little. Bad enough to have to force the money from Michael. Still and all, Ritzy's idea of threatening to use those papers against Lazaro...that was good. It had given him the extra clout.

Mario reached into his pocket to feel the boost of confidence that little piece of paper gave him - five grand, not six - but it wasn't a clean job. He thought about Ritzy's cut again and decided he might make some changes. But maybe not. With him, it was a point of honor. Because Ritz was the only guy... at this thought Mario's throat choked up...The only goomitch who'd ever shown him any real kindness. As soon as he got out of this hell hole he'd find a shack on some beach far away and invite Ritzy down for a couple days to celebrate.

Some creep in another cell coughed loudly and then

hocked one up. Mario half smiled. They got low class here? In Darien? He let out a big sigh. When were these Johnny Laws gonna' decide to do their questioning anyway? They still had his wallet and cell phone. Jeezus!

Suburban
State of Affairs

<u>Thursday Morning - Feb. 8th</u> - Ledgebrook Drive

Their phone rang twice before Carson came to. "Who could that be?" he mumbled. "It's not even six o'clock." He rolled to his other side and dragged the pillow over his head.

"Could only be school, at this hour." Then Dana hesitated, wondering if maybe it was that same creep, the breather. The phone rang a third time.

A muffled command came from under his pillow. "Answer it, Dana."

"Hello?" and then she heard a recorded voice announce that it was the Darien schools and..., "Yeah, OK, thanks," she responded like a fool to no one and hung up. Mmm, a chance to drift. She scrunched back under the covers. "It's a delayed opening. Winter storm is coming. Maybe schools will close." Remembering last night's love fest, she circled her arms round Carson's back and chest pul-

166

ling him close. Then she started rocking him back and forth.

"Lemme' alone." He was mumbling. She kept it up. "Lemme' alone," he said louder. "Are you nuts?" All of a sudden he threw off his covers and dived on top of her using both hands to hold her arms down. "Listen woman. You do as I say, ya' hear? Otherwise you're gonna' get one a' Carson's big pokes."

She couldn't help giving him a big smirk. "You don't have the stuff it takes, pardner."

"Oh yeah? Well, try this on for size." He shoved his groin against her and growled, "I don't, huh."

"That's just an ole territorial hard-on. Hardly worth pissing." The phone rang again.

"Shit." He looked out the window. "There's not one flake in the sky. What a sissy-ass school system." They both reached for the phone, but he beat her to it. "Yeah, hello?" Carson turned toward her, "Just a minute, Nancy," handed it over, and popped out of bed.

"Hi Nance," Dana said into the phone, wondering why she sounded so sparky this early in the morning. When Carson came out of the bathroom he was all combed and spruced.

"What did Nancy want?"

"She asked if I was going in at the regular time to catch up on stuff. She offered me a ride in case you want to take our car. Isn't that nice?" Carson was heading over to his chest of drawers where he pulled out a fresh shirt and started on the cardboard insert. This meant he was getting an early start into the city. So much for their wrestling match.

"Yeah, she's a good lady. So you won't have to come out tonight in this invisible snow storm to pick me up, right?" He stood there buttoning and grinning. Dana threw her feet to the floor and stood up. "Do you want anything for breakfast?"

"No. I should be able to catch the 6:37 if I get out of here in five minutes. What time is Nancy coming to pick you up?"

"Don't know yet. I'm supposed to call her back."

"That reminds me, honey. Go ahead and sign up for caller I.D. We can take a crimp in some other area of the budget. I want to be home tonight, like I said, but if this new monster snow storm should throw a wrench...he stood a moment, his fingers in mid-button, "turn on the radio, will ya'? I want to hear the weather."

Dana flicked their clock radio on, "New Canaan, New Fairfield, Newtown, Norwalk..." she turned it off. "They're just listing all the school districts that are de-layed. You can listen on your way to the station."

She watched him drive off and then called Nancy to say she'd be ready whenever she wanted to come by. Things were looking up, it seemed. Dana told herself to keep thinking positively. Was it only yesterday that she had listened to those audio tapes? It seemed days ago. Well, if they're of value to Hansen, good. If not, then better for her. This time, she promised herself *not* to mention her police visit to Nancy.

The view out their bedroom window was still frosted in white from the remnants of last week's snow, but all was quiet with not a flake in sight. This would provide great cause for Nancy to ride the system. Both of them were raised in upstate NY where people would laugh their heads off at a school delay based on bare ground. She smiled thinking of her brother when he got his driver's permit. Terry learned to drive through all that snow when he was sixteen and then taught her by whirling through unplowed parking lots at ten o'clock at night. The most fun was spinning those donuts. If Mom and Dad ever knew this stuff they'd have been beaten alive.

Dana sat down on the bed half dressed, thinking that she must call them again soon. That Thanksgiving when Terry "came out" with his partner was worse than awkward. It was painful. Dana shuddered to think about it. Even though Terry told her she'd been the crucial buffer and the one who managed to get everyone through the holiday, none of them would want a repeat. There had to be some way to change Mom and Dad's thinking. It's been more than a year now. How long does it take for parents to accept what makes their children happy? Dana stood up and turned to spiff up the bed remembering the last time she called home. Mom had started crying when Dana brought it up and then she said, "Your father refuses to discuss it." If only they could somehow break through that wall of prejudice.

Well! They love Carson. That's a relief. Dana pulled on a pair of velvet jeans and her light weight boots, just in case, and put on some coffee. She was gazing out the kitchen window when Nancy's car pulled into the driveway. As soon as she opened the door Nancy boogied in and started crowing over their morning bonus.

"Whoooeee! Weather man says maybe six inches. We just might get the whole day off, baby." She swooped around to Dana's back and gave her three quick, two-handed pats. Then with head high, feet astride, and hands on hips, she stood, waiting.

"Take off that jacket, girl," Dana commanded. "Let's celebrate with some coffee and bagels before going in, huh?"

"Good idea. And we won't leave here till we see the first flake. Deal?"

"Deal!"

Nancy hung her jacket over the chair and pulled one leg over the top of it to sit down. "Hey Dana. When's the next hockey game? We might get called into action again."

"Oh, brother. Make sure you never tell Carson about me trying to break up that fight in the parking lot." Dana poured some milk in a little pitcher. "Once we were walking down Amsterdam Avenue in The City, and I ran toward two hoodies. They were starting to push on each other. Carson screamed at me to get out of there. I don't know. It's some kind of instinct I have. He gets real upset."

"Jeez, Dana. Yeah, I agree with him. That could be dangerous. So hey, how are things going for you and Carson, anyway? Is he still working non-stop?"

"Yeah, pretty much." Dana poured the coffee and passed over Nancy's plate with bagel. "He was able to get home last night though. Late, but we had a good talk. If he can get this job done we might still be able to get away for a few days, probably not this weekend, but still."

Nancy nodded her head, bit into her bagel, enjoying a long chew and then swallowed. "Seriously though. You really got me into hockey. Is there another game tomorrow night, or Saturday?"

"I'm not sure; we can check at school."

"My God, what a night that was! I had no idea hockey could be so exciting. Really Dana, I'm glad you convinced me to go."

Dana pictured the ice rink where they'd been watching

the hockey game from Dana's favorite spot, standing right behind the protective glass, only a few feet from the Stamford goal. To be right on top of the action, to see the skaters racing toward their end and then feel them bang against the glass when they fought over the puck was Dana's idea of action. This one had been a crucial game. Darien's win over Stamford, 2 to 1 could put them into the play-offs.

She remembered how loud the crowd was. "I had to shout even though you were standing right next to me. Those kids were really ripped and out for blood, weren't they? I don't think one person was sitting in his seat." She turned to grab two napkins from the counter top. "First it was that slap shot, the one that swept high." Dana felt a secondary thrill just recalling it.

Nancy's eyes brightened. "God! The puck slammed so hard against the shield; we both had to duck. And then their gloves dropped and the fight broke out. The players were right there, practically on top of us. I still don't know who started that fight. It was so fast, what with trying to follow the puck."

"Yeah. Then came that burst of shouting from the bleachers. I remember someone yelling, 'He's kneeing him!' Over and over again. What an uproar. We couldn't even locate those guys in the stands, could we. Not until the security men started pushing through the crowd. Dana set her cup down and sat back. "It was a good thing they broke up that ruckus. I was afraid the whole crowd was getting a little wild."

"Yeah, and even getting out of the rink, with everyone smashed together and exclaiming over the game. One guy said he thought Darien had the game for sure when the third period started. He made some comment about

171

Stamford's sucky offense the first two periods and how pissed they were missing that last goal."

Dana nodded her head. "And remember that other guy? The one on my side yelling about how fuckin' lousy the reffing was?"

"Well, it's just a good thing Stamford didn't get their shot off those last few seconds before the end."

"Yeah. If they had, there'd have been some real trouble. I heard this one kid. These were his words. He said, 'What a shame security pulled Fenwick off that turd.'"

Nancy bit into her bagel with eager pleasure. "I'll bet Carson wishes he'd been there instead of watching a stupid basketball game with his friends."

"Probably. Have you seen the Knicks play this year?" Nancy shook her head. "*Bad!*"

"Really. But Dana, after the game, when you went over to the parking lot. Were they actually down on the ground punching each other?"

Dana chewed and then swallowed. She turned her head to one side recalling with some unease, how she'd wound her way through the cars toward those shouts and threats, "Don't shove me!" and "Fuck off, man!" But it was the adult voice from the other side of the commotion that had disturbed her. He was urging on a fight. His voice was deep and certainly not from around here. "Get'im, Jimmy! Get'im! You can beat the shit outa' him!" Dana hated it when adults egged kids on like that, and she yelled at him across the mob to stop it, but he'd kept it up. She was about to lose it when she heard him again, "Break 'is fuckin' ass! He's just anudah Dairy-Land dyke!" When she got close enough to actually see, two boys were down on the ground pounding each other. She called down in a firm voice for them to stop it, stop the fighting. Then she shouted into the crowd toward the jerk that he should stop it too. What she got through the darkness was, "Stay outa' this, Skirt!"

Fortunately, that's when four men cut through the crowd and managed to break it up, allowing Dana to find Nancy, and then go on to Maxwell's to meet Carson. "It was a fight all right. I'm really glad you looked for help Nancy; otherwise, who knows what would have happened?"

How close had she come to making a really dumb mistake? She'd heard a year ago that one of the women teachers at school tried to break up a fight in the halls. She got knocked down hard and came away with a lingering back injury. Dana hadn't told Carson about this latest folly of hers. If only Dana knew how much her interference would plague her in days to come, she would never have gone near the fight that night.

"Know what I heard?" Nancy wiped her mouth with the napkin. "After all the local buzz over the fighting that went on at that game? " Her eyes caught Dana's. "You know it's all the kids talked about in the school halls. Anyway, they're thinking of scheduling big rivalry games for after school instead of at night. I think it's so they don't come in all beered up and ready for a brawl. Good idea, huh?"

"Yeah, that sounds reasonable. Not as exciting maybe, but reasonable."

Nancy grinned, spreading her arms in a big stretch as she eased back in her chair. She dropped back down. "Anything new you know of in *the case*?"

"No. It's been pretty quiet." She practically interrupted herself with the next question. "Hey. You never told me

173

how late you stayed at Maxwell's Tuesday night. What did you think of Jay?"

"Well, he's attractive. But you know, in a salesman kind of way. Lots of enthusiasm, energy, and those guys love to look like they're listening to you when they're just wondering if they're gonna' score." She paused a minute. "It was fun, but...I don't know. Maybe I'm just too fussy. He suggested we 'carry on'. I left about 10:30. I don't think he'll call me."

"Well, Nancy? You're probably better off not getting involved with Jay. I think he's a player." Several snow-flakes drifting past the window caught Dana's eye. "Oh-ho! Look outside. I think it's snowing." They both got up to look out the window. It was pretty sparse, but it had definitely started. "Plus, he's still married. Carson bets he'll be moving back into the city soon, where there's more action."

"Know what? He's right. Everyone in this land of suburbia is married. Maybe I'll save up for a singles getaway or one of those Club Med vacations." They talked that scene while they finished with breakfast and poured coffee to go. Dana was thinking of the one single man she'd met recently. Maybe Nancy should have a look at one of Darien's law enforcers.

"All right." She said, "We're outa' here. Are you gonna' correct papers or what?"

"Yeah, and I just got a new idea for class I want to write up. It's a role-playing thing. Get the kids to pretend they're down in Caracas or maybe Bogota and get them to use a little conversational Spanish. I'd have the guys take turns trying to pick up a 'Spanish speaking girl who no habla ingles."

"Good one!"

"Oh, another thing, Dana. I just remembered. You know the health fair that was supposed to be held today? It'll probably be scheduled for tomorrow, which is actually better. The custodians will have more time to get all those tables arranged in the gym and we won't have to use our free periods to set up the booths. "Nice?"

"More good stuff, Nance. I'd forgotten all about the health fair. It runs through D and E periods, right? You know, having it on the last day before vacation is much better. The kids never want to work then anyway. And, to be honest, we just play act through each class, faking enthusiasm." They suited up for the wintry blasts and headed out the door. "Hey, I feel like we're starting vacation right *now*. Let's roll, girl!"

Hyatt Regency - Around 7:30

She felt cold around her shoulders. Clio rolled to her left side to pull the comforter up, and touched a bare arm. She reached around until she found the edge and yanked it, but it was yanked back. She frowned and opened her eyes a fraction. Then a little more. Pale light filtered in through the window. She found herself staring at a large naked back. This wasn't Michael. Her mind raced to last night. Oh that guy...the one at the bar! She lay there listening to his even breathing. What a quiet sleeper, not at all like Michael with all his grunting and snuffling. This guy, what's his name - oh, yeah Nick. He brought her here last night. But in whose car?

She lay there trying to recover events in their proper sequence. That gap between Silvio's and this hotel bothered her. And then she felt a small wave of fright. Ending up here might mean that her life had turned a bad corner. If Michael found out about this, it would be risky.

175

Except that on the phone he made it sound as though he didn't care if she came home again. She felt a lingering cut of anger. His stupid "shut-out" wouldn't last though, would it? A part of her believed that he was just tensed-up and acting that way on account of the company thing. She remembered him saying something about Hathaway getting called back in. Things might cool down and then he could go back to work. Yeah, he said it would when the investigation was over. There was a lot at stake here - millions. She wondered what kind of protection she had with their pre-nup. He could maybe lose a lot of money. She'd better find it and read it again.

Clio felt him shifting his weight. She wanted to figure a plan before he woke up. It would probably be best to treat it all lightly and give him a friendly good-bye. She looked at her ring finger. It was still bare, but in the morning light she could see where it made its pale indentation. Well, so what. It might not make any difference to this guy, one way or another. She could always say she was married and their night was a mistake.

He was shifting again. Then a mumbled, "Hey baby…" He rolled over. "Come over here," and he pulled her in close. His voice was deep and warm. "That was nice last night, huh?"

"Yeah, honey. Very nice. Do you know what time it is?"

"Why? What's your hurry? He gave her a warm kiss under her ear. We could just get cozy here and maybe ..." He left it unsaid. His free hand gently ran up her thigh and over her hip to her waist.

Clio slid her feet over the side of the bed. "Don't you have to go to work or something? I've gotta' go." She turned back. "Hey, did we come here in my car or yours?"

"Mine. Don't worry. I'll take you back to get yours, but what's your big hurry?"

She was already out of bed and scooping up some underwear from the floor. "I'll make us some coffee when I come out," and she closed the bathroom door behind her. Nick hooked his fingers together behind his neck and looked up at the ceiling. This chick was a hot one. He'd want to see her again. Okay, so he wouldn't rush anything. He'd ask for her phone number, see if she liked the idea of getting together again. Then take the next step.

When she came out of the bathroom, he was halfway dressed and standing next to the desk peering at the directions on the coffee pot. His chest was broad and he had big muscular arms. She noticed he wore a silver bracelet; maybe it was titanium. Links in the shape of iron crosses connected in a circle around his wrist. No tattoos. Whatever he did for a living must keep him in shape. "Okay, bathroom's free. I'll make the coffee, honey." She slipped by him and took the coffee pot from his hand.

Nick shrugged his shoulders. "Okay, be out in a minute." He scooped up some change and the keys to his car and dropped them into his pants pockets. "I don't want you runnin' off on me." He gave her a smile and a wink.

Nick was beginning to think that she might give him the brush, what with her brisk, business-like manner. When he came out of the bathroom, she was waiting near the door, with a paper coffee cup in hand and a coat hanging over one arm. Their conversation during the drive felt a bit stilted. Just about the weather and other generalities. They were soon within a mile of Silvio's, and snow was falling faster. Now she was saying something about needing to meet her sister. He'd think of something, though. Chicks liked to play hard to get; he knew that, but most all of them eventually caved. Nick's magic with women was part of his slick reputation. He was smooth and confident, also a little scary. This last was applied for the purpose of enhancement in bedrooms.

Clio was trying to keep this man's appeal in line. What a body! The last time she remembered being turned on to a man's body was years ago. And he had a kind of velvety manner. Nothing he'd said or done so far had put her off. They were going up Long Ridge now, driving past some big houses similar to her own. Her mind jerked back to reality. She would keep all personal questions to a minimum; it would be her safest avenue.

"So Clio, do you go to Silvio's much?"

"Not too much."

Ordinarily Nick didn't go that far north for a drink, but different locales was part of his new regime. "Yeah, I haven't been there much either. I mean will I see you there again sometime?"

"Maybe. I don't know." This wasn't going anywhere. He tried something safer. "How's the food there?"

"Really good." Her voice perked up. "You've gotta' try their veal scalloppine."

"I will." If she was into Italian food, he'd go there. "Sometimes I like to cook up a good dish of spaghetti and meat balls for dinner. Some garlic bread, a salad, and top it off with a bottle of Ruffino Chianti." Her head swiveled toward him, eyes wide. He turned toward her, smiling. "I like only the best Chianti. Not all the time, but for special occasions." He slowed down seeing Silvio's ahead on the left. "I sure would like to fix that for you sometime..." He waited for a response as he turned into the parking lot. The only car there was her Beemer, parked at the far end, with only a light covering of snow. He pulled up next to it. "How 'bout it?"

"You've been awful sweet, but I have a lot going on right now." Clio was looking for the car keys in her handbag. She pulled them out and turned his way. "Thanks honey," and gave him a kiss on the cheek.

"Wait a minute. At least give me your phone number. This is too good a thing. You can't just leave." He could see her hesitating. "If I wasn't so damned attracted to you, I'd never push like this."

"Okay. But don't call right away. I gotta' straighten some things out."

He quickly reached over and opened the glove compartment to pull out a pen and note pad. He handed them to her, and she wrote her number down. Right off, she opened the door and stepped out, dropping the pad and pen onto the seat, then flipped the door shut. Nick picked up the pad, looked at it, and then pushed the button to lower the passenger window.

"Hey, what's your last name, Clio?" She just smiled and turned her back to open the driver's door to her Beemer. Nick watched her slide in and the door slam shut. Oh well. He'd find that out later. And more. He sat there a moment picturing Clio at his place doing another strip dance for him. He'd have the right music ready next time.

Clio sat back and closed her eyes a minute. She was thinking about where she should go first. She could drive to her fitness center and kill an hour or so. No, she'd check in with Gemma first. She turned the key part way in the ignition to look at the clock - 8:20. So much had happened since yesterday. She wanted to get Gemma's take on Michael and this whole shitty Comp thing. Where had she put her copy of the pre-nup? Clio admitted to herself that the off-hand way she managed business matters might give her trouble some day. Well, she couldn't go home now and look for it. Michael was there and probably in another pissy mood. She'd test that out later in the day before deciding whether to go home or bunk in with Gemma.

She heard Nick's car wheels crunching on the stones as it backed out of its parking place. Was he sitting there all that time waiting for her to go first? He'd better not be trying to follow her. Christ! Talk about Michael getting paranoid. She watched as his Camaro pulled out of the lot and headed down toward Stamford. His name was Nick. Yeah, that was the name he told her last night. He was a smoothie. A little smile emerged. She could go back to using her maiden name. Clio Savini. It sure sounded a lot better than Lazaro. With a renewed lift to her spirits, she peered into the rear view mirror. She'd go to Gemma's and after that do a work-out at Body Sound. A little shiver ran through her. This chiffon dress would never work today. She'd borrow some jeans and a sweater from her sister, maybe go buy some kick-ass boots.

Hathaway Estate

Marion gazed across the kitchen seeing nothing, both hands holding a coffee cup that was vaguely warm. She hadn't slept well at all. Her mind was turned inward, in an attempt to understand this latest mess with Gordon.

Why was she allowing herself to play the role of a patsy in her marriage? Was it her love for him or a warped sense of fidelity? She hoped it wasn't something worse, a reluctance to become an independent woman. She knew of so many women in Darien who were stuck with lousy, even abusive husbands, because they couldn't let go of a country club life style.

Marion used to have such self-confidence. She worked as the business manager for an oncology center for six years, both before and after her marriage, until Collin was born. Ever since she had contented herself with keeping the house up and raising their boys. It would have been hard maintaining a job with Gordon traveling so much. And she didn't believe in having nannies. That whole image of the suburban matron held captive by a life of luxury left her cold.

When the phone rang, she decided to let Gordon pick it up. It was probably for him anyway, at this hour. Her mind went backward in time to September '05. This was when both boys went away to school, and Marion had begun to think of discontinuing her volunteer work and rejoining the work world. All of that was canceled by Gordon's affair. It had stunned her into a kind of paralyasis. It's true that she had insisted he move out, but then she took him back, and now... Marion dropped her head - it all starts again.

A heavy inertia was holding sway somehow. She realized it was an entrenched sense of loyalty that kept her hanging on. It must have taken hold early on, probably after her older sister died and her mother had her nervous breakdown. To preserve a semblance of family, Marion became the substitute mother to the two younger ones. She was their only mainstay. Certainly

Dad was hardly there. In her experience most all sur-
geons were virtually absent from their families, with the
hours they put in. Marion sighed. He was a remote
person by nature, and with his wife consuming jars of
tranquilizers, avoidance was a way to protect himself.

She looked out the window at snow blowing from the
limb of a tree. Another day of hibernating? No, that had
to change. She should really begin to research some job
opportunities. First look for something part time, and
see how that felt. It would give her a new focus. The
sound of Gordon's footsteps coming down the stairs
broke into her reverie.

He strode briskly into the kitchen and over to her chair.
Marion looked up at his face. "That was Peter Tompkins
on the phone," he said, smiling and leaning over to give
Marion a morning kiss. "He asked if I wanted to come
back in. I told him only if Barkley wasn't there; otherwise, I might blow his face off."

"And?"

"He's arranged for Barkley to spend a few days away
from the office, 'until the investigation puts him in the
clear' is what he said." Gordon slid his eyes skyward.
"That's a good one. The official word is that he's going
to St. Louis tomorrow for a - get this, logistics management conference."

Gordon stepped across to the bay window. "My feeling
is that the Feds are off my case, as far as Paula goes.
They're concentrating on bookkeeping and tax returns.
According to what Peter said, federal law dictates that
they have to prove not only fraud but the intent to commit
it as well. I don't know how they go about proving this;
the Feds aren't saying much of anything at the moment.
It'll be too bad for Comp if they *can* prove it. He turned

around with a smile. But at least I'm out of their spot-
light."

Marion studied his expression, wondering if she could
allow herself a feeling of relief. "So do you think you
should go back this soon? I mean, shouldn't Peter say
something to the people in your department? I imagine
everyone is wondering who they can put their trust in at
this point."

"I suppose that's true." Gordon stood, pondering.
"Paula's murderer is still out there."

"Yes. What's today, the 7th?"

"This is Thursday, the 8th. She was murdered last
Wednesday. I wonder if they have any new angles on
suspects. There's been so little in the papers lately. "

He walked over to the coffee pot. "Want some more?"

"Yes, please. I haven't made anything for breakfast yet.
What would you like?"

"Don't bother with anything, honey. I'll just slice up a
banana over cereal. Did you eat anything? I'll fix two, if
you like."

This was new. Well, he was being considerate. She
said okay even though it felt strange just sitting there, "So
are you going in?"

He was standing at the counter with his back to her
getting out bowls and reaching for the cereal boxes. "I
don't know. Maybe a cooling down day would be good.
I told Peter I'd think about it. What are you going to do?'

"Oh!" Marion stood up. " I just remembered. I have to
call one of the volunteers to tell her I'll be dropping off
stuff for the health fair. She's new and doesn't know the
M.O."

"Another one already? That must be three you've done
this winter."

"Yes. It's a big reach-out...on teen dating violence. I'd better make that call right now."

Gordon thought it was good that she was getting out of the house again, doing her thing. He listened as she arranged to make a drop-off at 10:30, somewhere in Stamford. She sat back down at the table and sipped her coffee. "I'm glad you're going to get out of the house," he said, "It'll be good for you."

"I've got to face the public some time." She took a spoonful of granola. "While I'm in Stamford I'll stop at DVC." This was a domestic violence crisis organization that Marion had devoted three years and a great deal of time to. It'll be interesting to see how the crew reacts to me - their 'lady in hiding'."

He didn't know how to respond to this.

"And to see what all I have to catch up with. It's been so long. At least I was able to set up the schedule of volunteers by computer from home. It kept my mind off some of the craziness going on around here. For a little bit, anyway."

"Are you still getting satisfaction working there? You've certainly put in the hours."

"I may be winding down a bit. I was thinking it might be time to go back to a paying job. The health field is crying for more workers."

"Well sure, if you would like to make that kind of a commitment. I mean, it's not necessary for financial reasons." He added jokingly, "I think I'll still have a job."

"It's not that. It's just time for me to put myself in a more independent state of mind."

This gave him pause. "Marion, you know I'd be happy to start back again with Chandler. I thought his suggestions were helpful.   And this time I won't let work cover our lives." After a moment of silence he added, "Right now my deepest commitment is to protect our marriage."

This was nice to hear, but couple therapy amidst all this other distraction was just too much. "Let's try to get through this other mess first. I want a return to normalcy, if there is such a thing. Then we'll talk about it." They finished their cereal and Marion went upstairs to gather laundry and make the bed. She needed to maintain some distance. It felt safer and strangely appropriate.

Taking Hold

Still Thursday, 9:00AM - Darien Police Station

Steve Hansen was getting restless. When were they going to get here? He didn't think he could hold Mario Boccanera much longer without an official charge. According to the FBI write-up, Mario was at the house for less than ten minutes collecting money that he said Lazaro owed him. But if that and a crow bar found on the floor of the front seat constituted an SAR, he'd better take a revised class on police procedures. Shit, who knew what kinds of legal tricks the FBI could work. The **S**uspicious **A**ctivity **R**eport that Agent Minicus referred to on the phone was an alternative, but Hansen wondered if it would hold up in court. Especially after he accepted their offer to come in willingly. The last thing Hansen wanted was to book Mario and then lose him on technical legal grounds.

He stood up and started pacing his office, reviewing the

186

facts one more time. First, Mario is stopped by two agents on Pebble Run, he's offered the option to come in for questioning, he grants consent, but then the city boys insist on coming up and doing an "investigative detention" which isn't supposed to go over six hours. Mario probably didn't know that, but still. He sits in a cell all night ranting about his right to a lawyer. This wait was getting Hansen more agitated with each passing minute.

Too bad it was the three letter guys who'd brought him in. Now they could claim him as their perp. Hansen also worried about the FBI's notion of "cooperation" with Darien police. Everyone knew that their practice of intelligence sharing with local law enforcers was a non-event, despite the post 9/11 claims. It didn't go past him that they might charge in and take over the whole case. He hadn't told them about Dana identifying Mario's voice on the audio tape, true. But that was his baby, and he had covered every legal procedure in taking it, right down to video-taping her reactions to each sample. All, so it would stand up in court. He'd have to tell her about that if they ever took it to court. The image of her standing at the door to his office came to mind. She was an attractive, nice person. He'd thought about her a couple times outside the case. He also realized that she wouldn't like the liberty he'd taken with a camera running. Too bad there were all these restrictions placed on cops today. Was it any wonder that criminals ever got convicted? He sank back down in his chair and stabbed a pencil into the cup on his desk. At the very least he might be able to use his "ear witness" as leverage, a chip to barter with these goons in an information trade.

His phone rang. It was the front desk, "They're here."

"Good. Send them in." Hansen walked up the hall to

greet them. Yep, there they were, the entire look: business suits, Brooks Brothers shirts, ties, and always the short cropped hair. It was almost laughable, but he kept his face straight as they introduced themselves, shaking hands first with Minicus, the one he'd spoken to last night, and an Agent Dell. "Why don't we go down here and talk in our meeting room where there's more space." On the way both Agents complained about the heavy traffic on I-95 and another damn snow storm impeding progress.

Hansen gestured toward some seats around a small table. "Yeah, you'd be surprised at the amount of reverse commuting nowadays. A lot of people come up from the city for basic jobs - landscaping, table waiting. And don't forget all those nail salons - ladies." This last comment drew a couple looks askance.

Minicus was the first to speak after they took off coats and sat down. "As you probably know, Detective Hansen, we have been in the process of a formal investigation at Comp-Coordinates in a joint effort with the SEC. We've succeeded in gathering evidence pointing to insider trading. But we also carry the burden of proof. Only when it becomes clear that top management is guilty of having committed conscious wrongdoing, can we bring civil charges against the people involved." He looked directly into Hansen's eyes. "But we're close. This is all under tight cover, you understand. For the past five days we've posted a watch at the Lazaro house. He could be up for indictment in a matter of days. It will help even more if this guy Boccanera can tell us anything. Did you already allow him to make the call to his lawyer?"

"Yes, he chose a public defender who is in court right

now...in Stamford, but he can break away mid-morning. We're ready to go here. You already know I'm the one who took Mario in for questioning on the murder weapon. That was a couple days ago, when I was in the city."

"Yes. The serial number was scratched out, I recall. Your forensic people did quick work. That's what we have to do to keep ahead of these skanks. Beat them with better technology."

Dell waved his Blackberry. "Yeah, with these we can do background checks now - from almost anywhere. Really speeds things up."

Hansen nodded as though he was impressed. "Frankly, when I talked to the guy, he didn't seem to have the smarts for any savvy corporate work. He's probably..."

Minicus broke in. "We know his connection to Lazaro. They're cousins. We're up on all his background, so I think the best way to go about this is for you to let Agent Dell and me take a shot at him first, and if necessary we'll give him back to you."

Hansen saw a take-over coming and began to get edgy. Weren't these guys supposed to be doing the white collar end? He decided to put it right out there. "I thought you said last night your people were eager to cooperate. What exactly does that mean?"

Minicus leaned back in his swivel chair and tilted his head toward his partner. "We have enough goods on this guinea to press him. We want to, shall we say, utilize what we have before his lawyer gets here. You can watch everything through the one way...and let us know which techniques are working, which aren't. Agent Dell here is a trained interrogator. "

Standing outside as an observer was not the assignment

Hansen had in mind, but what could he do? They were claiming bragging rights to information Hansen didn't have. Both hands came down on the table. "I guess that's the way it's gonna' be." He pushed his chair back and rose. "I'll tell them to bring Mario into the interrogation room. Be right back." As he walked to a phone in a nearby office, he thought that maybe it was better after all, if Mario didn't eyeball him right off. Let the Feds have a go, learn what they find out, and then spring his voice ID when the chance came.

Mario felt like he could use a shower and eight hours of sleep. Finally! They were going to ask some questions and then he'd get the hell out. He hoped the lawyer he'd spoken with earlier knew his job. This room they'd brought him to was tiny, and it was completely bare except for two other chairs and a small table. One wall was taken up with a big mirror. He wondered who was on the other side watching. Jeezus, after all that time waiting last night, here he was sitting by himself, waiting again.

Finally the door opened and two guys with ties on for Christ's sake walked in. "Sorry you had to wait so long, Mario. We had to come up from the city. God-awful traffic on 95." He gestured toward his partner, "This is Agent Dell and I'm Agent Minicus. We've been told that you consented to answering a few questions we have, so let's get started."

"Yeah, but where's my lawyer."

"He'll be here Mario. You haven't been charged with anything yet, so it's not time to worry." This was a ploy Minicus was exercising under approval from a senior officer. They'd convinced their regional chief that access to an attorney might interfere with gaining evidence

important to their investigation. It was made on somewhat thin ground, but worth a go. At least it could buy
them some time. He continued, "Your name is Mario
Boccanero and you live at 1436 Jerome Avenue, Apt. 4B
in the city. Is that right?"

Mario nodded his head.

"You're a Bronx boy, huh. Lived there long?"

"Yeah, all my life."

"So last night you drove up to see your cousin. You say
he owed you some money." Again the nod. "Did that
work out for you? Did he pay up?"

Mario didn't want to talk about the check in his pocket.
He looked up, frowning, and said, "Look I'm supposed
ta' have a lawyer heah. If you guys wanna' know about
my cousin, ask him."

"We will; you can be sure of that. But understand that
it could be in your favor to give us a few answers. Your
cousin is under investigation. You probably know that
already. And you are not exactly standing on firm
ground." Minicus's voice took on a firmer tone. "We
know that a Detective Hansen brought you in two days
ago under suspicion of murder."

Mario practically leaped out of his chair. "Wait a
minute! Wait a minute! That gun he had isn't mine! I
told him that! And I didn't murder anyone. I told you
Feds that last night! They let me go!"

This pissed Hansen off. Why did they have to mention
his name? He could see Mario's resentment soaring.
Any further contact he might get with his suspect would
only aggravate him more.

He watched Agent Dell, who'd been standing near the
door, step forward and pull a spare chair around to
Mario's side of the table. Dell spoke in a soft voice, "We

know, we know." He sat down and after a moment, asked brightly, "So Mario. What kind of work do you do?" No response. "This is not a life-threatening question we're asking. Let's try again. What do you do for work?"

"I'm not employed right now."

Dell looked down at some papers. "We see here that you were asked by Detective Hansen where you were on the night of January 31st. You said you were at home watching TV, but there was no one around who can prove that's where you were. I'm wondering. Since that time, has anything or anyone come to mind who could place you there? Any phone calls? Any contacts at all?"

With his eyes to the floor Mario just shook his head. "I don't have anything more to say." Then he looked up. "I know my rights. I'm not talkin' till my lawyer comes."

Minicus took over. "We've done some homework, Mario. We know your whole history: your birth weight, your grades in high school, the names of all the guineas you hung out with in the neighborhood, the whole of it, right on up to your job at Hercules Hauling, five weeks of unemployment checks, and then the temp job you started at Comp-Coordinates on January 26th. Everything you've been up to for the past couple of weeks."

This last bit, Minicus added on, was a lie. No one had followed Mario before the Metz murder, and even though the Darien police were now holding his keys and cell phone, tracking contacts on his phone would be off limits until they'd placed a formal charge. As it stood, they didn't have enough evidence to do that.

Mario's mind was racing, along with his heart. How could they have been following me? I'da known about it. They'da already pulled me in, even before finding that gun. Shit, even that night, when she saw me following her. If she called the cops, I'da been picked up, maybe given a warning. *Some*thing.

Dell's chair squeaked as he leaned forward, "Mario, you rented a car and drove all the way out to Stamford to pick up some money Lazaro owed you. It must've been a decent amount. I mean to go to all that trouble. I want you to think hard about your situation here. You could be doing yourself a big favor by cooperating with us. Michael Lazaro owed you money. What did you do for him? Office work, a handyman job, what?" Dell waited. He looked up at Minicus and then back to Mario. "Look, you haven't been charged with murder or any other crime here. Do you understand that? And it won't matter if you worked in your cousin's accounting department. It's like I said. We can make it easier for you if you just answer a few questions." He waited for an answer. Nothing. Then Dell stood up and leaned down in Mario's face, "Are you going to be stupid enough to cover for him if you're innocent?"

Mario stared at a nick on the table top and slowly shook his head. These pricks and all their fucking history gathering. Now he was burning. Hell no! He was not going to rat on Ritzy. Or his cousin either. "I've said all I'm gonna' say. Now let me outa' here. Either that or get me my lawyer."

The two agents rose to their feet and started toward the door. "You sit there a while and think about it some more." Dell and Minicus walked out.

Outside, Hansen couldn't help but feel a small triumph. So Club Fed couldn't get Mario to talk. Maybe now was the time to put his game into play. "So he wouldn't break, huh?" Both agents looked directly at him and turned on little, sideways smiles. Placing his hands on his hips, Hansen gazed down at the floor and said, "It kind of surprised me really. I mean he's a simple sort of guy."

Agent Minicus looked steadily at Hansen. "Won't be long. Just let him sit a while."

"Yeah," Dell said, "simple all right, but with an animal loyalty. I'm thinking that he comes from the old school. Don't forget - his whole family background is Sicilian." He glanced up at Hansen and asked, "Did you see any-thing?"

"Uh well, it was looking pretty good there for a bit; he looked scared at one point, when you told him you knew about everything he'd been doing recently. There's gotta' be something he's hiding."

"Yup. And it's more than that temp work he did at Comp. You know what I think? I think Lazaro hired him to keep tabs on Paula Metz. But it just doesn't figure in my mind that he killed her. Look at his police record. Those charges are diddly-squat, starting with loitering, attempted car theft. When was that, some fifteen years ago? And in 2005 he's nabbed for issuing worthless checks. Then there's your effort on the gun Steve, which goes nowhere because he says he 'lost it last summer' and the stupid state law ruins that for us." Dell turned to his partner. "Frank...his face - did you see it? When you talked about him being under suspicion for murder...he went ballistic. I gotta' say, I've seen a lot of liars in my time, but his whole face registered innocence."

Hansen spoke up. "I don't know. I think he's lying." The conviction in his voice was firmer than he'd planned, causing an awkward silence. He quickly changed the subject. "So what's next? I think you're gonna need a formal charge here. It's going on ten o'clock. We can't keep him detained much longer. Defense will cite the police here for abuse."

Minicus looked long at the detective's face. "What makes you so convinced he's lying?"

Steve figured that waiting any longer might work against him, so he came out with it. "After I questioned Mario about the gun, I created a WAV file using voice prints from the interview video."

"Yeah? And so?"

"I have a witness who was at the train station that night. She recognized his voice."

"And *now* you're telling us about this? What the fuck is going on here?" Minicus was fuming.

"Hey!" Steve Hansen was just as mad. "You Feds come up here after making us wait all night and then take over our perp. What do ya' think?"

"Listen to me. A woman's been murdered. We need to find her killer. Now if the FBI is in a position to have the most comprehensive means of doing that, we should be the ones in charge here. Does that make sense to you? Huh? Just how many murder cases have you investigated, detective?"

Hansen didn't want to give them that answer. He felt a huge sinking sensation. He was going to lose his case.

"Now bring out that tape, if you don't mind. We might want to listen to it, to make sure it was done right." Mincus looked up at his partner, shaking his head.

"And give us the name of your witness." Dell was speaking to Hansen's back as he headed down the hall. "We could have used this earlier, you know." His voice rose with each receding step, "It could've saved us some time!"

*

195

Gemma's Apartment - After 10:00

Clio was feeling much more comfortable, now that she was dressed in Gemma's sweats and some warm, woolen socks. "Do you want another cup a' coffee?" Gemma was calling from the kitchen. "No, I'm good." What a relief to see her sister managing on her own and moving around easily. It would be five weeks now since the hysterectomy. She'd probably be able to get a job pretty soon. Then Michael would finally shut-up. Didn't he have any charity in his heart? It amazed her that rich people could be so cagey with a few thousand bucks.

Ever since last fall, when Clio had encouraged Gemma to move to Stamford and then helped her locate this little apartment, they'd grown closer. Up until then, they'd lived fairly separate lives. Four years' difference in age and living in distant cities had kept them from seeing much of each other. That and other reasons. Gemma had never approved of her older sister working at a strip joint, and Clio didn't like the creep Gemma lived with. Yeah, he was good looking all right, but what difference does that make when you live with a stupid bully?

It wasn't until she'd gotten the call from Mercy Hospital and seen Gemma's battered face that Clio understood how much of a brute Ellis really was. What a shocker that had been. She still wondered how Gemma had kept his bad ass treatment of her a secret the whole time she'd lived with him. It wasn't till they'd moved her down to Stamford that Gemma would even discuss it. That one night when she told Clio the whole crummy story, Gemma insisted afterwards that she never wanted to talk about it again.

He was just like all those bastards, Clio thought; they're all the same. They get drunk, find something to get pissed-off about, and then start beating up on their women. Gemma said a couple times she threatened to move out, but it only got him madder. He'd tell her she could never make it on her own, didn't have any skills. Was she gonna' go crying to her mommy and daddy? Well, Mom and Dad would never have let her live in peace if she'd gone home to them. Clio knew that much. Gemma finally explained why she'd never gone for help, or even mentioned it to anyone. She said it was on account of the shame.

Clio sat staring at her feet resting on the coffee table. She could understand a certain amount of the shame Gemma felt even though it had worked against her. In most ways though, the two were complete opposites. She would never allow any man to push her around. There were times when she wondered if she could ever love anyone...long term, anyway. Gemma, on the other hand, was a push-over for affection. She'd been that way all her life. Poor kid. First a busted nose and face and then in less than two months she's gotta' have a hysterectomy. "Hey, get outa' the kitchen!" Clio called, "I'll clean up in there later. I want to talk to you about Michael."

Gemma came into the living room drying a glass with a dish towel. "My mind hasn't changed. I don't think you should go back there yet. Not if he's being such a jerk. You said that yourself."

Clio nodded her head. "Yeah. I was thinking though. What if the worst happens? What if he loses his job? I mean, he might even go to jail if they convict him of fraud."

"He said that?"

"No, not the jail part, but his whole company is swarming with FBI, the Wall Street types. Right now he's worried mostly about losing his job."

"I still say let him tough it out on his own, through the weekend, anyway. It sounds from the way you talked before, like that's what he wants anyway. He hasn't called you, has he?"

"No."

"So there."

"I guess I'm just curious. At some point I want to go back for some clothes." More importantly she wanted to locate that pre-nup document. "Are you sure you don't mind if I stay here a couple days?"

"Of course not. That is, if you don't mind sharing my queen size." Gemma perched on the arm of the couch. "Hey, I want to know more about this other dude you were with last night." She gave her sister a good-natured nudge on her shoulder. "What if Michael finds out you're at bars picking up guys?"

"He probably doesn't even care at the moment."

"But you said you gave this Nick guy your cell number. I don't know Clio. You really have to be more careful, especially when you're out drinking. What if this guy had robbed you or something?" Just then the doorbell rang. "Oh, that must be the DVC lady dropping off the stuff for the fair." Gemma set the glass down and answered the door. "Hi. You're right on time."

"Hello, Gemma." Marion lifted two bags up. "See? There's not a huge amount to tote around. If you have a minute, I'll just go over the setting up and what to expect while you're there." She took a step in. "I didn't even know that they delayed school openings till I started driving over. I thought it would be good though if the materials were here for you. We're hoping they'll schedule the fair for tomorrow."

"Yes, I heard about the school delays. So far, it doesn't look very serious out there.

"C'mon in and meet my sister." They walked through the little foyer and into the living room. "Clio, this is the lady I told you about from DVC, Mrs. Hathaway."

"Oh, please. Call me Marion." Her eyes lingered on Clio for several seconds. "I feel like we've met some-where before. Yes! Your name. I remember now. Clio is such a distinctive name." Marion's voice had tightened somewhat with the tension she was feeling.

"We have?" Clio rose from the couch and gave her hand a little wave of hello. She looked closer at Marion's face trying to place her.

Where do I go from here, was all Marion could think about. She half turned to Gemma and then changed her mind and turned back. "I believe it was at the company Christmas party. Aren't you Michael Lazaro's wife?"

Clio let out a big guffaw. "Well, put a needle in me!" She plopped back down. "If this isn't one humongous coincidence, I don't know what is." The three women found themselves nodding awkwardly. Clio broke the tension, "So are we the innocent wives of a couple of lawbreakers?" They both laughed. Gemma stood in position, wide-eyed.

"Let's keep it to 'suspects' for the moment," Marion replied.

"Yes, uh...good idea."

Gemma pulled a ladder-back chair forward and motioned toward the sofa. "Well, for goodness sake, let's all sit down. I want to know more about this. She looked at Marion. "That is, if you have the time."

Marion was still smiling and half shaking her head. At the same time she was cautioning herself to take care with what and how she said anything. "I do have to get back to the office. I have a lot of catching up to do. As you may have learned from the papers, we've had to keep close to home for the past week."

"You can say that again. I've nearly gone bat-shit. Oh, excuse me." Clio remembered that she was talking to Darien high society. "I just meant that it's been a pretty crummy bunch of days. I'm glad Gemma's here to get me out of the house for a while."

"Yes, that's nice. Well, let me go over a few things with you, Gemma. You haven't done a health fair yet, have you."

She shook her head. "No this is my first assignment. I finished certification just last week. My sister knows that I've been attending classes."

"Yeah," Clio added, "it's been good for Gemma, having something to do while she's been getting her strength back. You know she had a hysterectomy five weeks ago?"

Marion turned to Gemma. "No, I wasn't aware of that. Are you sure maintaining our booth for a several hours is going to be all right?"

"Oh, I'll be fine. In another week the doctor says I'll be able to exercise and everything."

"Terrific. There will be students at the booth to help you." She leaned down to open one of the bags. "Actually, all you have to do at the high school is get there about fifteen, twenty minutes before the fair starts and arrange these pamphlets and give-aways on the table." She looked up at a window. "They predict only four to six inches today, so I'm pretty sure we'll be on for tomorrow. I'll confirm that with you early tomorrow when we hear from the school."

"Okay, that will be fine."

Clio was stretching one hand toward a bunch of pamphlets. "These look interesting. Look at this one, Gemma. 'What You Need to Know about Dating Violence'. We should have had this when we were in high school. Yeah, my sister told me that your hotline has helped out a lot of women." She thumbed through the pamphlet. "And you have a shelter?"

"Mm, hmm. For mothers and their children too. A temporary, but safe haven. Of course its location is kept secret... for their protection."

"Jeez, what are all those lollipops for?" Gemma was still looking in the bag. "There must be a hundred Dum-Dums in here."

"Oh, you've got to have those out on your table. Teenagers seize on them. See, with all the other organizations representing you have to attract kids to your booth. We hope to sign up some junior and senior girls for certification classes. You'll be good at providing them with your own impressions on that, Gemma. That other bag just holds more duplicate material. You can look through it all later if you like." Marion sat back. "Do you have any questions?"

"No, I don't think so. It seems pretty clear. You said another volunteer would be coming to pick up these bags then at the end of the day?"

Marion nodded her head and placed both hands on her knees. "Well, if that's all, I'd better head back."

"I have a question, if you don't mind." Marion steeled herself, hoping Clio would keep it on the present topic. "What do you hear about that investigation at Comp? Do you think the financial department is in big trouble? I mean, could it affect a lot of people's jobs?"

Marion was staring down at the floor. "I can't say anything for sure, Clio. I think everyone there is feeling pretty tense." She picked her head up and smiled. "This is my first day out of the house, and look at us, sitting here talking about it. There's no escape." She hoped they'd get her drift. Turning her head, she said, "It's so good of you to help us, Gemma. I think you'll enjoy being at the high school. The kids make it more interesting than it would be at an ordinary health fair." She stood up and pulled on her coat. "So nice to meet you both."

As soon as the door closed, Gemma twirled around and whispered, "Did you ever?"

"No! What I can't get over - she's a nice lady. When I read about Gordon Hathaway in the *DISPATCH*, I imagined her as one of those executive trophy wives with heavy diamond rings, bridge parties and golf dates. You know the type I mean - treatments at beauty parlors and tanning salons every week."

"You don't remember her from the Christmas party?"

"No, I was uncomfterble' with all those people. And I prahbly drank too much. What I remember is Michael getting all pissed-off." Both women stared off into space, caught up in their own thoughts. Clio practically jumped off the sofa. "C'mon, Sister Suzy. Let's go to Saks before the driving gets too bad. I need to buy some boots."

Gemma gave a little chuckle, " I thought you were gonna' do your Body Sound thing."

"Yeah, maybe later. Or maybe I'll go home and get some clothes, check out the scene there." She rolled her eyes in mockery. "See if the FBI is hiding in the bushes."

*

Back at the Station - Same Time

By the time he'd reached his office, Hansen was burning with anger and frustration. He slammed the door to his closet just to hear the noise. Next he kicked his chair and watched it skid backward and knock against the window sill. After standing in place for a full minute he pulled the chair back and slumped into it. Now what. He'd have to hand over the only hard evidence tied to this killer and watch the FBI run with it. There was simply no other choice. He reached into the bottom drawer, pulled out the packet, shook his head sadly and headed back.

They were standing right where he'd left them, deep in conversation. "Let's see what you have there." Minicus pulled out both the audio file and the video of Dana in the lab from when she listened to the voice samples. "Okay, this should stand up in court. You had probable cause, what with the gun registration." He pulled out a group of folded papers and flipped them open. "These are the notes you took from your interview? With, let's see, Dana Redman?"

"Yes, that was last Sunday. I asked her to come to the train station, so she could walk me through her side of it. The next sheet, in back there, shows a drawing of her position in relation to the platform...where Paula Metz went down. That was after the first gun shot when Dana Redman had an exchange with this guy. You can see it all there. What they said." He looked at his watch. "You know, his lawyer may walk in any minute now. I'm worried that we're losing time. And maybe our suspect."

"We were just talking about that. The front desk said he's already on his way." Minicus handed the packet back to Hansen. "Hold this for the time being. We'll see if he's changed his mind about cooperating. If not, we'll go to Plan B. Let's go, partner." Minicus opened the door to the interrogation room. Hansen stood in place a moment mystified, but then took up watch outside.

Dell started, "Time's up, Mario. Have you changed your mind? You gonna' talk to us?"

Mario had been sitting with an elbow propped on the table and his chin cupped in one hand when they came in. He'd been remembering how mad his father used to get whenever he found something that'd gone wrong. He'd fire one question after another at Mario. "Weren't you right there when you weren't supposed to be? Huh? Huh? Didn't I tell you never to go there?" He'd put all these accusations into the form of questions and never let up. Mario would stand there waiting for it all to finish, never saying a word the whole time. His dad always ended with the same damn thing. "Godammit, do I gotta' get an ice pick? You're about as thick as concrete. Answer me!" Then he'd raise his arm, "I'll give you what for!" And the arm would come down. Well, screw these Feds and their gang-bang. They'd get nothing from him.

"Look at me Mario." Dell tried again. "You are not a dumb person. We know that. And we believe everyone deserves a second chance. That's why we let you reconsider this opportunity. If you tell us what Lazaro was paying you for, we'd be willing to cut you a deal."

Two whole minutes went by as they waited for some response. "Okay. That's it." Minicus and Dell walked out. They were part way down the hall, before gesturing a "follow us" to Hansen, "Let's go back to your meeting room where we can talk, Lieutenant."

Hansen couldn't believe what he'd just seen. They'd accomplished absolutely nothing. He stared at their backs. "You didn't even tell him we have a witness! What was the point?" Minicus raised one hand to stall any more queries.

Back in the conference room Minicus explained. "All right. This is where we're going. We're not ready to press charges. An SAR might not stick. We think we're better off letting him go and then tracking his every move. There's a chance he'll lead us to something. We'll get a search warrant using the audio-tape and your witness as probable cause. I think we can wire his apartment and have everything set by tonight... tomorrow morning at the latest." Hansen sat staring first at one then the other.

Dell added for explanation, "Look Steve, he's a bullheaded, small time crook who might just lead us to some solid evidence."

"So I should release his public defender?" They nodded.

"We'll tell Boccanera he's being released on a formal caution. We want him to think he's finished with us and free to move about; it'll give him a little self-confidence."

"Let me get this straight. Am I going to be tracking him or is that you guys too?"

"Our guys will take care of it, since he's headed back to the Bronx. We'll count on you to handle whatever needs to be done here, in Darien. Oh, and it'd be a good idea to contact this Dana Redman, make sure she's handy. What does she do? Does she work?"

"She's a teacher at the high school here."

"Sounds good. Would she represent well in court?"

"Yes, but she told me she's going away on vacation starting this weekend."

Frank Minicus thought a minute. He wasn't fond of

using this kind of witness, not as evidence in murder cases. Too often their testimony didn't stand up in court. There were dozens of reasons defense could use to puncture their reliability, particularly in this case: bad or scant overall lighting, poor angle for viewing the face, snow and wind blowing, a nearsighted witness. On top of all that, most witnesses were subject to memory fade over time. But it was all they had at the moment. "Maybe you should call her. Tell her to be available...till Saturday, in case we need to talk to her."

"All right. Schools are closed today, so she's probably home. I'll try to reach her there." After a momentary pause Hansen asked, "What happens next?" He was hoping they would just go back to the city, continue with their white collar investigation and stay away from his case.

Minicus glanced over at Dell, "We need to ask if you'll let us use one of your offices. Maybe even this conference room for a couple days." He turned his head toward Hansen, smiling, "If it's all right with you people. As soon as our task force at Comp finds enough for an indictment on Michael Lazaro, we'll get consent from a Federal Magistrate for a search warrant on his place in North Stamford. Then we can go in, get his computers, phones, any documents he's been stashing." Then Minicus looked out the window. "This snow and all; it'd be a lot easier working right from here."

Hansen's chest went empty. What a takeover. Still, there was no way he could refuse their request. This was not what he had figured on, but then nothing else had figured his way either.

Breaking Away

Cruising Stamford - Same Thursday Morning

After a Western omelet at Carley's Diner, Ritzy picked up some dry cleaning and was in his car rolling along through the swirling snow, alone in his thoughts. He asked himself where he should go, what he should do next. Last night's conquest was better than a good distraction. He smiled to himself; it was the perfect remedy for a man in need. He'd get back to that babe, Clio. But now what to do. There was nothing from Mario yet.

Mario was hired by Lazaro's company to do office work. That part was reassuring, but did he even find his way out of the city? Ritzy remembered thinking at the time of his call that getting Mario to rent a car, drive it up to Stamford, and collect from his cousin might've been too much to expect from him. He sounded eager to get the dough though. But if there was no call in the next couple of hours, Ritzy would try to get in touch with him.

He was counting on these pre-paid phones to be what the Boss claimed. Last year **T** ordered everyone to go out and buy one. They were supposed to be untraceable. Even still, look how **T** ended up - stuck at home wearing an ankle bracelet till his trial.

It was going on three weeks now with no job, no assignments – well, except for getting that bag she was carrying. He hated feeling at loose ends. Maybe he should head back toward town and check in with Scampi. He was practically the only contact Ritzy still had from the old job. Poor guy was all alone trying to maintain operations surrounded by incompetents. With **T** on his way to jail, the fucking Federal Marshals were in Danbury as well, working right out of one of his buildings. Out of all **T**'s carting and hauling jobs, only one business office was left at *Stamford Waste*. To think that all the rest up there was being taken over and run by the Feds was more than Ritzy could stomach.

That and then **T** going over the hockey union's salary cap. It ruined life for a lot of guys who played for his hockey team. Now they've disbanded the **D**anbury **T**rashers. He pitied those guys, because **T**'s hockey team would never get back on the ice again. Those guys would have to look for real work now. It was a sad state of affairs. But in Ritzy's mind, with sports you're supposed to follow the rules. **T** shouldn't have gone over the salary cap. And paying their wives for non-existent jobs is not your standard kind of bonus.

Ever since that loss to the Kalamazoo Wings, play had been suspended for the season. Now Ritzy had to content himself with high school hockey. Truth be known, it made for pretty good ice time. Scampi's kid had some real promise, and he was only 16 years old. If they got another win, they'd be in the play-offs. Ritzy remembered Scampi saying the next game was Friday, but did he say where? First he'd go home and shower. Later, he'd swing over to **Stamford Waste** and see what the news was with Scampi

*

It was almost eleven o'clock, and he still hadn't heard from Mario; never even got back to him after Ritzy had left that message. Screw him. That jamook must've fucked it up somehow. Ritzy wagged his head back and forth. Mario just didn't have it in him to be an enforcer. You've got to be able to put some muscle into a job like that. So Lazaro must not've paid up, not without those papers in his hands. There had to be some way to make this ball-breaker pay off. Ritzy sat on the sofa with a cup of instant in one hand, his phone in the other. He could always think better with both hands full.

There was a shake-down here somewhere; he knew it. With a different kind of plan he might just parlay that hit into cash. He still had the papers. They were right there in his desk, and they were worth several large ones. Ritzy already knew where Lazaro lived. Christ, he'd found it right there on whitepages.com. And he had the blood to make his own brand of threat work, but he wanted to keep off the grounds; he didn't want to do a face-to-face exchange. His instinct told him to make it play from a distance. Who knew. The place might still be under watch, what with that investigation going on and all. He remembered reading that Feds were all over those VP's estates.

Ritzy stood up and walked into the bedroom, then back again, squeezing his phone with each step. It would come, he knew it. And then it did. Yeah! Those Hispanic guys at ***Stamford Waste***...they used to talk about sending money home all the time. How'd they do it? Ritzy stood there motionless trying to recreate their conversation. Most of it was in Spanish...dinero and mi casa he recognized. And then it clicked. He bolted to the computer and Googled "sending cash western union".

Amazing. There were tons of places right in town: variety stores, news stores, check cashing places that could be used for pick-up. All you needed was a driver's license and the payer's info with a money transfer code number. Ritz would keep his own identity concealed by using his other driver's license, the forged one **B**ig **T** had arranged for last year. Okay, that took care of his end, but he'd have to figure out how to deal with those papers.

First, Lazaro would want proof that he was in possession of them. No fax machine here, but he could use Scampi's. No, better yet, he could send it as an attachment from one of *their* computers. Mario must have Lazaro's e-mail address. He'd send Lazaro a sample page that would identify it as one of those documents from her bag.

Yeah, Ritzy was getting excited. He could make this work; he knew it. The only tricky part would be in convincing him to transfer the money *before* sending him all that paperwork. There were a couple ways to make that work. One not so bloody as the other. He preferred that one. The important part was to get the words right. He would have to think this through, even write it out. For this, he'd have to make sure every corner was covered.

The more he thought about it, the more he liked the idea of getting those papers out of the house. It was actually to his advantage. If the wrong people found them here, they'd link him to the Metz woman.

Heading Back to the Bronx - Late Morning

Some jerk in back of him was crawling up his behind. Christ, what a god-awful way to travel. As if he hadn't gone through enough already. Mario was hunched forward, going 35 miles per hour down I-95 through a blind of snow. It was bad enough having to drive up to Stamford in the dark last night. Now he had this G.D. snow to get through. Mario tried to console himself. If he got the car back okay, he wouldn't have to pay for two days' worth.

Good thing Ritzy had taught him how to drive. So many years ago. He used to say that a man had to be able to drive a car and shoot craps. But no one should have to drive in such conditions like this. At the same time he was thinking that nobody'd ever worked so hard for a stupid five grand. He'd give Ritzy only two. Mario felt he'd gone through enough already. He was actually proud of himself. He hadn't given in to those pigs, not even an inch, and now he was free to go...with a friggin' formal caution, whatever the hell that meant. "You're goddamn right I'll be cautious, you sons a' bitches," he yelled at the windshield. The car in front suddenly appeared closer; he came back to the moment and slowed down. From now on he'd keep his eyes peeled on those red tail lights. Its New York license plate gave him a feeling of comfort; he was headed home. One of those Darien cops told him he could get back to the Bronx by just staying on 95. He said it turned into the Cross Bronx Expressway, if that didn't beat all. And then it went all the way across to the Major Deegan. So if that was true, he could get off at the 4B exit and take Tremont Ave. right up to the Budget Rent-a-Car.

A white blur whooshed by on his left. How some of these guys in the other two lanes could speed ahead passing other cars he couldn't comprehend. They'll probably get themselves killed, along with a bunch of innocents. Mario didn't want to take his hands off the steering wheel to turn on the radio even though some music might be nice. Another thing crossed his mind. He'd been so anxious to get out of the police station and into his car that he'd forgotten to check his phone. Maybe Ritzy was trying to call him. Well, he wasn't about to get off this death row till he was safe in the Bronx. Then he'd call Ritzy and tell him about last night. He had the money; that's all that counted.

It took him two miserable hours to get to the rental. When he finally pulled the car to a halt, he dropped his head and gave the sign of the cross to whoever was in charge up there. Mario was exhausted and starving to death. That cheap egg and cheese McMuffin they'd given him for breakfast was what...five, six hours ago? He pulled his phone out of a jacket pocket and flipped it open. When his messages came up, sure enough there was one from Ritzy.

"Hey Mario, what's goin' on? I haven't heard from you. Listen, as soon as you can, call me back. I need Lazaro's e-mail address."

That was it? What the hell. Why did he want that? Mario sat a moment, thinking. Did Lazaro give him his e-mail or was it just his cell number he got, way back when? It seemed like a month had gone by since that first meeting at Comp. He looked at his watch, 1:05. He'd make the call after turning in the car. It was just a ten minute walk home.

Despite the cold slush of snow on his feet, walking

through the old neighborhood again began to work its charm. A gathering sense of calm coursed through his muscles, easing the tension in his neck. Morris Park would always be home, but right now any place hot and sunny sounded a lot better. Just as he took the stairs up the stoop he remembered that Lazaro's info was right there in the contacts option on his cell. He already had it out and was punching in Ritzy's number as he entered his apartment.

"Hey Ritz. I just got back. Wait'll you hear who I spent the night with last night."

"Jeezus Mario. Don't make me guess. Sophia Loren?"

"No. The Darien police."

"What!!"

"Not to worry. They let me off this morning and they got nothin' outa' me."

"What do you mean? What'd they pick you up for then?"

"I was just drivin' back from Michael's house; it was around..."

Ritzy broke in. He didn't want to take the chance of cops tracking Mario's calls. "Let me call you back on my phone. It'd be better."

Mario shook his head. The world was going too fast here. He flopped into an old couch and had just put his feet up on a yellowed hassock when his cell rang.

"Okay. Start at the beginning. Did that push on Lazaro work?"

"Yeah, that part went fine. I got a check from him; I just gotta' cash it. Ya' see I was drivin' back down his road when the Feds pulled me over. They've been watching Michael's house. They told me I could get arrested for suspicious activity or somethin' if I didn't agree to come into the station and answer some questions. Those fucks kept me there all night and most of the morning. Ritzy, I never told 'em anything except that I was collecting some money Michael owed me. Ya' know, like from a bet. I swear. You'd a' been proud of me."

Ritz was just shaking his head. What was it with this guy? He never, ever got through a job simply. But it sounded as though he was out of trouble, at least for the moment. Best thing would be to get Mario elsewhere and soon. "All right, good Mario. You've been a real stand-up guy. Now listen to me. Just cash the check and use it to go somewhere down South, ya' hear? Spend some time in the islands. Anywhere but here, till this whole thing cools down. And don't worry about my share for now. I got another plan."

Mario couldn't believe his ears. Good ole' Ritz. "Are you sure about that?"

"Yeah. I just need Lazaro's e-mail address. Have you got it?"

"Yeah. It's...wait a minit. I gotta' go to the contacts." He started to press the home screen button but then said, "Wait. Are we gonna' be disconnected?"

"Mario, first you put us on hold. Then go to your address book." He waited a second and then decided differently, "Never mind. Mario? You there?"

"Yeah. I just..."

"I'll call you back in a few minutes. You go look it up." Ritzy wondered if Mario would ever be able to go beyond the Bronx. Just the way he talked was a GPS giveaway. Good thing Ritzy had spent enough time in Stamford to lose most of that New Yorkese.

"Okay, okay." God, he was tired. Mario hit End, pressed the address book icon and there was Lazaro's name. His e-mail address was right after the cell number. Phew. He walked into the kitchen to look for a pencil and some paper and wrote it down. Now he was ready for when the phone rang again. In a day or two he'd be in a jet air plane flying to the sun.

*

Outside, sitting in a Ford Crown Victoria were two city Agents biding their time until the consent from their Federal Magistrate came through. Once they had their search warrant they could go to work, but they'd have to wait for Mario to leave the building. One Agent would follow him and the other would get inside and bug the apartment. "You know, with this snow and his bein' in a cell all night, we might be here for a while.

"Yeah, he'll probably be sleeping all afternoon. I know I would."

*

Going Home - Mid Afternoon

As she turned up Pebble Run, Clio found herself squinting her eyes. She was scanning the neighborhood trying to see if the black SUVs Michael was always talking about were still around. Nothing, just a Con Ed truck near the Fielding's house. She hoped the storm hadn't cut off electricity. What she couldn't know was that the men in that van were the same two Agents who had picked up Mario the night before and were waiting now for the go-ahead to enter the Lazaro house.

Their driveway hadn't been plowed yet. As Clio turned into it, she pushed down on the accelerator, urging the Beemer to make it up the incline. She had to admit that Michael was right about getting a four-wheel drive. It

215

really did good in the snow. Maybe things were better with Michael now, what with the FBI gone. She was glad she'd decided not to make a test call before coming back. See him face-to-face. Then decide if Gemma was right about leaving him alone. When she stepped out of the car, her new boots sank into a couple inches of snow. See? She congratulated herself. Those sling backs woulda' been torture in this.

Inside, the house was gloomy and silent. "Michael!" And again, "Michael!" She heard a toilet flush from the second floor. Standing in the foyer she waited, looking up. Pretty soon he appeared at the top of the stairs and started down muttering under his breath. Jeezus, he was wearing the same damn clothes he had on yesterday. Clio pulled off her coat reminding herself to be nice. "Hi honey. Miss me?" He didn't say anything, just brushed past her. "I didn't see any FBI cars out there. Do ya' think they're gone?" He walked on, heading into the living room, completely ignoring her. "I asked you a question, Michael. Are you gonna' answer me?"

"What are you doing back here? I thought you were making your own plans."

"Well maybe I have." She put both hands on her hips and thrust her face forward.

"Michael, look at me." When he turned around, she said sweetly, "I thought you'd at least give me a smile...or maybe tell me what's going on. Didn't you say something about Barkley? Something or other might change?"

"Nothing's changed. I'm still on leave." He turned back. "Are you satisfied now?"

"I'll be satisfied," her voice was rising, "when I know what our future is gonna' be, and I'm talking about you and me both. We're still married, last I knew, and I got a

216

right to know what's goin' on!"

"I know about as much as you do. Nothing. All I do is sit around waiting for the ax to fall from somewhere." He proceeded through the foyer. "You might as well find better company to be with, because it's no picnic here." By this time he was into the living room and out of sight.

"I'll do that!" Clio spun around and clomped up the stairs. In their bedroom she opened every drawer visible. Using her fingers as strainers, she sifted through bras, pajamas, jewelry, cosmetics, summer clothes, the works - in search of her copy of their pre-nup.

From downstairs she heard Michael shouting something about what the hell she was doing. She ignored him. Next she frisked the sweaters and corduroys on every shelf in their closet, but came up with nothing. In a rage, she pulled out a duffle bag and large suitcase. "Goddamn son of a bitch. Now I gotta' ask him for it." She pulled favorite outfits from their hangers and lounge wear from the chest of drawers, and threw them in the suitcase. The duffle bag she filled with shoes and cosmetics.

By the time she'd finished packing and slamming all the drawers back into place, another idea came to her. She'd get their address book from the kitchen drawer and look through it, see if one of the names rang a bell. Then she'd call him and ask for a copy.

With her bags at the front door and the address book stuffed into her hand bag she felt ready to leave the bastard with his own foul mood for company. But she couldn't go without a parting shot. There he was, as usual, in his lounge chair flicking through one of those boring investment magazines. "Well, I hope you find something in there that pays money, because we're gonna' need it."

"Oh shut up, Clio. Go on, get out of here. Go to your sister's or something."

"I am going to do just that." She stood poised, waiting for effect. "And maybe more." As she headed for the front door, the phone rang. "I'll get it."

"No!!" Michael burst out of his chair. "I know it's for me!" She stood glowering at him and walked toward the phone anyway, not listening to him.

"Don't you answer that!" he yelled. And then it was a race. They were grappling with the receiver, Clio almost laughing with the game. He pulled it out of her hand and whispered a forceful, "Get your ass out of here!"

His hand was over the receiver, but he could hear a voice saying, "Your time is up, Mr. Lazaro. You have till 9:00 tomorrow morning."

"What?" And then he demanded, "Who is this!"

"Now listen carefully to what I'm going to say." Clio had picked up her bags and was already out the door.

In Nancy's Car - That Evening

"It was really nice of you to help me get a jump start." She caught Dana's eye, "I mean it. I didn't pick you up this morning with a design to put you to work."

"Nancy, remember? It was my idea. Besides, the gods gave us this bonus day. Why not put it to good use? But I am curious. Doesn't the landlord normally have the responsibility to keep a place up?"

"That's true most of the time. I made a deal with them to paint it myself if they'd cut the rent by $25 a month. They're kind of old. I think they were just sick of doing it themselves. And of course I wowed them with my personality."

"So you haven't thrown any wild parties yet?"

218

"Not yet."

They had spent the afternoon in Nancy's garage apartment shoving furniture to the middle of two rooms, taking down all the pictures, and had finished filling holes and cracks in the walls with spackle. The ceiling of one bedroom was even painted. With their winter gear on, they were back in Nancy's Honda heading toward town, but driving slowly through back roads that had been plowed only once. "There must be four, five inches out there."

Dana was thinking about Nancy's stamina. "You sure are devoting a lot of time to the health fair. I didn't realize how much arranging and organization it takes. How'd you get roped into doing this fair? Did someone at school ask you to do it?"

"Oh you know Carrie." This was the school nurse. "She's a riot. We have the same lunch period. She was talking about it one day last month and asked if I'd help out. It doesn't require a lot of time, and you know we've gotta' make a good impression being new teachers at school." She changed subjects. "Weren't the girls good to come in today? Now I don't have to figure out their schedules tomorrow or arrange to get them excused from class. It's all done."

"Those slogans she put up for DVC are great - 'Love Is Not Shoves'...What was the other one?"

"Don't Be a Silent Victim."

"Oh yeah, and I was thinking about those two girls. The one with red hair and funky clothes...Margie, right?" Nancy nodded. "She intrigues me. I've seen her around town. You said she lives with just her mother. Do you think there's a domestic violence background there?"

"Could be. I don't really know. Both girls have

219

completed their certification, I know that much. They went through the DVC program where you spend a lot of hours learning how to handle abuse cases. They didn't talk a great deal about it. Someone told me all their volunteers sign a commitment to confidentiality. Which only seems right. Anyway, they're pretty enthusiastic about doing their volunteer work right at the school."

As they drove slowly through the back roads of town, Dana thought of how nice it felt to do something good for a close friend for a change, something helpful. She hadn't thought once about the Paula Metz case. It suddenly occurred to her that she should check her phone to see if Carson had called. Generally she left it in her car while she was at school. Out of habit, she'd ignored it all day. In fact she'd forgotten it was even there, in her school bag. Maybe she should wait till she got home to call Carson. He would have a better idea of his train time by then. She was even thinking that he shouldn't bother making the effort. Driving at night through this would be slippery and slow going. Up ahead they saw flashing lights and a long line of cars on their side of the road. Nancy slowed down. "It looks like someone tried to take a curve too fast."

"Too bad for us. It looks like we'll be sitting here for a while."

"Aw, I can try..." She checked the lane for oncoming traffic. "Nope. We'll wait a little. It's kinda' hard to turn around here."

Dana pulled her cell out of her school bag. She'd decided to call Carson. He picked up quickly and asked how she was doing. She told him where they were and then said she thought it was silly for him to try to come out.

There was a pause while he thought that over. "Dana, are you sure about this? I could leave as soon as I finish this last bunch and get the 6:07."

"No, that's silly. Once we get past this accident we're not far from the station. Nancy will drop me at the car. Did you park in the usual spot?"

"Yes. But Dana, let me think. It's about...the fifth car from the end in the third row." He paused while She repeated it. "Are you sure?" he asked, "Is this really all right with you?"

"Sure, I'm sure. If you have an open invitation to stay at Rick's, you might as well use it. I'll call you from home around 8:30, 9:00. Is that a good time?"

"Should be. I can see myself putting in three more hours tops." His voice sparked with some enthusiasm. "Dana, if I can get up to December's accounts by tomorrow, I might just be able to finish the whole thing off by Sunday."

"Great! Go for it!" Dana had such a good feeling as she closed the phone. Once he finished this internal investigation they'd finally be able to relax and enjoy themselves. "How's it look up there? Any movement?"

"No, not yet. You know I could try to turn this baby around and we could go back to my place, have a little dinner. Tomorrow morning I could drop you at the station before school."

"Naw, we're too close and it's out of the way for you. Look! The first car is moving." They inched forward and finally passed a station wagon that had slammed into a telephone pole. Flashing lights allowed them to see two EMTs carrying someone on a stretcher to an ambulance.

"Well, that's a warning for anyone," Nancy said. "Poor guy. I hope he makes it."

221

Finding the Saturn was not as easy as she'd expected. They were all buried under snow. But Nancy pulled a broom out of her trunk and started whisking. Dana poked fun at her "Upstate-preparedness", but soon found herself grateful. They had it all brushed off her car in no time. "See ya' round the campus," Nancy said getting back into her car.

"Oh, I'll bring my fourth period class in - to see how you're doing tomorrow, okay? Maybe I can help out somewhere."

"Good on! Hey, what about tomorrow night? Want to try for another game? I talked to one of the custodians who lives in Stamford. It's a Division II battle between Stamford and Westhill, their biggest rival. And Darien will play the winner in the play-offs."

"Oh, that should be a hot one. But I better play it by ear." It occurred to Dana that nothing else seemed to be going on, and it was their first night of vacation. "Hell, I don't see why not. What time's the game? Maybe Carson can come with us, or at least meet us afterwards at Maxwell's."

"Great! It starts at 6:00. See ya'. And thanks again for all your help today."

The house stood completely dark. Dana wished that she had left a light on before leaving that morning. Their shovel was sticking out of a pile of snow next to the front door, so she cleared the walk. At least it was nice and warm coming inside. After putting on all the lamps, she walked into the kitchen and noticed two messages on the machine. What Dana had not felt all day whooshed back over her. Nuts! She forgot all about signing up for caller ID. What if those two were from that breather creep again?

She stepped across to the wall phone and stared at it before pressing the play button. A recorded voice announced, "Due to a winter storm, the earlier decision for a delayed opening has been changed. All Darien schools will be closed for the full day. Repeat. All Darien schools will... "She pressed delete. The next voice started, "Dana, I thought you might be home today. This is Detective Hansen calling. I've been asked to alert you to the possibility of coming in for further questioning, here at the station. I realize that you're going away, but we may need to talk to you before you leave. I think you said it might be Saturday. If you get in by 6:00, please give me a call. The number here is 662-5330, ext. 4. Or you can use my cell number. It's 654-8478. You can call that any time if you get in late."

She stood looking at the wall and then punched play to listen again. On the second listening of Hansen's message she fastened onto the word "possibility". Okay, maybe they won't need her. What more did they want? She'd given them as much as was there.

The clock above the kitchen table read 5:44. With a sinking feeling she decided to do her civic duty. But would this ever end? First she had to get rid of this outer wear. Off came the scarf, the jacket and boots. Her mind was chugging. Had something new developed? She saw herself casting back and forth, between wanting to be a nobody and the desire to know the inside story. Well, she'd been good and kept her mouth shut today. There was that much. Dana found herself smiling at a certain self-recognition; her curiosity would probably override any misgiving she had about serving as a witness.

She picked up the receiver telling herself to be happy the breather creep had not called and punched in Hansen's office number. "Hi, it's Dana. I just got in."

"Oh, thanks for calling back. I thought you'd be stuck at home today."

"No, a couple of us went in to work. We don't mind driving in the snow. So what's up?"

Hansen gave a little sigh and then explained that the FBI had visited Darien to do some further investigation on the Metz case. They had read her statement and might want to ask some more questions before she went away. He did not mention Mario's detention and release that morning. "So Dana. If you can break away tomorrow or at least come in after school lets out, I'd sure appreciate it."

"Well yes, but your message said that coming in was a 'possibility'. Now you make it sound certain."

"I have something I'd like you to do for me, Dana. It won't take long, I promise."

Hansen had a new plan, one of his own making. Even though the night shift had tried to take a picture along with fingerprints the night before, Mario had objected loudly, claiming he wasn't under arrest; they couldn't do that. Using the video tape of that original interrogation, Hansen captured a still of Mario's face and with a little editing using Photoshop, zoomed and cropped for a close-up. His picture was now with five others in a photo array. Maybe this was not in the strictest of police protocol, but it was sure worth a try. For his own peace of mind.

If Dana identified him as the one at the train station, he'd have his man. Hopefully this could be done apart from Dell and Minicus. With luck, they'd get their go-ahead on the search warrant for the Lazaro house and be jumping on that tomorrow.

It took Dana by surprise when Hansen mentioned that he had a photo array he'd like her to take a look at. His voice sounded in earnest. "It'll be my last request, Teach." She didn't say anything. "I'll be out and about a good bit tomorrow, so you should probably use my cell phone number. I left that number, right? 654-8478?"

"Yes. It's here in the message you left."

"Just call me when you pin down a good time to come in. Can you do that?"

"Okay, but it'll be after 3:00. No, you better make that closer to 4:00 – 4:30."

"Right. I'll plan to be back at the station by then. And thanks again."

After placing the receiver back on the base, Dana stood there for a moment, thinking. So the FBI was on the Metz case now. Weren't they supposed to be doing the white collar part? This could be interesting. On the other hand....well, who knows. She wrote his cell number on a sticky note and stuck it in her pants pocket. They were still good for another day. She didn't drop one bit of spackle on them. Dana sat down for a minute, staring at the kitchen wall, "Tomorrow and tomorrow and tomorrow," she sighed, wondering if it would bring something more than all this nagging uncertainty.

Put into Play

<u>**Ritzy's Place**</u> **- Thursday Evening**

Ritzy sank into the sofa with a can of Bud feeling the glow of absolute satisfaction. He was the enforcer supremo now. Everything had gone off exactly right. First he congratulated himself on staying away from Lazaro's house. What a pig sty that would've been if he'd gone there like Mario did last night. And then working from **Stamford Waste** was a smart move. Fortunately, there was still one set of offices left, and Scampi gave him free use. Using their computer would keep his own name and address under cover.

He was thinking how creepy it is now, driving through all those empty buildings, like going through a grave yard instead of commuting to the home office. Jesus! What did Scampi say? The Feds were gonna' put those buildings up for auction! And so who gets the money for *that*, huh? What a travesty. Was it the friggin' Feds who would be reaping the benefits here? All of it was beyond his comprehension.

Big-**T's** whole enterprise was left with only one building to work out of. There was Scampi running the remnants and overseeing a skeleton staff of jerks. All because **T** and his other big earners were swept up on racketeering charges. Thank God Ritzy had slid under the Fed's view. Being only an "associate", he was still too fresh to be taken seriously. It was kind of ironic and all. Only a couple months ago he was longing to be part of The Family, ready to take the vow. Now he was out and having to find work on his own.

Admittedly he was a figure in hiding so to speak, but so far Darien's Finest didn't seem to have a clue. He pictured again that woman with the scarf, crouching down there with the hub caps. He still worried about that, but Christ it happened over a week ago, and still there was nothing about witnesses in the papers. He kept trying not to think about that fuck-up at the station, but it was hard not to. No one was ever going know about that. The only one who knew he was even connected to Paula Metz was Mario. Ritzy had to hand it to his old pal. He at least knew how to keep his mouth shut. Jesus, if the **F**irst **B**unch of **I**diots let *him* go, Ritzy had a right to breathe easy. One corner of his mouth curved up with a smile. They wouldn't be able to link him to Lazaro either, not now, with his other "identity", the one **B**ig-**T** had made for him.

Ritzy sat back breathing a deep sigh of self-satisfaction. His e-mail with that attached sample page started things off just right. Simple and direct. With a smile he recited that part of his message out loud to the opposite wall, "Your complete set from the bag is still to come - for the right price. Will phone details in two hours." Hunnh. He swallowed the remains of his beer and strolled back into the kitchen for a fresh one. Yes, he'd taken a chance on timing. Lazaro might not be the type to check his e-mail on an hourly basis. But he also figured that a spooked executive stuck at home was going be at the computer looking for company news. And he was right on that account; it all worked according to plan.

Ritzy reached into the frig and cracked open a new can. Then, from his hip pocket, he pulled out the script he'd written, so he could enjoy this particular phone conversation all over again. "Your time is up, Mr. Lazaro. You have till nine o'clock tomorrow morning. Now listen carefully to what I'm going to say."

Then of course Lazaro wanted to know who it was. "I'm the one who sent you a sample page, Mr. Lazaro. Every one of those papers is going either to the SEC or the FBI. I haven't decided who should get the credit yet." This was only to add a little drama. Ritz wouldn't give the friggin FBI a scrap. He remembered picking up on a slight, silent pause at the other end. Ritzy had done all his homework, just in case Lazaro tried to test him out. He knew all about SEC's Northeast Regional Office now; it was right there in Battery Park, in the World Financial Center. And he'd read the contact information. There was even a link for whistle-blowers on their web-site. Of course he'd use his own style of self-protection; he had no use for theirs.

Ritzy read out the next line, "That is, unless you prefer this set of papers to go to you instead...for a price." That was when Lazaro told him in his loud, whiney voice that he'd already been bilked with fake papers and he wasn't going to throw away any more money. But at the same time, his voice didn't have that ring of self-assurance. Getting that sample accounting page had ruined the happy-ending fantasy Lazaro created after Mario ran off in the dark.

Michael had spent some hopeful moments imagining that there really weren't any papers in her overnight bag after all, and it was just a bluff Mario had pulled to get his money. He'd thought that Paula might have come out to Darien that night for a tryst with Gordon. Now, in the light of day, he could see how absurd that was. Hathaway would never play so close to home. The voice on the phone broke up his thoughts.

"For ten Gs... that's ten thousand dollars you can shred them, burn them, put 'em in a vault, for all I care. What's it gonna' be?"

Lazaro had to think fast. If the FBI investigation nailed him for fraud, that was one thing. But to get slapped with complicity in a murder charge because of what happened to Paula Metz? That had to be avoided at all costs. Who knew what Paula might have added as notes that would be incriminating. He had to get those papers back. It was his only protection. This time he'd make sure they were in his hands before paying a dime. He put this demand to voice.

"Naw, naw," Ritzy countered. He smiled remembering that next line. "We're doing this my way. Now here's what you're going to do, Mr. Lazaro. You will sit down at your computer and bring up 'sending cash through Western Union'. The whole thing is right there. It's all a matter of following the directions. Look into Stamford's locations till you find Ely's News and Variety right there on Hope Street. Are you writing this down?"

That's when Lazaro cut in, mad as hell, insisting that

nothing would happen until he had the papers in his hands.

Ritzy looked out the kitchen window and took a big swig. He swallowed before reading the script in his hand out loud again, using the same menacing tone he'd used with Lazaro on the phone. "You either operate according to my plan or you'll end up like Paula Metz. Believe me, I can make it happen. Only this time the whack will go a lot slower. Think about it. You'll be sucking your own blood for one last breath."

Once Lazaro caved, it was a matter of spelling out the procedure. It took a couple of minutes for Lazaro to write down the transfer details and read them back correctly, but it had worked. That's when Ritzy wrapped up the directions, reminding Lazaro, "Don't forget, your deadline is 9:00 AM." And then he delivered his 'Touch of the Ritz'.

"Now then Mr. Lazaro, you need to know that I'm a man of honor. I believe it is an advantage to both of us if we end this transaction in a mutually satisfactory manner." After this pronouncement came his guarantee. "As soon as I pick up the money transfer at Ely's News, I will see to it that you receive your papers, sent either to your home or to a mailing address of your choice. *And* I will use a messenger service to provide for same day delivery." Ah, the pledge of a true gentleman. Ritzy read out his last line. "Now it's my turn to write, Mr. Lazaro. How should the mailing address read?" He looked up from the script and smiled.

Beautiful. He'd be heading down to Ely's Variety in the morning and driving back ten Gs richer. Ritzy took another big slug from his can. He looked at it. "Hey, maybe this is my last night drinking Bud." At the same time the image of a thick, juicy steak popped up. "I don't have that," he muttered. What he did have though, was some penne, and there was half a jar of vodka sauce left in the refrigerator. He'd see if that bag of mixed greens was still good. Yeah, stay home tonight. Keep it all low-key. Watch "CSI" or maybe there was something good on ESPN. Quiet, safe, and sober. That way there'd be no chance of a screw-up. His big reward was to come. Settling back on the sofa again, he put some attention to better, warmer days ahead. He'd take a little vacation, go south like Mario.

A sweet notion popped into mind. Maybe Clio would like to join him. Yeah! Of course she'd have to share a little in the cost, but she must have money somewhere, what with driving that Beemer. On impulse he flipped open his cell. She might like to know he still had her in mind. Then he remembered her saying she had some things to straighten out and not to call right away. Maybe he was getting ahead of himself here. Yeah, he'd wait. It'd be better all round

The Hathaway Estate - Same Time

Marion found Gordon in the den sitting comfortably on the velvet love seat reading before a roaring fire. All he needed to perfect the picture was a Labrador retriever at his feet. To come in and see him in such a cozy, domestic scene was unusual. She had always been the one at home doing the greeting. She walked over to the hearth and rotated her hands above the flames. "Oh, this feels good. Did you stay home all day?"

"Yes, I was able to get a good bit of computer work done, and I made some phone calls. How did your day go? I was a little worried about you driving in this snow."

"Oh, I took it easy. I was at the Center during the heaviest part. I see that you've shoveled the front path." Her voice took on a note of enthusiasm, "Gordon, you'll never guess who I ran into this morning." She turned from the fire to face him as he looked up with raised eyebrows.

"Do I have to guess?"

"Clio Lazaro! She was there at her sister's apartment when I dropped off the bags for the health fair. Do you remember her? She was at the Comp Christmas party."

"Oh, yeah, Lazaro's wife. She's the zoftig one with the huge ear rings. She kind of stands out in a crowd."

"Yes, she wore those stiletto heels that nearly caved, under a very unsteady walk."

Gordon gave out a little chuckle. "I remember. Michael ushered her out pretty early that night. What a twosome they make: mouse meets peacock."

"Well, when *I* saw her, she was dressed in sweats and wooly orange socks - not so sexy. Her sister introduced her as Clio with no last name. I'd never have put it together if it weren't for that unusual first name." Marion turned again toward the fire. "It gave me pause, I can tell you that, what with Michael Lazaro getting pitched out and all. I didn't quite know what to say."

"I can imagine. Well, what did you think of her?" He thumped the cushion next to him. "Sit down and tell me about it."

"First of all," Marion turned to face him, "she didn't remember me from the party. I guess she was too soused. But then I had to laugh, because when she finally figured out who I was, she said something like, "So are we the innocent wives of a couple of lawbreakers?"

"Really?" Gordon smiled. "Well, she has a sense of humor. And," he added, "it sounds like she's keeping up with the local news."

"Then she made a sarcastic comment about being trapped in her house for days on account of all this." Marion walked over to the love seat and flopped down. "Well, her words were more colorful. She said she was going bat-shit."

Gordon shook his head, smiling. "I can't imagine living in the same house with Lazaro; from what I hear he's hard enough to work for. What do you think ever brought them together? He's one of those dull accountant types, scrawny, almost bald. He's certainly not...what do they say now, a hotty?"

Marion gave him a coy look, "Money, honey?" They smiled at each other and nodded an 'uh-huh'.

A sudden awareness of domestic intimacy broke into this moment of warmth. Eighteen years of close living and similar values, all smothered under a week's load of high stress, had popped up to the conscious level. They sat in silence, neither one knowing where to go next. Marion caught herself falling into a familiar pattern. The seduction of love recaptured was something so strong. She was no longer sure that she could guard herself against it.

Gordon simply felt helpless. Finally he asked, "Would you like to go out for dinner? You've put in a whole day's work. We could go to the club, if you like." He noticed a doubtful expression gathering on her face. He quickly added, "Or maybe you'd rather go some place where we're less conspicuous."

Marion dropped both shoulders and cocked her head to one side, thinking. "Oh, I don't know. I can probably find something easy to put together. We could eat here by the fire."

"Sure. Anything you'd like."

Her head was down now. She was studying her hands. "Did you get any more news about the investigation?" Another question quickly followed, "Did Peter Tompkins have anything new to say?"

"Yes, the FBI is still all over the place, but Peter thinks they should be out by the end of the week. I called him back this morning to say I'd be coming in tomorrow, which is fine with him. I also asked if he was planning to make any kind of statement to the various departments." Gordon turned to look at his wife. Now she was studying a finger nail. "Peter's mindset right now is to stay cool and calm. He told me that unless this investigation becomes a bigger issue, he's going to make little of it."

"Really? Well, I guess that's probably a smart political stance. Kind of self-righteous maybe, but a protective one for Comp. What about your department though? Will you want to say anything to them?"

"Probably not. I won't make any announcements, if that's what you mean. Several e-mails have come in from my staff, a lot of them commiserating with what I'm being put through. They all say they'll be glad when it's over with."

"Imagine that," she said looking at the ceiling.

He leaned closer and lifted her hand, palm up, to his cheek. "Stay with me, please Marion. I need you." When she met his gaze, he felt that she just might be there again.

Heading to the DoubleTree - Around 7:30

"He said it was about a mile and a half up Route 1, on

the right." The snow had finally stopped, making visibility a lot easier. They were tired and hungry. Dell started jabbering about his wife's constant complaints. He was never home, his mind was always on the job, there was no time to be a family anymore.

Minicus let him drone on, half listening. He was worried about the timing. For one thing, they hadn't come up with a subpoena for Lazaro yet. He'd been hoping they could get into his house by tomorrow morning, but now it looked like obtaining the subpoena and a search warrant wouldn't happen till later in the day. Minicus did not want to drag this into the weekend, if he could help it. His team in New York said they were close, but still had a few more steps to take in the invest-tigation. He'd taken pains writing up a procedural blue-print for them to follow, but they were somewhat new to working on an investigation of this magnitude. Despite his communications that afternoon, he wondered if they were getting bogged down with unnecessary duplications.

His other frustration was the report from their tail on Mario. Apparently they were still sitting outside Mario's apartment, waiting for him to come out so they could get in there. They said he was probably sleeping off his "overnight" at the Darien police station. The snow storm, in point of fact, had probably kept a lot of people indoors, even in the Bronx. If he could count on Dell's gut feel-ing, Mario was the one who'd lead them to Paula's killer. He was their ace-in-the-hole. Minicus gave his head a slow shake; but the schmuck was in fucking hibernation.

Dell spoke up. "There it is; you see it? God, I could use a drink. Jack and Ricky said there was a good sports' bar in Norwalk, just up the Post Road." These were the same two Agents who had picked up Mario on Pebble

Run. Now they were back in place doing tonight's shift, ensconced in the Con Ed utility van. He was confident that Jack and Ricky were fully equipped and ready to move on the house as soon as the order came in.

They pulled up the driveway and found a parking spot right in front. Grabbing their duffles from the back seat, Minicus checked again with Dell on what, if any action had gone down at the Lazaro house. "So if I'm right, the only person who went inside was his wife? You're sure of that I.D.?"

"Yeah, Clio Lazaro. They've been married about three years. We did a run on her. Nothing stands out. She was inside the house for about half an hour and then came out rolling a big suitcase and carrying a canvas duffle. She was driving a silver BMW. They didn't follow her. Because you said for them to stay on the scene."

Minicus gave a short nod. "And there was nobody else."

" Right."

They were almost to the entrance. " Okay Buddy, we'll drop our bags here and then head up to...what was the name of that tavern?"

"O'Malley's. They're supposed to have a great shepherd's pie. Oh! And they mentioned a beef and Guinness stew. Jesus, I gotta' stop talking food."

"Yeah, shaddup' Dell."

Gemma's Apartment - Going on 9:00 PM

With every commercial break the same topic came up for discussion - Michael's shitty attitude. "Lemme' tell you Gemma, it's always the same. Like with TV shows - I can never watch any boy/girl shows with him. He says they're 'mindless'. You know what he's watching now?

CNN news and then it'll be reruns of CSI. Every week. I hate this writers' strike. '30 Rock' is gone, 'Dancing with the Stars', 'Desperate House-wives', everything. Our only choices are sports and old movies. And reruns."

"I know. That's why I always look for what movies are on." Gemma stood up and walked toward the foyer. "I was thinking that your suitcase might fit on the floor of the hall closet, if I put your boots and shoes in a box or something. We could stow it in the bathtub when we're not taking a shower." She turned around and headed back through the living room.

"Yeah, that would work. I think my duffel bag is still in your bedroom somewhere. We can use that." Gemma had already disappeared. Clio called, "I'll fill it up next commercial!"

Trying to find space at Gemma's for her clothes and shit was impossible. Her closet was the size of a couple of coffins and all the bureau drawers were maxed-out. This meant living out of her suitcase, lying out there on the living room floor, because there was no room for it in Gemma's bedroom. Clio had forgotten what it was like to live small.

Moving in with her sister wasn't the breeze she thought it would be, but it was a hell of a lot better than putting up with Michael's nasty moods. Out of left field, an image of Nick popped up. It was of him standing in the hotel room that morning, half dressed, reading the coffee pot. Had she been too cool, too stand-offish with him? The very thought of another night with him sent warm bubbles through her body. What if he didn't call her like he said he would? She didn't even know his last name.

Gemma returned from the bedroom carrying the duffel. "Once we get our stuff all squared away we can go out and celebrate. Hey whadaya' say, Clio. Tomorrow night let's do some TGIF prowling, huh?" She had practically growled the prowl part.

"Sure, fine by me." Clio chuckled. "You've already got me wondering what I can wear. Hey, sit down; here's the movie." Gemma joined Clio on the couch, feet up on that old coffee table of Clio's from her former single life. She had made Michael bring it up from the basement and load it in her car when Gemma moved to Stamford. It brought back memories of a life style she had put into past tense and was glad to be out of.

When her cell phone rang, she was taken by surprise. Was this - maybe Nick? Her home number shone from the screen. No, just Michael, "Clio, it's me. I want you to do something for me." She couldn't believe it. Not even a hello, how're things going. "Are you there?" She said nothing. "Hello, hello!"

"What is it Michael. You're interrupting our movie."

"For Christ's sake Clio. You gotta' help me out here. This is important!"

"So what is it." Her voice was flat.

"Tomorrow a package is coming to Gemma's address by courier messenger. They guarantee it'll get there by 2:00 PM at the latest. It's addressed to her, so she'll have to sign for it. But I want you to hang onto it for me. Will you do that?"

"She's working tomorrow."

"What do you mean she's working. She didn't have a job, last I knew."

"She's working a health fair at the high school. In Darien." Clio added an insincere, "Sorry."

Michael was getting exasperated. "Well, for God's sake, YOU sign for it, just use her name!"

"You mean I gotta' sit around here all day waiting for your dumb package? Why don't you have it sent there?"

Michael gasped for breath and the strength to contain his fury. "I CAN'T DO THAT! Clio, please! This is a matter of the highest priority. You could be saving my..." He almost said life but decided to say, job."

"Awright, awright. Shit. After the way you treated me today, I told myself I'd never come back to that house again."

"We're talking about our future, Clio. If I'm a little pre-occupied right now it's for a damn good reason. Now can I count on you to do this for me? I promise I'll make it up to you."

"Aw*right*! I said I'd do it. But I'm not coming back there till you know how to treat me nice, y'hear?"

"Call me tomorrow as soon you get it." He added, "Please."

"Didjya' hear me...?" But he'd already hung up.

Gemma pushed mute on the TV remote. "Wow, what was that all about?"

"Oh he wants me to stay here all day to sign for a package. It's addressed to you. I don't know, Gemma. This whole mess sucks."

"It sounds kinda' shady. Why is he using *my* address? Maybe you should stay out of it, y'know?"

"It's not anything dangerous. I just can't...I don't know. I can't ignore him. He sounds desperate." She stood up and walked round the table. "I'm getting myself a glass of that Chardonnay. Want one?"

Gemma shook her head. She was taken up with imagining all kinds of things that could be in the package: a gun, a bomb, a severed hand. This was crazy, she knew, but something was wrong here. When Clio came back in she said, "I want you to call me tomorrow if anything weird happens here."

"Oh, Gemma, it's probably nothing but a bunch of boring papers. Take it easy. I know him; his life is paper and numbers."

"I guess you're right. But still."

Clio sat back down, looking at the TV screen. Halle Berry's character had turned from a shy graphics designer into the lithe, sexy "Catwoman" who could leap between skyscrapers. She was doing just that at the moment.

"So are we done with the movie?"

"No. Are you kidding? He's not gonna' ruin the *whole* day for me."

Friday - February 9th - The Health Fair

Dana's sophomores came pouring into "D" period begging her. "Pleeeeez Miss Redman, can we go to the Health Fair, pleeeez?" She stood there smiling, shaking her head, saying nothing. They were jabbering away about the free food, the back and neck massages, shooting baskets to break some kind of record.

"They said jump rope is next, you guys. And then I heard they're gonna' do tennis."

She wondered how much hype was going on here. How could they manage all this action in a crowded gym?

"All right everyone, take your seats." Dana waited while they continued with who said what when. "The bell rang!" She cried out, over the din.

There was a collective sigh and then the sound of their chairs scraping across the floor. Unless they were doing group work, Dana liked having desks arranged in a circle to give her classes the feel of a seminar.

"We're still missing four people. Anyone know where Julie is, or Ray?"

"Yeah, she's not here."

"I see that Mark."

"No. I mean she left yesterday." With a big grin, "She started her vacation early."

"What about the others? Anyone know?" Her question drew several shakes of the head.

"Okay, here's what we'll do. Give it two more minutes to see if they're coming. Barry, make a note for me, will you?" She placed a blank white sheet of paper on his desk and waited for him to take out a pen. "D period class is in the gym getting healthy." A huge cheer went up and three kids jumped out of their chairs. "I said TWO minutes!" They sat back down grudgingly.

There were no late-comers, but she scotch-taped the note to the door anyway, locked it, and followed her speeding group down the hall, "WALK!" She yelled.

Inside the gym Dana searched for Nancy in the crowd, but didn't spot her. From the looks of it, this fair was a big hit. Her kids were right; it was all here. In a corner to her left, a bunch of boys were rooting someone on as he aimed and shot a basketball toward a rigged net. She walked over to see how this simple pastime connected to a health theme. A man was wearing a white tee shirt sporting a red insignia for the American Heart Association. He was handing off the ball and starting a timer for the next kid. It must be they're promoting exercise to get those blood vessels surging. And there to the side was a string of girls waiting for the boys to finish so they could start with their jump ropes to beat the clock.

Dana continued walking and canvassing the various

241

booths, keeping an eye out for her kids - to make sure they weren't acting like jerks. So far, so good. One girl was sitting astride a massage chair with two black cushions to press her face into. A group of girls watched her get a soothing rubdown on her back and neck. She could go for one of those, herself.

Up ahead she recognized the back of Nancy's head, so she ambled by two tables offering little plastic cups of yogurt topped with granola, encouraging kids to start their day in a healthy way. Next was a table with safety brochures about alcohol abuse and the hazards of DUI. But the table was empty. She looked above for some indication of sponsorship. On the wall was a Darien Police placard. Well, that's interesting. She guessed the cops were either taking a break or off taking care of criminal matters.

Nancy was leaning over the DVC table talking to a woman sitting next to Margie, the funky red-head who had helped them set up. "How's it going?" She asked coming up behind Nancy.

"Oh! Hey Dana, hi! You remember Margie here, right? And this is Gemma Savini. They're holding down the fort for DVC." They all exchanged hellos and shook hands. Nancy continued, "I was just given the job of telling Gemma that they're not allowed to hand out lollipops." She rolled her eyes upward. "It doesn't send the right health message. Can you beat that? I remember when that was my only reason for going to the dentist."

Gemma nodded, saying that they were told to put them away. Now the only draw was their teenster Margie, whose friends would come over to say hi. She spoke up. "You know what? I see a bunch over there from my class. I'll go over and tell them to come take our dating survey." Grinning, she threw them a backward glance. "And maybe steal a couple cups of that yogurt for our table to give away."

Dana looked across the gym as Margie took off. "This place is throbbing with action. Do you remember it being such a big deal last year?"

"I don't think it was. But then it's the last day before vacation and with tonight's game and all...everybody's in a party mood. Oh, Dana. I was just saying to Gemma that some of us are going to the Terry Connors Rink for tonight's game. She's brand new to Stamford. Her sister is staying with her for a few days, so I said we could meet them there if they'd like to go too.

Dana glanced down at Gemma, who was holding her hands together, smiling shyly. She had a dark, appealing, Neapolitan look to her. "That's a great idea. And we can hit Maxwell's afterward if you like. Oh Nancy, I talked to Carson last night, and he said he'd meet us there - probably not at the game." Dana stuck her arm out toward Gemma and wiggled her fingers. "We can do some shcmoozing, you know? Introduce you around."

Gemma grinned. "That sounds like real fun. Thanks a lot."

She asked Nancy if there was anything she could do to help out in the twenty minutes left of the period. Nancy shook her head but said maybe a hand after school to clear out stuff would be great. Dana sauntered off to make sure all her kids were still "keeping healthy". Sometimes an assembly or fair like this gave them a chance to sneak out for a smoke.

*

Conference Room, Darien Police Station - 1:30

Minicus was fed up. He'd been on the phone all morning trying to make headway at one site or another but he'd been frustrated by all three. Now his boss was talking about having him set up a new task force for a savings and loan scandal at another corporate office in Manhattan. He was so close here; if only he could get a break.

When Dell came back from the bathroom he barked an order at him, "Put another call in to our Bronx watch, will ya?"

"I just did; it was less than half an hour ago. And stop worrying. They'll let us know as soon as they can get in."

"I can't believe that two-bit guinea hasn't come out yet. It's been what, 25-26 hours he's been holed up in there?"

"You're soundin' a little cranky, Minnie. How about we take a break and get something to eat? There's a little place just up the Post Road. Uncle Mack's I think it's called."

"No, you go. I've got to stick by the fax here; those warrants might come through. Bring me back a pastrami on rye and a Coke, will ya?"

He wondered about these Italians. How could they sit inside their houses for days on end? Lazaro was one for the books. He hadn't gone anywhere at all. Of course a geek like that probably spends all day crunching numbers. He probably started already on his last year's tax return, fudging his income. If Dell was right about Lazaro, he was their key link to the killer.

They were still within that two week span of optimum time when something could break. Agent Minicus felt he had a real opportunity here. Not only would he flatten those Comp thieves; that was close to being sealed. But he might just get Paula Metz's murderer. What a "sweet shop" that would be for him. He'd seen the Darien detective only in passing that morning. He felt a little sorry for him, but not much. Minicus could tell yesterday that he was grinding his teeth over losing position on the case. Maybe Hansen was out on some other assignment. Although it was a low priority, Minicus would remind him to bring in that witness of his, Dana something or other. Might as well leave no stone unturned.

Once more he pressed the home office number at Federal Plaza. "Agent Minicus here. Are we even close?"

"Okay, we're just seeing...yeah, the subpoena's been approved. Still waiting on the Lazaro search warrant. That shouldn't be too long though. They told me 'his magistrate' would attend to it first thing. Soon as he gets back from lunch. Don't worry; I'll call you soon as I see it...and then fax both of them."

"Right! I'll be here waiting." Good. That makes it one down, one to go. His shoulders slumped with relief. Within the hour, baby. Make it happen. He wanted Dell to hurry up now and get back.

Gemma's Apartment - 1:30

Clio stared out the third floor window at the street below getting more and more exasperated. She had gone through their phone book three separate times looking for that lawyer's name, but nothing looked familiar. Now she wondered if it had ever been written down. She checked the small table clock once again. Less than half an hour more and she'd be out of there and straight home to insist that Michael get her a copy of their pre-nup. Turning

245

back toward the living room she forced herself to think about something else.

There was one good thing - seeing Gemma's face when she left this morning. She was smartly dressed and looking cheerier than Clio had seen her in months. For the first time it felt as though her ordeal was over and the move to Stamford was opening up a better life for her. Clio felt that maybe her own was turning a corner. And she wanted it to be a good one. A vision of yesterday morning reappeared. This time it was of the two of them under that warm hotel comforter just waking up. It was when he pulled her next to him and said how nice it'd been the night before.

Oh, she'd have to stop this fantasy foo-foo. He was probably a one night stand, and that's all. Clio picked up a box of crackers she'd been munching from and immediately set it back down. Why hadn't she made herself a decent sandwich? Next she pulled out her cell phone thinking that she might call one of her old buddies from The Zebra Club, just to catch up on the news there. It had been months since she'd connected with any of them. In some respects she asked herself why she'd put that life so far behind her. When the phone rang her hand jumped. But the ring wasn't hers; it was Gemma's land line on the hall table. After the second ring she checked the screen. Oh, it was from Michael. "I *said* I'd call you." She grumbled. "Nothing's come yet and I'm getting sick of waiting around."

Michael mumbled a 'bloody Christ', fearing that he might have been scammed again. If so, he'd lose it altogether. "Clio, we've still got about twenty minutes to go. Don't let me down."

"Well then, tell me just what's so important in this

package that you gotta' have it sent here, huh?"

"They're papers, Clio, papers. That's all you need to know."

"Yeah? I bet they're ones you have to hide, right? I'm telling you Michael, I don't like you using me and my sister this way. And I'm at the point where I want some guarantees. It's about my future I'm talking about. Like, what happens to me if you go bust?"

"Shut-up, Clio. There is no future unless I get..." Just then the doorbell rang.

"Well dearie me," she said, "there goes the doorbell. I'll answer it if you tell me that lawyer's name, the one who did our pre-nup."

"Jesus! Answer the door, Clio. ANSWER THE DOOR!"

She stood still, saying nothing. The bell rang again. "You hear it? Tell me his name!"

"For Christ's sake! Amberson! His name is Charles Amberson! Now answer the door!"

Clio put the phone back down on the table and opened the door. "Gemma Sullavini?" the messenger asked, extending a wired pen for her electronic signature. "Yeah, close enough," she said, "Sign this thing here?" Clio had never seen this kind of hand held machine before.

"Yes, right here." He pointed to a tiny screen. She signed and he handed over the package. It looked to be a size that would hold a bunch of papers. She could hear Michael's voice coming from behind, through the phone.

"Was that it?" A pause. "Was that it?"

She put the phone to her ear and closed the door. "Yeah. It's addressed to Gemma. I signed her name." She looked at the return address. "Jeez. It came from right here in Stamford."

"That's the one! Good! I'll be over to get it as soon as I finish something I'm doing here. Hang onto it!"

"You mean I gotta' wait again? Fuck that!"

"Clio, please. I won't be more than half an hour. It takes fifteen, twenty minutes to drive down there. You know that." This was true. "I just want to make sure of one thing."

She turned and gazed into the living room, considering. She'd waited this long. Going along might pay off later for her. She sighed and agreed. Once she'd set the package and phone down, Clio told herself that Gemma would be home by 2:30 or 3:00 anyway, and then she would be free to break out of this hold down. She wanted to pick up some groceries and that face cream she'd forgotten to pack.

Now hunger was really taking over. Clio walked into the kitchen and checked through the "deli" drawer of the refrigerator. A little ham was still there and some Swiss cheese. She built herself a sandwich and cracked open a diet Pepsi. Just as she settled onto the sofa, her cell phone bopped a call.

"Hey Clio; it's Nick. How ya' doin'?"

A thrill surged through her, leaving her almost breathless. "Oh, Nick. Nice to hear from you. I'm fine. How are you?"

"I'm ready to party, Baby. I feel like I just won the lottery. Want to join me?" Everything had gone perfectly at Ely's. All they wanted was the transfer number Lazaro had faxed to the computer at *Stamford Waste* and to see his driver's license, which of course was his new one with the "Ricky" ID.

Clio caught herself before leaping at the opportunity.

"Uh, well I can't tonight if that's what you're talking about. I already have plans." She almost said with her sister, but again checked herself.

"Oh, too bad. Well how about tomorrow night? Saturday. You busy?"

"No, I'm not." She remembered the offer he had made, "So is this for one of your famous spaghetti dinners or did you have something else in mind?"

"What I really have in mind is about a week of sun in Puerto Rico. Wanna' come?"

She laughed and said it sounded real nice; but maybe they should start smaller - for right now."

"Sure. I said I'd make some spaghetti for you, didn't I? I'll go out and get the fixings right now. The sauce always tastes better if it sits overnight. How about around 6:00 - 6:30?"

"Great. But you'll have to give me directions."

"Sure. I'll give you a call tomorrow, late afternoon." Then he added, " To make sure no other guys have gotten to you first." She was taken a little by surprise until she heard, "Just kidding. You and me? We're a combo."

She laughed giving her head a little shake. "You're a real character, Nick. Ya' know that? Talk to you tomorrow then... Oh!" She caught herself. "Why don't you give me your phone number too, just in case. Let me get a pencil." She grabbed her pocket book and scraped the bottom for a pen. "And are you gonna' tell me your last name?"

"It's Rizzo, Nick Rizzo at your service, madam."

She pulled a magazine forward from a pile on the coffee table. "Okay, shoot." With that done, she shifted her voice to the old 'Zebra come-on tone'. "See you tomorrow then. Can't wait."

Clio leaned back and gazed out and beyond the hall to the door. Holy Mary, Mother of God. Her life *was* turning. She looked down at her ring finger. The wedding ring? It can stay packed in her suitcase. A smile curved up and the room brightened. She sat there a moment longer still holding onto the phone, feeling the glow.

Face-Off

<u>Darien </u> - School's Out: late afternoon

By the time she had finished figuring lesson plans for the first week back and then helping Nancy clean up, it was already after 4:00. As she drove away from school along Darien's freshly cleared back roads, she noticed how the winter days of February were finally getting longer - and brighter. The sun was low in the sky spreading a gold and pink glow on the snow. Long shadows cast by trees standing on the lawns of handsome, country estates set their own replicas on a white land-scape. What a quietly beautiful scene. It enhanced her own feeling of release from duty, from tests and papers to grade, from responsibility. In that moment Dana glided into vacation mode. She told herself to drift, to savor the float.

It didn't last long. Within ten minutes she was in town and turning up Hecker Avenue for the police station and sensing her high mood leveling out. In a way it was funny. Coming into the reception area, announcing herself to the officer behind the glass, and waiting for the door to buzz her in felt almost routine. If it turned out the FBI wanted to question her, what more could they ferret out than that first Lt. Frampton and then Steve Hansen?

At the sound of the buzz she opened the door, and saw him walking toward her from down the hall, but it was not with his usual, energetic stride. "Hi Dana", he said, "Are you glad to be out?"

"You bet I am. The day went past pretty fast though. How are you?"

"Oh, okay. It's good of you to come in." He looked tired. "You must be excited about going on vacation tomorrow."

"It turns out that we won't be leaving till Monday. Carson has to finish a big project in the city."

"Oh. Too bad." He turned and proceeded back, down the hall. "I don't think this will take long," he said, "If you'll follow me, I have that photo array set up back here."

She followed. "What about the FBI? Do they need to talk to me?"

"No. Not today, anyway. They're busy with something in Stamford."

"Oh." Dana hoped it would be the same over the weekend too. "Well, that's good, I guess."

They entered a small room full of file cabinets and a work table with six manila folders, all laid out on its surface. "Would you like me to take your jacket? I can put it on this chair."

"That's okay. You said this wouldn't take long." She started unwinding her scarf, "I'll just toss this over here," and she chucked it on the chair.

He turned on one of his old smiles, "Is that 'Blue and White Wave' scarf required apparel when you teach at Darien High?"

Dana grinned. "No, but I do wear it for storms and hockey games. Ice rinks are pretty cold, you know."

"Right." After a moment's hesitation, his expression turned serious and he commenced to explain police procedure. He would serve as the impartial witness. He stated that any of her verbal reactions as each photo was uncovered had to be recorded. She looked at him. This seemed more important, at least in a legal way, than the audio ID had been. But his face registered little, only a faint smile.

He turned to pick up a clip board from the top of a file cabinet and from it read several official statements, like how it was as important to clear innocent people as it was to identify the guilty. Also that a person's appearance can change with a hair style or facial hair. When he read out that a picture of the perpetrator might or might not be amongst the present photos, Dana was puzzled. Why then had he asked her to do this? It also began to feel a bit daunting. She could be putting the finger on someone, maybe mistakenly.

He finished by assuring her that regardless of whether she identified someone or not, the police would continue to investigate the crime. Finally, he pointed his finger to the left and instructed her to start at the far end of the table. She was to open each folder separately and study the picture inside carefully. "Take all the time you need." He then took a few steps back to lean against the wall, clipboard and pen in hand. "Any time you're ready."

The first was of a dark-haired, middle-aged man with a

square jaw that struck no familiar chord. She closed that folder. The next was also dark-haired, but with a rather gaunt, lean look, maybe a few years younger than the first. His eyes were close-set, which didn't feel right. By the fifth photograph Dana concluded that this collection had been grouped for type. All had black hair and appeared to be of either Italian or Hispanic background. They were between their late 30s and 50. She could not say that any of these faces was the one she remembered, vague as that memory might be after ten days. In her mind's eye was a face with good, balanced features that none of these men possessed. Of course he had worn a hat, but the dark hair seemed right. The sixth picture gave her pause, but his nose looked like it had been badly broken. No, not right. She closed that folder and went back to number one and through all of them again, to make sure.

"I'm sorry, Steve, I really don't feel a match." He couldn't hide a brief but definite look of disappointment.

"Well!" he said emphatically, pulling himself upright. "You sure made my job easy. I didn't have to write a word." He looked at the form on the clipboard, thought a minute, and then asked her to sign it, even though there was nothing entered under witness's comments.

As she handed back the pen, she asked, "Are you allowed to tell me anything? I mean was your suspect in there?"

"Here's the thing. I could tell you if you picked the suspect, but I'm not allowed to make any statements beyond that... OR gestures, for that matter."

"Oh." She glanced down at the floor. "I guess I haven't been much help."

"Dana, what is - is. You did your best."

She picked up her scarf and he held the door open. Neither one of them said anything as they walked back toward the waiting room. Dana was feeling inexplicably blank and kind of sad. What was it like to work hard on a case and get nowhere. Just then she decided to try something kooky.

She whirled around and smiled. He looked surprised. "Hey listen," she said, "you should take some time off for a little recreation." He stood there perplexed. "Some friends of mine are going to this big hockey game in Stamford tonight and then we're gathering afterwards at Maxwell's for some beers. Want to join us?"

"Uh, probably not. There's some follow-up work I have to do here."

This didn't sound convincing. "Oh come on. There'll be some great single women and a few good guys." After a brief pause she said enthusiastically, "C'mon! Branch out."

"That's nice of you, Dana." He smiled, pleased that she'd included him. "I don't know. Maybe. It all depends on what goes down here and in Stamford."

"The game is at Terry Connors Rink. It starts at 6:00. Stamford against Westhill. It'll be a hot one." He half smiled and shrugged.

She turned and called back, "We'll look for you!"

Terry Connors Rink - End of Second Period

Nancy suggested that they hit the snack bar for a dog and Coke. It was a good idea, because one or two of the others they'd invited might be acting on a similar notion. Dana couldn't help but be a little embarrassed that her big social set-up was looking like an empty party bag. It would have been such fun to watch Steve Hansen's reaction to Nancy, her bright Upstater vs. Gemma, the dark Italian and her sister. During the game she kept turning her head toward the entranceway checking for him. Nancy didn't know that Dana had invited "The Detective"; she had been on the lookout for Gemma. At least Carson would be there to meet them after the game. He was shooting for the 7:37. Dana had asked him if Jay would be coming up, or if he preferred trolling the city now.

The score was Stamford 3-1, and it had held there for the whole second period. Slick, speedy passing had turned into blind passing with no particular strategy. Westhill was freezing the puck a lot to keep it out of Stamford's grip and this tactic often stopped play in order to set up another face-off. The crowd's loud and enthusiastic cheering first period had fallen into an eerie quiet, particularly with Westhill spectators. Dana was glad to stand up and walk a bit.

This snack bar turned out to be a glorified concession stand with a few tables to sit at, but at least there was a hot dog lady. They were standing in line, waiting to place an order. The room was jammed . "Are you having what I'm having?" Nancy pulled out a wallet from her jacket pocket.

"Sure." Dana pointed to her pocket. "I'm good for the beers later."

"Stop it, Dana It's the least I can do after all the help you gave me yesterday. AND today."

"Okay, okay." She turned around to check out the crowd. "Hey, isn't that Gemma coming in the door?"

"Oh yeah! Hey, Gemma!" She waved her hand above several heads. "Over here!"

She smiled and gave a nod of recognition. As soon as

she'd threaded her way over, the chatter hit fast: "I was worried we'd missed you"; "Yeah we were looking for you too"; "Can I get something for you here?"; "No, I'm good"; "So did your sister come too?" and so on. With snack trays in hand they followed Gemma out and through a thinning crowd to the other side of the rink where Stamford High's fans were sitting. Right then the home team - Stamford, came skating out to huge cheers. Westhill was already on the ice sweeping round one half of the rink at a fast clip. Dana and Nancy had been cheering from the Westhill section before, hoping they'd knock Stamford out of the play-offs. Actually, Dana thought Stamford's side would be a happier place to sit, although she wouldn't have a good view of the entrance. She told herself to just enjoy the rest of the game. Maybe Steve Hansen would show up at Maxwell's.

Gemma explained, as they stepped up the stairs of the bleachers, that her sister was sitting with a friend she'd run into unexpectedly, some new guy she was dating who roots for a friend's kid, a player. A whistle sounded to signal the drop and another cheer went up. They weaved their way through knees and squeezed in. Gemma took a seat and then turned their way to introduce Clio on her left and next to her, Nick the friend. They all said brief hellos and turned to watch the action. Dana was wondering if Westhill's coach had succeeded in firing up his team, so that they'd have a game here.

Both teams appeared to be reenergized by the intermission, and thus far Westhill was playing a good defensive game, but they needed a goal. After twelve minutes of ice time neither team had scored. Over the crowd Dana heard Clio asking her friend a question about someone on Stamford's team. Even though she had one of those voices that carries, Dana couldn't make out all that she said. One word "Enforcer" came through. Dana watched as Clio looked back to the ice and nod her head. She leaned over Nancy's shoulder, "Gemma, did she say 'enforcer'?"

"Yeah, from what Nick says, his friend's son is the team's enforcer." She smiled. "It's usually the biggest guy on the team." Dana frowned, a little puzzled. Gemma continued, "I guess he's supposed to protect his teammates from getting bashed." She pointed down to one of the players. "There he is - number 17, the large one fighting for the puck."

Nancy cut in, "Well, he got it. Look at him go. Wow! These guys have to be plenty aggressive to play this game."

With Stamford blazing down the ice and into the attacking zone, Dana gave out a little sigh. Please, not another goal. This game would turn into a push-over. Defense held on though. She looked up at the timer. Only three minutes remaining. She was beginning to thirst for a beer. She also had to get to a bathroom. Maybe she should go now before everyone else got the same idea.

Just then a voice to her left yelled, "Get'im Joey! Get'im!" Dana's skin tightened. Her head jerked left. Clio's friend Nick was standing up with his fists pumping up and down. "You stupid slow-whistles. He speared 'im! He speared 'im!"

She was caught between an ugly recognition and that "speared'im" term he used.

Clio yelled up at him. "What? Wha'd he do?"

Nick turned to respond. "He jabbed Joey. With his stick blade. *Two* times!" They turned back to the ice.

Other fans stood up and started yelling. Dana sat frozen as recognition battled fear. The whole Stamford crowd was now on its feet yelling at the refs. Nick was still screaming something about the stupid ref. His voice! It was the same as that guy's two weeks ago, at the fight in the parking lot. The whistle blew and a penalty was called. She wanted a closer look at his face but she didn't want to appear obvious. What if he recognized her?

A major penalty meant Westhill would be down one player. No game left. She turned to Nancy to say she'd meet her right outside the door - she had to go to the bathroom.

Nancy gave her a funny look. "Don't you want to wait till the end? There's only a minute or so to go."

Nick turned in their direction with a smile to say something and stopped. The smile closed down as he looked at Dana's face and then stared at her scarf. There it was. Nick looked up again, but turned his head back slowly, mumbling something.

He was the one! And at the station too. "See you outside by the door," Dana called as she started pushing her way to the bleacher stairs. She scampered down, never looking back, and passed quickly around the end of the rink toward the concession area. If she remembered correctly there were bathrooms nearby. How was she going to handle this? Would he be going with them to Maxwell's? Some of the crowd was already filtering out as the buzzer sounded the end of the game. Maybe she should have dragged Nancy with her. But the others would have wondered why they were leaving so suddenly. Dana needed some time to think.

With a quick intake of breath she slapped her pants' pocket and then shoved her hand inside. Yes! It was still there from last night. Hansen's cell phone number. She'd call him from inside one of the stalls and then call Nancy and tell her to send the others on to meet up at Maxwell's.

Inside, she had to hit the john first. Fortunately, one door stood ajar. She swept in and let go. With that need taken care of, Dana punched in Hansen's number and listened to it ring twice.

He picked up. "Steve Hansen."

"It's Dana. I'm at the rink. Where are you now Lieutenant?"

"Dana Redman?" His voice registered surprise.

"Yes. Listen. I saw the same man who was at the train station. Just now. We're here at the game. I'm scared 'cuz he looked like he recognized me too. Are you any-where nearby?"

"I'm still at the station. Why don't you come directly here?"

"No, that wouldn't work. The game just ended. My friend drove. See, he's part of this group I'm with. They're all waiting for me outside, and we're supposed to go on to Maxwell's. Can you go there now?"

"Yes, I'm close by. I'll be there waiting for you. Keep your cool, Teach." He added, "And don't give my career away, okay?'

"Got it!" She flipped her phone shut and hustled out of the stall and through a gathering line of teenage girls heading in. It was good she came in when she did. No need to call Nancy.

Dana was out and making her way down the little hall to the rink area when something poked into her back. A voice spoke roughly in her ear, "Keep walking and do exactly what I say or this .45 is gonna' shred your spine. Got me?" Dana started to turn her head. "Don't look back! Do exactly as I say."

It was him. Her heart leaped into her throat. She took hesitant steps trying to make her brain function. How could she get out of this?

"C'mon, c'mon. Keep moving. Turn right." They were walking rink side now, through an oncoming crowd. The Zamboni came into sight from the far end and wheeled onto the ice.

"Turn right again. Now!" He poked her into the snack bar. "Keep going toward the back where that door is, to the left."

Ten to twelve people were standing around talking, but they paid no attention to the two. He had one hand on her left shoulder now, guiding the direction as they began to weave their way through tables on the far side of the room. Dana thought of diving under one of the tables, but decided they wouldn't give much cover. Even if she did, he might start shooting at all of them. Her eyes darted right and left in an attempt to catch someone's attention as they passed through, but no one looked their way. They angled across to the far end.

Beyond the snack machines and concession stand a woman was leaning over, her back to them. He shoved the gun harder into Dana's back. They were about ten feet from the back door behind the counter. It was standing part way open, showing a slim rectangle of darkness outside. He grabbed her left arm and propelled her ahead. The woman's voice behind called out, "Hey, you can't go out that way!"

They were through and outside, standing on a bed of gravel. Dana tried to turn, to wave at the woman, yell, do something, but he slammed the door shut and gripped her arm tighter. "You make a sound and I'll let you have it."

Then he swung her back around and pushed her forward. A heavy whirring from fans overhead covered sounds from the crowd inside. Dim light coming from a far off lamp revealed a high chain link fence. They were standing in an enclosed rectangle, maybe 20 by 40 forty feet long. She could make out two dumpsters, coils of hoses, oil drums and other equipment.

Damn! Dana was hoping there would be cars parked back here and that she could make a run for it, but all she was able to see beyond the fence was snow piled high and black sky. He force-walked her to the right along the fence, in search of an outlet. They reached that end. Nothing.

"Fuck!" he snarled and turned her back the other way. She was trying to picture how far they were from the entrance, where Nancy would be standing. Oh God, Dana thought. What if she tries to call? Dana didn't want her phone to ring or for him to get a hold of it. They had turned back and were almost to the opposite end when a desperate idea switched on. It took effort but she forced confidence into her voice, "You'll never get away with this. My friend called the police."

"Shut-up. You're a liar." There he stopped. He'd found the gateway out. "Open it up!"

Dana rattled it ineffectively. "It won't open."

Both his hands came forward. "Jesus!" He started jerking on the latch to make it open.

"She *did* call them*!*"

"You fuckin' bitch!" His arm flew up and came down, cracking her hard on the side of her head. "Shut up!" She half-dropped to her knees but caught herself and at the same time jammed her hand into her jacket pocket to grab the phone. Then she saw his leg come up. He delivered a hard kick, but she got only the end of it. Dana went down anyway and rolled to one side, her back to him. Her thumb ran over the phone till recognition hit. She pressed the off button. Then a sharp tug jerked her neck up. His hands were yanking at her scarf. In a quick motion he wound it once more around her neck.

The gun. Where was it? He tugged her to her feet and started pulling the scarf tighter and tighter. Dana began to gasp. "Please, please." He applied more force. She could pull no air in at all. He squeezed harder.

"This is how you're gonna' die you meddling bitch." He pulled even tighter. Dana felt herself beginning to go black when suddenly he eased off. She gulped in a huge batch of air. Her knees buckled. "Are you gonna' keep your mouth shut?" He tightened the scarf again and yanked her up to eye level. She was hanging there by her neck. "Huh? Huh?" He let go of his hold and she dropped to all fours gasping for breath.

A ragged "Yes" came out.

"Just remember, I'm out there." The gate swung open knocking against her hip. He leaned over her and squeezed out one more menacing threat. "And now I know who you are." Then he took off.

Dana lay there, on her side, listening to the clump of his feet running off and around the end of the building. Then, for open air and sky, she rolled to her back. Over the drone of fans above she could make out the distant sound of horns tooting and cars backing and wheeling out of the parking lot, a welcome reminder that she was still alive. The cold gathered in and she began to shiver. She waited though, till she stopped panting and to make sure he was really gone before pulling herself up. Dana lurched to the fence and clung to it with her fingers,

263

assessing the damage. There didn't seem to be any permanent harm, physically. She didn't get that bullet in her spine. Dana was grateful for that, but she also felt a little foolish. He must have been faking a gun all that time. When her breathing returned to normal, she wondered why he'd stopped choking her. Maybe he just wanted to get the hell out. She staggered out of the enclosure guided by ambient light shining from the parking lot. Nancy would be worried.

Coming round the front of the building, Dana scanned the area for any signs of him, but figured he'd taken off by now. A last stream of headlights pointed the way through the exit and on, up the road. Catching sight of Nancy, she began to trot. Nancy was standing to one side of the entrance craning her head to the left, then out toward her car. They had left Dana's parked in back of Maxwell's earlier. She called out in a kind of croak, "Nancy, I'm over here!"

Nancy started walking toward her, "Dana! Where've you been? Were you sick or something?"

"No..." She leaned over supporting herself with both hands on her knees, afraid that she'd start crying. After a big intake of breath she blurted, "I got mugged," and pointed, "back there."

"Jesus, are you OK?"

"Yeah, I'm just a little shaky. Come on, let's get out of here. I'll tell you about it in the car."

On the way back to Darien, Dana gave her a fairly scant version of what happened, not mentioning Nick. Nancy was having a hard time believing she'd gone through such a scare. Shouldn't she be calling the police?

"He didn't get anything, Nancy. I never carry my wallet to games. He didn't even get the two twenties I stuffed in my pocket." She quickly asked about the group. Would they be coming to Maxwell's? Nancy told her just Clio and Gemma, and that Nick had left right before the end whistle. He was meeting his friends for beers in Stamford. With some relief Dana added that she didn't want to talk about what happened until after she saw Carson, to get his opinion.

She sat on her hands to warm them and to hide the trembling. So he had never intended to join them. Good, but she wondered about Clio. How was she a friend of his? Dana let this go though, deciding to let her detective take over any investigative questioning.

Nancy went on about how they had waited outside for her, chatting. Apparently, it was only the night before that Clio had met Nick. She'd been surprised to see him at the game. She continued, "I told them to go on ahead and we'd meet them there. Clio knows where Maxwell's is." Then Nancy started to tease Dana about her engagement with danger at hockey games. With this, Dana urged her not to say anything about her encounter. She emphasized wanting to talk to Carson first. And anyway, the guy hadn't hurt her or robbed her of anything.

Dana suddenly remembered to turn her phone back on and to check for messages. The first was from Nancy asking what was taking so long in the bathroom, a long line? The next was from Steve Hansen saying he was at Maxwell's waiting for them. Were they on their way? Nothing from Carson, so he must have caught his train. No reason to call him, then. His train wasn't due for another fifteen minutes or so. And he had a two block walk from the station.

They were pulling into the back lot looking for a parking space. Hopefully, she'd be able to catch a few minutes with Steve before joining the others.

Maxwell's
You could hardly find your way through the crowd to
order a beer. They spotted Gemma and Clio half way
down the bar, in the midst of the crowd. It was TGIF, big
time. Dana scanned across heads to the far end, but
didn't see Steve. A sudden tap on her shoulder startled
her. She craned her neck around to see who it was. A
few feet back was Steve motioning with his arm for her
to follow him. Dana called above the din, "Nancy!
Order me a Bass, will ya? I see an old friend. Be with
you in a minute." Nancy frowned a little but nodded and
moved forward.

Dana followed Steve's head as they threaded their way
back, toward Maxwell's entrance which divided the bar
from the restaurant. Two separate sets of doors framed a
kind of foyer that created a quiet waiting place. They sat
down on a bench between two Island Pines decorated
with tiny lights. Perfect, she thought. Steve asked immediately, "Is he here?"

"No, he didn't come. He's not coming." They needed
to keep this brief. "I'll tell you this quickly so we can get
back inside. First, I recognized his voice from two weeks
ago. It was after a hockey game. He was real loud, egg-
ing these boys to fight. Oh, and his girl friend Clio is
with us. I don't know much about her, except that she
just met this guy Nick recently. You can find out more
from her. Apparently he follows the team. A friend's son
plays for Stamford. I don't want you to leave though
unless I have some kind of protection. He grabbed me as
I came out of the bathroom, pushed me outside. He's
threatened me."

"What?" He gave Dana an intent look. "How?"

"He threatened to kill me. He told me he knew who I was, and he would be 'out there' in case I said anything." Steve's eyes stared ahead. "And he half strangled me with my scarf."

"We have to move on this. His name is Nick?"

"Yes. I don't know his last name. You'll have to find that out from the others. Oh! They don't know about what happened to me. My friend Nancy is inside now with them. They're sisters, Gemma and Clio. We should go in before they begin to wonder where I am...again."

"OK. You take it easy now. Let me take the lead." He stood up and put his hand on her shoulder. "Don't worry Dana. I'll see that you get round the clock protection. What kind of car are you driving?" She told him a maroon Saturn sedan. He patted her on the back. "Let's go."

They walked back in, summoning a pretense of casual, Friday night socializing. Nancy caught sight of them and waved. "Hey, *there* you are!" She said, pushing forward a Bass.

"Thanks. I just ran into Steve here." Dana glanced back in his direction. "I want you to meet Gemma and Clio, her sister. And this is my school buddy, Nancy." Dana put her hand on Nancy's shoulder. "This is Steve, everybody." She turned his way again to deliver a spark for conversation. "You said you were living in Norwalk now, right?"

"Yeah." He raised his voice over the bar noise. "I hear you've all just come from Terry Connors Rink."

This launched a brief summary of the game, which didn't amount to much, and then Clio asked Steve how the bars in Norwalk compared to Darien's."

"I guess this," he waved a gesture of his hand sideways, "by comparison, is an upscale crowd."

Dana decided to cut in here, looking at the sisters, "So I understand your friend Nick couldn't come?"

"No," Clio answered. "He's with some buddies in Stamford."

"Oh, too bad. Well, he certainly seemed to know a lot about their team."

She shrugged. "I never followed the game myself."

Gemma picked up. "He told us about his friend's son who plays for Stamford. He's the team's 'enforcer.'" And she smiled glancing up at Steve.

"I guess every team's got one," he agreed. "Hockey's a great game to watch in person. I don't like watching it on TV though." Nancy nodded her head. "I've gone to a few of the high school games. Used to play myself." At this he paused, lifting his head, thinking. "Nick..." he started to say and paused again, for effect. "You know what? I might have met him. Uh... I remember a month or so ago. I was at a game up in Trumbull. We were standing behind Stamford's goal watching the game. He kept talking about the various players on their team. Yeah, and his friend's son. I'm trying to remember his last name."

"Nick's or the player's?" This was Gemma. She looked eager to be of help.

"Nick's."

"Oh, I don't know." She glanced at her sister. "Clio, do you?" Dana held her breath.

"Yeah, it's Rizzo." She cocked her head looking at Steve, "Sound right?"

"*That's* it. He lives in Stamford, right?"

Steve thought he saw Clio's head begin to come down

in a nod, but Carson's voice broke in from behind. "Hey, everybody, Hi! Been having a good time?"

"Oh honey, I'm glad you got here." He gave her a little kiss. Then Dana panicked. He might recognize Steve's last name. She'd have to keep the intros to first names only. She went ahead with that form and it went off fine.

"So who else needs a drink?" he asked. "I know I could use one. How about I do this round?"

There were a few protests, but Dana jumped in to take orders. Beers all round except for Steve and Clio. She didn't know why but her request for a glass of Chianti amused her. "Come on Carson, I'll go with you. You'll need more than two hands." As they waited for their order at the bar, Dana told him that Steve was Lt. Hansen and he was doing a follow-up on some guy Clio knew. "No one else knows he's a detective and they're not supposed to yet, okay?"

Carson shrugged his shoulders and smiled. "Sure. Cops and robbers. I'm game." Then he frowned. "Does this have anything to do with you?"

"I'm fine." She had gulped down that first beer and was feeling the release of some of the pent-up tension she'd been holding. Keeping up this brave front was getting to her though. "I'll tell you all about it when we leave. Oh, did you get a hold of Jay?"

"Yes, he's going to stay in the city over the weekend. Fresher material, I guess."

Dana had to smile, thinking that he'd probably never change. Maybe Sally was better off on her own. She covered Carson's hand with hers. "Did you have anything at all to eat?"

"I grabbed a sub at Grand Central. And a beer." He smiled and asked, "Did you?"

"Just a hot dog, but I'm okay for now." In truth, home and a bed suddenly sounded good. She wondered how long she could last. "Carson? If they want to carry on late, I don't think I'm up for it, that all right with you?"

He looked a little surprised. "I thought you'd be in the partying mood, your last day and all, but that's fine by me. It's been a long week." The bartender placed four beers and the glass of Chianti before them. "Oh, but Dana," His eyes widened and with a smile, he cocked his head. "I did get a lot accomplished." Carson paid up and they were on their way.

The first thing she noticed getting back to the group was that Steve wasn't there, even though the group had grown in size. Two new guys had joined the ladies and were going full tilt on some issue. Jay, or no Jay she thought, new faces always bring on the curious. Dana spoke softly to Nancy. "Did Steve leave?"

"No, he said he'd be right back."

The taller one of the two newcomers interrupted the other one, "Yeah? Well that's the *real* world. These white communities are disconnected from the rest of the world. They come out of their ivy league colleges not knowing how to relate to different types of people." Dana was surprised that they'd gotten onto such a weighty topic. Maybe this guy was trying to make an impression on these new "Italian sisters" from Stamford. As they continued, she gathered that the debate was over who got the better high school education: kids in elite, highly competitive schools like New Canaan and Darien or the ones attending less academic ones but with the broader, mixed population of bordering cities.

Both she and Nancy exchanged amused glances but kept quiet. Just listening was more fun. Steve rejoined them, sidling through to stand next to Gemma. Then they turned away a bit to carry on a separate conversation. She looked quite animated and responsive. Dana wondered if he was "on the job" getting information or just flirting. She looked younger than her sister and closer to Steve's age, but why wasn't he homing in on Clio, if it was information he wanted?

The debate eventually exhausted itself, coming to no provable conclusion and then turned to more conventional topics. Carson started talking about the snow storm today and how glad he was to commute by train. "Anything on rubber wheels around here," he said, "seems to cause delays and accidents." Nancy joked that in time global warming would take care of any heavy snow falls. Someone else complained that there should be a better bus line to Stamford. Dana was having trouble investing interest in any of this. One of the two new guys squeezed in next to Clio, supposedly to lean his weary body against the bar. Dana gave Carson the "let's go" look, and they polished off the rest of their beer.

"Hey guys," she said. "I'm afraid Carson and I have to beat it. Believe it or not, he's back in the city tomorrow morning. More work. We've hardly seen each other all week." They did smiles and handshakes before going. She turned in Steve's direction and looked up, her face a question.

He said, "Great to see you again, Dana. I'll give you a call about that project you have." He leaned across to shake her hand and said in an undertone, "Everything's taken care of. You'll be safe."

"Okay everyone," she called. "See you again soon, I hope."

They were moving out when she heard Nancy calling

after her, "Hey don't go anywhere without getting my permission first!" Dana raised her hand and waggled fingers in the air, pleased that they weren't deserting her. There was still an extra guy for her to talk to.

The air outside was cold and refreshing, but with that leave-taking accomplished, a wave of exhaustion passed through her. Dana led the way into the back parking lot to where she'd parked their car earlier. Carson said from behind. "So you were serious before. I thought you'd want to stay out later tonight." Dana just shook her head.

She pulled out the car keys and clicked the unlock button. "Honey, would you drive?" She handed him the set.

They were cranking the heat up and pulling onto the street when he said, "Okay. Now tell me about this Lt. Hansen. Why was he here tonight?" Dana's attention was on a car that had pulled out of the lot and followed them to the first stop light. Was this the 'protection' Steve had alluded to? It stayed with them as she described to Carson everything from 4:00 that afternoon on. They had reached home and were sitting in their own driveway still talking by the time she got them up to the scene at Maxwell's.

"My God, Dana!" He reached over and pulled her close. She broke down. It took her a few minutes to regain composure. Finally, she wiped her eyes and sat back up. She turned her head far to the right and fixed on a car parked on the other side of their street. Light from a full moon was enough for her to make out two silhouettes sitting in the front seat. "I think we have a look-out here." Carson turned his head with a question on his face. "A car was following behind us." She opened her car door a little.

"No!" Carson gasped and grabbed her arm. Just then their headlights blinked off and on two times.

"It's okay honey, it's a police car."

Carson said, "Jesus, I didn't even notice it; I was so intent on what you were telling me." He shook his head. "Dana, I am not letting you out of my sight until this fuck head is behind bars."

Dana smiled and squeezed his arm. "Let's talk about that inside where it's warm."

Heading to Darien Police Station

As soon as Steve Hansen could break free of the group, he drove the short distance to headquarters. Everything he needed to get this going would be right there. The run-down on Rizzo was already in progress. After checking on that, he'd get the warrant for his arrest. He also wanted to connect with Minicus. Find out what progress they'd made with Lazaro - this was to make sure they weren't already ahead of him. After serving the search warrant and making Lazaro's arrest they'd shifted their work place to the Stamford police station, since that's where he was being detained. As far as Hansen knew, the arrest was still on civil charges, nothing criminal. At least not yet. Last he heard, they were trying to get a voluntary statement from him.

Despite a long, frustrating day, at that moment Steve felt he was back in the game. Yeah, he was juiced. This was the real thing. Let Club Fed focus on Lazaro and that mishap Mario. He thought about that afternoon, watching Dana pass through his photo array. It had sent his high hopes plummeting. Man, he had gotten that one wrong. Counted on her voice recognition matching Mario's picture. All because of those audio tapes. Dana must have recognized a similar quality in their voices. He wondered if Nick Rizzo had grown up in the Bronx too.

Tonight though. What a great job she'd done at Maxwell's. And at the rink! She'd be okay now. He had dispatched a squad car to keep watch, and they called from her address to say all was quiet.

He was turning onto Hecker and heading up to the station when it occurred to him that he should make a follow-up plan with Gemma. Plan it now, while he was alone and could think. Once in the station, he'd get drawn in too many directions. It had been an instinctive decision to focus attention on Gemma. She appeared to take an interest in him and was eager to please, certainly more so than her sister. If they weren't able to collar Rizzo tonight, he'd have to move step-by-step very carefully on a different plan for tomorrow, with Gemma.

With his new "girl friend's" phone number in his pocket, he'd left around 10:00, saying he had a job to finish up; he had just stopped in for a break. Before leaving he asked Gemma if it would be all right for him to give her a call sometime soon. The big smile appeared when he turned to her and said, "Let's make that tomorrow." So with more luck and a smooth manner, he'd get a chance to talk to Clio too. *May*be. He was counting on her as his big link, gambling that she wasn't in any imminent danger. If Dana's account of Clio and Nick's relationship was a recent one, he could let go of the idea that she might be in league with him. So far no one had asked what he did for a living; he'd already decided on that answer - he was an accountant. But if the circumstances changed, he'd have to show up in official status.

A lot depended on results tonight. He was getting out

of his car at this point and wondering what possible kind of date he could contrive that would allow him to call Gemma in the morning. What was even open at 11:00 besides some diner? He'd have to think of something plausible *and* good. She said she liked animals. There was always the nature center. This made him laugh. Hey, a stroll along their trails and then brunch.

Once inside, Hansen was given the run-down on "Nicholas Rizzo". They had done it, using both variations: Nick and Nicholas. There were two in Stamford and one in Danbury. Every one of them had clean slates except for a couple speeding and parking tickets. One of the addresses in Stamford was down in the Shippan area facing onto Long Island Sound. Hansen didn't think this guy would be living on an estate, but he didn't want to brush over any possibilities. The other address was part of an apartment complex closer to town. This same guy drove a 2002 red Camaro, one of their last. Now Hansen recalled Gemma mentioning that her sister had met Nick only the night before, at Silvio's in North Stamford. That whole crowd tonight seemed to like talking about restaurants in the area. She was wondering if he'd ever eaten there. Great Italian food, of course. His gut said, this Rizzo was the one.

The first order of business was to get a warrant for arrest. If he was already at home, they'd need it to get inside. He would have to get a detailed description of the attack on Dana and to write down the exact wording of his threat. He picked up the phone to call her. She sounded tired but gave a full account. The charge would be Assault & Battery compounded with a threat of death. Her last words were, "If you get him, I better be the first one to know about it."

That accomplished, he contacted Forensics. By now the rink would be shut down for the night, but he could send a crew over anyway, to go over that fenced in area in back. Any physical evidence they might find would be a plus.

Finally, he called the Stamford station to ask if either Minicus or Dell was still there. Both had left for the day. He learned from one of their detectives that they'd been able to enter the Lazaro house around two that afternoon and placed him under arrest. The charges were still the same - all civil. They'd searched the house and confiscated the usual stuff; his files, computers, phones. The Stamford detective told Steve that Lazaro would be held there until his court date, set for the following Monday, the 12th. Steve thought about that. It meant big headlines in tomorrow's papers and more hyped news coverage, just what he hated. "Okay Hank, thanks a lot."

Best to move now, he thought. He'd take a drive over to that Stamford address tonight and see if they could spot a red Camaro parked in the complex. He thought about who was on night duty, hoping Officers Blake and Hernandez were available. If Rizzo appeared outside at all, they'd be able to make an arrest then and there. Once again Hansen felt handcuffed by the law. Without the warrant it meant they couldn't enter the apartment unless Rizzo gave consent. "Good ole' number 4 in our Constitution, ladies and gentlemen," he muttered as he stood up and strode to the front desk. In his mind a bust-in would feel good, real good.

The Get-Away
If it hadn't been for fucking White Plains he'd have been gone by now. After that mad dash home, packing,

and hitting an ATM, Nick raced down the Merritt Parkway to Westchester Airport. There, he found the ticket counter, already closed for the night. He was told it was too late for any flights going out, even from La Guardia. There was nothing else to do but drive down there and look for a motel nearby. Some guy standing near the counter told him about a hotel right across from the airport, on Ditmars Blvd. He'd go for that.

So far no one seemed to be on his tail. He was pretty sure he'd squeezed that bitch's mouth shut. It nagged at him driving down to Queens. Was she lying about that friend of hers, that she'd called the cops? He thought about calling Clio to find out if she'd met up with them at that bar, or if anything was said about it, but decided to wait. He should get away from this whole place.

It was pretty late by the time he checked in, but he wanted to book a reservation for Puerto Rico using his other I.D. He'd make it a one-way ticket to leave him open - for what, he didn't know. They even had a kiosk where you could print out your boarding pass, right there in the hotel lobby. A couple of scotches and a decent night's sleep would put him in a calmer state of mind.

Saturday Morning - February 10th - At The Marriott

Waking up in the hotel room reminded him of that last time with Clio. Christ. Was it only a couple days ago? Too bad he wouldn't have her company down there where all they spoke was Spanish. He'd never even been out of the country before. Maybe he'd call her, see if he could change her mind. He brewed a cup of their crummy coffee and put on the Weather Channel hoping to see if he'd be flying into 80 degree sunshine and no rain for

277

the next week. After a shave and shower he began to get antsy. The flight was hours away and it was still only nine o'clock. He would pack and check out, because sitting around in this room waiting was a drag.

Downstairs he asked if there were any private parking garages nearby. Lucky for him, they had self-parking that cost him only $19 a day, right there at the hotel. Their shuttle to the airport ran every twenty minutes. So what if he got there early. He'd get an assigned seat number, check his bag, and chill out at one of the airport coffee shops.

He smiled as he stepped off the shuttle. As far as he personally was concerned, everything was lookin' good to go. The sun was out, snow was melting, and his cash flow was flush. A new life was starting up for "Ricky Montrose". Who knew? He might even connect with Mario at some point; they could start up a little business of their own. He crossed over to Spirit's entrance and followed the signs up the escalator to ticketing to check his bag. He didn't even have to wait in line.

Beyond Girl Talk

<u>Gemma's Apartment</u> - Saturday morning

They were still going on about their new guy friends. "I like the way he asked for my number - like, real polite. And then when he said he'd call today, I was like, Yes!" Gemma jabbered on, "Don't you think he's nice looking? I mean, not a stand-out-in-the-crowd look, just...nice."

Clio grinned as she leaned over to give Gemma a pat on the shoulder. "We are two, new-found chicks, Gemma, and it's about time. I was getting fed up with being a shut-in, weren't you? Everything that's happening now? Is *good*!" She got up from the couch. "Want another cup of coffee?"

"Sure," she handed Clio her empty and sat back, staring into the gray TV screen. Gemma told herself to take it down a peg. She'd done this before - gotten all jazzed up and stupidly let herself plow ahead with runaway hopes. This time coming back to reality was easy, what with the reminder of her condition. A hysterectomy meant no children, unless she adopted. How many guys did that eliminate? She consoled herself in a whisper, "Take one thing at a time."

Clio returned with two steaming cups. "You know what I think? I'm thinking the best thing I've done recently is move in with you. Even if it's only for a week or two. Really. It's given me a chance to look at who I've been living with for the past three years. And it's all because I wanted to have nice things...and no money worries, for once." She took a sip of her coffee. "I mean he never even showed up yesterday to pick up that goddamn package. After making me wait all day for it. Sometimes Gemma I want to snuff him out like you would a cigarette." She looked over at her sister, feeling a little ashamed of herself.

Gemma pulled her head back a bit astonished at Clio's blistering style. She thought a moment. "I have to say I wondered about that too. If it was so important, why didn't he come for it? But you should probably wait and see what he says today. Maybe there's a good reason."

"Well, I'm not going out of my way to be his big helper anymore, not after the way he's been treating me. I want to have some laughs for a change."

"That's good and all, but go slow. I don't know. Nick seems really cool, but ..." Gemma shrugged her shoulders. "We both should go slow."

"Well that's exactly what I told him! I didn't tell you about this yet. But during the half, or whatever you call that period thing, when you met Nancy and Dana in the snack bar? He was going on about me coming on a vacation with him. To Puerto Rico, no less. He says you don't need a passport to go there. Like that's the big convincer. Well, I told him a spaghetti dinner is good enough for the time being." She gave Gemma a look of triumph. "So see?"

"Way to go, Clio. For you, that's restraint! You should really hold off... at least for a while, till you see what happens with Michael and this thing with his company."

"Yeah, yeah. I told myself, first thing Monday morning to call that lawyer and find out how much I'm protected. Because see, now I have questions I would never have dreamed up when we first put that pre-nup together. I wish I was..." Gemma's phone rang.

She jumped up. "Oh...do you think that's him?" and ran toward the door. "No, no. What am I saying? It's too early." She picked her phone up from the hall table. "Hello?"

"Hi, Gemma. It's Steve. We met last night. I hope I'm not calling too early..."

"No, no. That's fine. It's after 9:30. Did you get your job finished last night?"

"Uh, yeah. That's all done. What I was wondering... it's a nice day for a change. The sun's out. How would you like to take a walk? I was thinking of the Stamford Nature Center. They have a nice farm there. And then we could go for something to eat?" He was afraid she might laugh at him. "I've heard it's much nicer before the Saturday crowd gets there, with their kids and all. They have some great trails."

"Well, sure. Sounds like fun. You say they have trails? Will I need hiking boots?"

"No, no. Regular ones will do just fine. There may still be some snow left on the trails. Hey, that's terrific. So I'll pick you up. Did you say you live in Stamford?"

"Uh, huh. The easiest way is to come down 95. I'm off

281

Canal Street." She gave him the address and apartment number.

"Got it. Is half an hour too soon? The Center is a ways up; it's close to the New York border."

"Sure. That's fine by me."

Gemma was digging her boots out of the closet, but at the same time complaining about a different call, one that Nick had made only moments ago. "I don't know, Clio. He's sounding a little crazy. You were good to stick to your guns."

"What I don't get is this sudden need to take off." Clio clunked down on the sofa. "I mean, what's the big hurry? He says... just last night, at the game, he's says he's made this great spaghetti sauce for us, and now he's tryin' to persuade me to come with him to Puerto Rico! Today!"

Gemma was shaking her head as she sat down in a chair to zip up a boot. She suddenly looked up, "You're kidding. Today? You mean he's canceling out on your dinner date?

"Yeah. What a rip, huh?" She sank onto the couch, trying to find some humor. "Oh well, I didn't bring any summer clothes with me anyway. Can you believe he thought I'd just pack up and meet him at the airport?"

"No! That's balls for ya'." She stood up. "But Clio, I thought I heard you say at the end you'd think about it."

"Oh, don't worry. I'm not going, not on such short notice."

"You know, I feel sorta' bad leaving you..." The bell rang. Gemma's head turned to the door. "There he is. Right on time."

She opened the door with a big smile, "Come on in. I'm all booted up. I just have to find some gloves."

As Steve stepped in, Clio waved from the couch. He

took another couple steps through the short hall. "Hi, Clio." He smiled. "So did you two stay late last night?"

"Naw. We left Nancy with those other two guys to choose from."

Steve smiled and nodded, "Fair enough." He waited a beat. "So I guess you're spending some time with Nick then this weekend?"

Gemma flipped into the conversation, "Would you believe he just invited her to go with him to Puerto Rico?" She searched in her pockets, "Ah-ha!" she said, pulling her gloves out, "Here they are," and continued, "*But*, she turned him down." She gave Clio a high salute with the flick of a glove.

Holy shit, Steve thought, This is fast. His face went quickly from astonished to concerned. "So you're not going. Is that right?" he asked. With Clio's shake of the head he turned to Gemma and placed one arm around her shoulder. "I have to ask you something very important. Both of you." He looked back at Clio. "Can we sit down? I need to talk to you. It's serious."

A heavy stillness filled the room until Gemma spoke up, "I don't understand what's happening here."

"Please, let me explain." He unzipped his jacket and started to reach inside for his badge but then changed his mind. "Can we sit down?" Gemma joined Clio on the couch and Steve swung an old wooden captain's chair around to the other side of the coffee table. "Last night Dana called me from the rink after she'd had a frighten-ing experience." He paused a moment, deciding to move through this gradually. "She wanted my help, but she didn't want to make a scene. Clio, apparently your friend Nick grabbed her as she came out of the ladies room and forced her outside, behind the rink."

"What?" Clio snapped forward from the sofa back. "You gotta' be nuts! We were there! Why didn't she say anything about it?" She sat there glaring, ready to pounce.

"I'll tell you. Just let me talk, okay? Dana told me that she recognized him from a time before, at a previous hockey game in Darien where there was an encounter, a fight of some sort after the game. But that's not all. She also saw him at the train station the night Paula Metz was murdered. She was scared."

"Why didn't she call the police then?" Clio turned to look at Gemma. "Something's wrong here." Her sister sat very still staring straight ahead, like a kid watching 'Dawn of the Dead'.

Steve answered Clio. "She did," and pulled out his badge. First he turned to Gemma, "I'm sorry to come in here like this, Gemma." He held his badge forward for both to see. "I'm Lt. Steve Hansen, Darien Police. We need to find Nick Rizzo as soon as possible. He's dangerous."

Clio shook her head in disgust. "This beats it all. You come here for a date with my sister - SUPPOSEDLY! And then you want us to help you find MY date!"

Gemma moved her arm forward to restrain Clio. "Hold on, hold on. Think about it, Clio. What do you know about Nick Rizzo? You just met him. Now the police are looking for him."

Steve leaned forward, his forearms resting on his knees. He looked directly at Clio, "When did Nick ask you about going to Puerto Rico? What time was this?"

"Shit, it was just before you came." She shook her head, "And to think I was half sorry not to be going with him."

He was wondering why Rizzo made the call in the first place. Was he testing her to find out if Dana had talked? "Think back Clio. Did he ask you about Maxwell's? I mean who you met up with, if Dana and Nancy were there?"

"Yeah, he asked who all was there. Did I pick up any new guys, just some teasing. I told him Gemma thought she met someone nice."

"But nothing was said about Dana?"

"No. I just said she went home early with her husband."

"And then he asked you about going to Puerto Rico. Did he give you any particulars? Departure time? Airport?"

"He said it was an early afternoon flight, but there was still time if I could get there around noon...But you know what? He wanted me to drive *myself* down to La Guardia." She was going back over what he'd said. "That kinda' queered it for me. He told me he wasn't in Stamford; he'd have to meet me at the airport, and then he went on about what a great time we'd have. I wouldn't need a passport or anything, just a little spending money. Hunh! Cuz' next he says, 'Or maybe a lot!' Then he gives me one of his ha-ha's."

Steve zeroed in on Rizzo not being in Stamford. He must have taken off last night and stayed somewhere else. That was why they'd had no luck finding him at his apartment. He switched back to the moment. "But he didn't mention which flight or even an airline?"

"No. Because I told him I didn't think it was a good idea for me to go; it was all too sudden."

"And that was it? You just said goodbye?"

Gemma broke in, "I heard her say she'd think about it."

Clio glared at her.

Steve sat back. His mind was racing with a plan. Did he dare? He shot a glance at Clio. "What if you were to change your mind?"

"What the fuck?" She looked at him and then stood up and circled in back of Hansen.

He craned his head around, "Just to point him out at the airport, Clio. Not to go with him. I promise, we would make sure that you'd be completely safe. You have to understand; the only way we can make an arrest is with someone who can identify him. Dana is the only other person who could do that, and I frankly don't think she could go through anything more. Not after last night."

"Yeah?" Clio was prowling around the living room at this point. "Well, why should *I*?"

"Because he threatened to kill her. She believes he was the one who shot Paula Metz." They watched Clio look at the floor, turn away, take a few steps and turn back.

"You'd be completely covered. We'd see to it."

It was all so much to take in. And yet despite the risk, she felt a hook pulling at her. This was just like in the movies; it was an adventure, with some excitement for a change. She paced the floor. But wait. She stood still. What would Michael think of this? No, no. Hold on. He'd totally freak out. If he was cleared and got his job back, she'd have screwed up the whole marital relation-ship by working with the police. Clio shook her head. "I can't do this." They waited. "There's too much at stake." She looked over at Gemma, who sat there frown-ing.

"You sure?" Steve asked, "You wouldn't have to approach him at all, just point him out to us."

"I'll do it," Gemma said quietly. Steve's head turned

back to the sofa.

"Stay out of it, Gemma. This isn't your responsibility."

"Oh yeah? Well, I'm your sister. You're living here now. What if he came back and started calling you? He could be one of those stalkers."

Steve broke in. "I have an idea - if you're willing. But Clio, it depends on if you can get back to him. Do you have his phone number?"

She stood in place, numbed out. Then she walked over to the coffee table and picked up *People* magazine and flipped it over. "It's here."

"Okay!" he was excited. "All you have to do is call him up and tell him you've changed your mind; you've decided you want to go. If you can just get us the airline and flight number, we're golden." He turned to Gemma. "You sure you're willing to do this?"

"I'm sure," she said and then brushed both of her hands sideways over her eyes, covering a state of disbelief. She looked up. "You call him, Clio. You can do this."

Clio stood still, thinking, "Yeah, I guess so." She pulled out her cell, paused, and then threw a warning look back at them, "But I don't want you guys lookin' at me while I'm talking," and proceeded to the kitchen.

Steve tore off Nick's number and then checked his watch - 10:25. He hoped they had enough time. He'd have to decide how to put this together, because he'd need back-up. With Clio's voice in the background, Steve turned toward Gemma. "I feel bad about how this turned out. I don't want you to think I'm just using you." She was looking down, her hands clenched at her sides. "Not at all," he went on, "You're a great lady." She sat there saying nothing. "Will you agree to a rain-check?"

Gemma had been thinking about her stupid life and

287

how lousy her choices in men were. "We'll see," she said. "I don't know. Let's just get through this."

Finally Clio's voice went quiet. She strode back into the living room, "The flight's at 1:35." She cocked her head to one side and frowned, 'Spirit Airlines'? I've never heard of it, have you? He said it's some new vacation kind of plane."

Steve stood up. "Did you get the flight number and destination?"

"He said 601 - to Puerto Rico."

"But to San Juan, right?"

"I don't know; it's just an island isn't it?"

"Never mind. As long as we've got the flight number, we can check it out."

"Anyway, I'm supposed to meet him in the Central Terminal, wherever that is. He said Spirit's easy to spot and there are garage entrances just on the left. If I park on ground level, I can walk straight across. He'll meet me at Spirit's check-in."

"Okay then. What time did he say you should meet?"

"At noon."

Steve wanted to get down to his car and make some phone calls. He looked again at his watch. "It'll take about 45 minutes to get to La Guardia. Good thing it's Saturday. You're sure he said at noon?" He stood up.

"Yeah, that way we'd have time to grab a sandwich after we checked in."

He looked at Gemma. "You might want to wear...I don't know. Whatever a woman wears on a plane to go south." He started forward, toward the door. "And pack a bag or two."

Clio blocked his way, with her legs planted apart and hands clamped on her hips. "She's not going unless I go too." Her eyes held fast to his. "And look!" She ran over to the hall closet and slid the door open. On the floor her suitcase lay open, spilling over with clothes. "See? We're already packed."

Steve rolled his eyes to the ceiling. "You beauties beat them all." He started for the door. "I'll be down in my car getting back-up for us. Just come down when you're ready, but be quick. I'm in the black Toyota, right out front."

On Their Way

His first call went in to the Darien station requesting a back-up team. He wanted them in plain clothes, no uniforms. They were to meet him at Gemma's address as soon as possible so that they could get down to La Guardia. He waited, tapping his fingers on the steering wheel while they verified Clio's flight info. It all checked out. He was directed to Concourse B, in Central Terminal. Steve then repeated his no uniforms order. They confirmed and projected a ten to fifteen minute ETA. Next Steve called the Stamford police station to see if Minicus had come up with anything new. Surely they'd have checked through Lazaro's computer and phone calls by now. He wanted to know if any hits from Mario had turned up. Could be he knew Rizzo. As he waited for the extension number to connect, it occurred to him that this tangle with the FBI was turning into a game of who was ahead of who. A voice came on, "Agent Minicus here.

"This is Steve Hansen - remember? The detective in Darien? Just calling to see if you got anything from Lazaro's house that ties us into the Metz case."

"Not a whole lot yet. Right now my team is focusing

on his recent banking transactions."

"What about phone calls?"

"Well, we tracked a call that Mario made from the city - that was the night of the 27th". His voice took on some emphasis. "It was from East Village, right near where Paula Metz used to live. Another was from Grand Central, the night of the murder, which is mighty interesting. The last one he made was from outside Lazaro's house - the night we brought him in. We'll be checking Lazaro's office e-mails and records as well." He sucked in some air and breathed out a sigh. "So far, there's nothing that ties him directly to the murder, but the whole thing reeks of complicity. We're working on Lazaro now. I think we can wear him down."

"Yeah, it's probably just a matter of time. Any other calls? Any he made from home?"

"There's not much really. A couple back and forth to Comp-Coordinates, their CFO."

"That's it then?"

"One came to Lazaro's house Thursday around 5:00, but we weren't able to trace it. And then he made a couple yesterday to Stamford. We'll look into that. What about you, anything?"

"Right now I'm cross-checking a possible lead." Steve thought of his other question. "You still have that bug on Mario?" He listened to a tiny gap of silence.

"Of course! What's this all about Hansen? Do you know something we don't?"

Just then, Steve caught sight of Gemma holding the door open for Clio, who was coming out and heading for the steps, dragging a big suitcase behind her.

"I think I have a lead, but a call just came in, and I gotta' go. I'll keep you posted." He flipped his phone shut and got out of the car to help with the bags.

Clio was striding briskly down the walk and had overtaken her sister. At the curb she handed the bag over to Steve. "Too bad we're not going any place real, huh? I'd like to hit Las Vegas right about now." She glanced at Gemma and then at his car. "Do we both sit in back, arrested style?"

He shook his head, smiling. "Dear ladies, sit however you like." He loaded the suitcase and slammed the trunk shut. Then he placed one hand on the roof and gave them a serious look. "But listen now. You've got to be tough about this, and ready. I mean for anything. This guy is on the run, and he may be carrying a gun."

He saw the Darien response car speed up the street and pull to a stop alongside his Toyota. Steve stepped up to their passenger window and leaned in. Hernandez and Blake had gotten the call. This was good. "Here's the plan: we're going to La Guardia's Central Terminal. It's Concourse B we want: Spirit Airlines. He hoped that area was laid out the way he had it pictured in his mind. We'll park just opposite on ground level. If need be we'll use two of those spots inside, the ones they sometimes reserve for limousines. They should be near the exit. I'll lay out our plan on the way down."

"Got it." Hernandez said, "We found out it's flight 601 to Fort Lauderdale; then they connect for San Juan. Want us to lead?"

"Okay. I'll drive the ladies. Don't run the siren unless we have to get through a traffic pile-up on the way down. Oh," he gestured toward his car, "meet Gemma, the one in front and Clio Savini. They're the ones who can point out Nick Rizzo for us."

The two cops smiled and called to Hansen, "Okay, let's

head out." By the time they'd passed through Greenwich Hansen had gathered his strategy. He reached toward the console and picked up his two-way radio to deliver the plan, step-by-step to Blake and Hernandez. Steve would go in with Gemma to decide on the best place for her to stand watch. It should be close to the Spirit entrance, but near the back wall and out of sight. He would stand forward, near the check-in lines and in her line of sight, to get her signal. She would first brush a hand off her right shoulder and then nod in Rizzo's direction. Hernandez would also be inside, positioning himself alongside another entrance, one a little farther down in case Rizzo tried to make a run for it.

Outside, Clio and Blake would take up watch near the passageway leading out of the garage, opposite the central island, with Clio shielding herself part way behind a pillar. This was in case Rizzo arrived after the designnated time. That way they'd have full view of taxi and shuttle drop-offs. If she spotted him getting out of a cab Blake would call Steve for a heads up and then he'd follow Rizzo inside.

"Is this clear to everyone?" he asked and looked sideways to include Gemma. They all agreed and closed out. "Clio, you've got your cell with you, don't you?" She said yes, of course. Then he asked Gemma again. "Are you still okay with this? Any questions?"

She looked hesitant. "I was just thinking about that big, luggy suitcase. I'm standing there by some wall looking all around for him. I don't know. They're always telling you to keep your eye on your luggage. What if I have to run or something?"

Clio spoke out from the back seat, "I don't think you even need it. I'll have it outside, and if he catches sight of me somehow, I'll just give him a wave, ya' know? With a suitcase, I'll look legit." Steve nodded in agreement. By this time, Clio was so into the kick of it that she had wiped Michael from her mind.

They sat back and watched the scenery flow by as they passed through the border entering NY State, then on beyond New Rochelle, each imagining possible scenes in the roles they'd be playing. Some heroic, others in shades of peril. It was as though they'd been placed on location as extras in an action scene for some film.

Steve was thinking about Clio's conversation with Nick in the kitchen. Did he really believe that she'd change her mind like that? And was he convinced that Dana never mentioned what had happened at the rink? He broke into the quiet. "Before we get there, I need to have you fill me in on some of the background here. Like, how long have you known Dana and Nancy? And how did you meet up with Nick?"

Gemma spoke up first. "We haven't known them long at all. It was just yesterday. I was volunteering at a health fair at Darien High School. Nancy showed me around and introduced me to some of the people. One girl, a student, helped set up the booth and sat with me to promote DVC. It was my first time volunteering." She looked out the window, recalling the scene. "There were a whole lot of kids there. And then Dana stopped by to say hi. We got to talking and somebody came up with the idea of the hockey game. They invited us to meet them at the rink and then go for some drinks afterwards at Maxwell's. That's about it, right Clio?" She turned toward the back seat.

"Yeah, Gemma told me these two teachers were supposed to come. I didn't actually meet them till they came over for that last part of the game."

"And what about Nick? How did that come about, Clio?

"I just spotted him in the bleachers walking down this aisle close by, so I called out to him. I was really surprised to see him there. We both were. Anyway, he decided to come sit with me."

"But how'd you meet him in the first place?"

Clio wanted to keep this part short. "At a place in North Stamford called Silvio's."

"Yeah? Then what?"

"We had a couple, three drinks. I don't know. We were attracted to each other. He dressed nice, and he was a gentleman." Clio paused, "He offered to drive me...he thought maybe I had one too many."

"And?"

She shrugged her shoulders. "We ended up at the Hyatt."

"Yeah? Under his name? Yours?" No answer came from the back. "Okay, well can you tell me what kind of car he drove?"

"It was red, one of those sporty jobs."

"He tell you about himself, what kind of work he does?"

"Jesus! All these questions. No, he didn't. Quit grillin' me, will ya'? I wasn't in a talkative mood."

"Okay, okay. This'll be the last one; it's easy. Describe what he looks like so we can all have a general picture of him once we're at the airport."

Gemma looked back at Clio, who sat with her arms folded across her chest, frowning, "I'll tell you, and if Clio disagrees she can speak up."

"Wait a minute; let me get this to my guys up ahead."

He turned on the two-way. "It's Steve. You should have a picture of what Rizzo looks like before we get down there. Gemma's going to describe him. Ready? Go ahead Gemma."

"Well, he's tall, about six feet, or maybe a little more. He has dark, almost black hair and brown eyes. Would you say he's about 40, maybe 43, Clio? But in good shape." She nodded from the back seat. "He's good looking - the masculine type."

"A mustache? Any tattoos or other things you can think of?"

Gemma shook her head. "Not any I could see." She turned to look at Clio again, smiling and raising her eyebrows. "You saw more of his...him than I did. Anything stand out?"

Clio thought back. That same picture of Nick at the hotel popped back, of him holding up the coffee pot. "It's nothing much, just a silverish bracelet he wears. It has these iron crosses that link together."

Gemma said she saw it too when he was standing up at the game shaking his fist.

"Okay, that should be good enough. Got it?" He flicked off the radio. "Just settle back now. No more questions." So far traffic had been light and they'd made good time. Blake and Hernandez continued ahead of them down Hutchinson Parkway. It was as they approached the Whitestone Bridge that Steve began to feel a little twitchy. Was he going too fast with this?

Why was Rizzo still hanging around? In his place, Steve would have been across a couple state lines by now. Something was keeping him in the area. Was it money? Maybe he had to get a hold of a stash before leaving. But the other question was why he wanted Clio to go too.

The vigor he had felt at the outset was beginning to recede. As he headed toward position in line for EZ-Pass, caution started to seep in. He thought about the possibility of Rizzo being armed and in the midst of a crowded airport. He pulled out his cell phone and placed another call to Minicus. Stamford's front desk told him he'd gone out, did Hansen want his cell number? As soon as Minicus picked up, Steve gave his position and a quick summary of the essential information. Could they send a team for additional back-up?

Minicus's voice was angry, "What kind of shit game are you playing anyway, Hansen? You tryin' to one-up me?"

"No. I had to move fast on this. Hey, do you want in on it or not? It's a definite lead on the Metz murder."

"Yeah, well we called your station and followed up on your work last night. Even though you have a warrant for Nick Rizzo's arrest, he's crossed the state line. That makes him a fugitive Lt. Hansen, and *that* puts us in."

"Okay, but just call Port of Authority Police at La Guardia, will ya? Tell them to place a stake-out on Nick Rizzo. Maybe they can stop him before he checks a bag or goes through security. And listen to me, please. We put together a good set-up once we get to the airport. Both these women with me can identify him. Just don't take over the place. You'll tip him off. Keep back at least until noon."

"I'll check for one of our chase cars in that area. Who else is with you for back-up?"

"Hernandez and Blake from our department. I'll be at Spirit check-in with Gemma. They'll be stationed at two other spots." Hansen worried that they might screw it up by sending one of their "NINJA" SWAT teams over before he could get everyone placed. "Did you get anything from Lazaro?" He was through the gate and merging into lanes for the bridge.

"Here's one for you. The one named Clio in your car is Lazaro's wife. We traced that Stamford call he made to a Gemma Savini, her sister. We were just about to go over there."

"Holy Christ! Hang tight a minute. I'll see what's going on with that. I'll call right back." Steve gave a moment's thought to pulling over, but he was afraid of losing time.

Clio was in the back seat anyway asking, "What? What's going on?"

"The FBI has arrested Michael Lazaro on a civil charge for stock fraud."

"He's in jail?" She got a nod. "Sweet jingling Jeezus." Her fists pressed against her forehead. "Christ almighty."

Gemma craned her neck around to look at her sister. Clio sat in a dazed trance with her mouth hanging open.

Steve waited a minute to allow this stunner to sink in. "And here I thought you and Gemma lived together."

"Only since Thursday. I couldn't stand being in that house with him anymore."

Steve didn't know how to react. His brain was congested with the episodes of a two day soap opera: first, a one-night stand with Rizzo, next a move to Gemma's, and then a ticket to Puerto Rico. Now both of these guys were either in or headed for jail.

Gemma blurted out. "Clio, remember yesterday? That must be why he never picked up that package. The police got to him first." She shook her head, "The dirty bastard."

Hansen asked, "A package from him was sent to you?"

Clio answered. "Yeah, he said it was just papers, but he

sent them to Gemma's, prahbly' so he wouldn't have to use our home address."

"We should hand it over to the police, Clio, don't you think?"

A tiny speck of betrayal made its way through Clio's sentiments, but it didn't last long. They talked about how they'd have to hand them over to investigators anyway, so they agreed to release the package to Hansen when they got back to the apartment. Besides, in Clio's mind it was pointless to play a wifey protective number. She knew he'd hate her for it the rest of his life, regardless. Jesus. What kind of life would she have now? She asked Steve what it meant if you were found guilty for civil crimes. Would he have to serve twenty years in that Danbury prison?

"That's where most white collar criminals spend their time, but only if it's a huge amount of money and committed over a long period of time. Take one thing at a time, Clio. Lazaro's court date will come up soon; it's likely to be in a couple days. He'll be indicted on civil charges, and he'll probably be able to meet bail and go home." In his own mind Steve decided not to mention the possibility of more serious charges, ones that might come later having to do with complicity in the Metz case.

Hansen called Minicus a third time to report their decision to hand over the package at Gemma's. They drove in silence, Hansen focusing his attention for the turn-off to La Guardia.

Take-Off

<u>La Guardia</u> - Midmorning

  Nick was telling himself that sitting around waiting for
Clio was a lot more entertaining than sitting around
counting down time till take-off. He was sipping his
third cup of coffee at one of those tiny tables in the Food
Court and picturing her in that silky animal print dress
with those hips swaying back and forth. Then a warmer
picture of the two of them sprang to mind. They were
lying under some palm trees sipping Mojitos watching
the waves sweep onto a white sandy beach. Nothing
ahead but the blue horizon of the Atlantic cutting across
the sky.

  Yeah for sure, making that call this morning had been
the right move. Best of all, he found out that nothing had
been said to her crowd at Maxwell's, so he could relax on
that score. Then, when he blurted out his plan for them
both to take the trip together, it surprised even himself.

As soon as he said it, he imagined her reaction. Too sudden a change of plans, not enough time to get ready. He hesitated when it came to asking her to make her own way down. He didn't really expect her to agree to the whole thing, even though he apologized and promised to make it up to her. But Christ! Half an hour later she's back to him saying she'd like to see Puerto Rico, but only if he promises to show her a good time. This dame was all right. He liked her spunk.

As soon as they hung up, he rode the escalator up to the ticketing counter to book another seat, but he was too late; they could only get her on stand-by. What a fucking shaft. They said her name was first on the list, and they thought she had a good chance of getting on. Small consolation. Nick was worried. She'd get all the way down here and then find out she didn't have a seat. Boy, would that piss her off. He'd have to think of some better alternative. Maybe let her get on the plane first. No, they'd be checking the tickets at the boarding gate.

Another smaller idea came to mind. He'd go outside in a little bit and wait for her there. Clio would like it if he greeted her coming out of the parking lot and carried her bags in for her. Yeah, that would start things out right. He'd sweet talk her. If there was one thing he could always count on it was his style with the ladies. You just had to treat 'em nice...as though they deserved it.

Nick was riding down the escalator again checking his watch for the umpteenth time - 11:25, when his phone rang. He pulled it out. For sure it was Clio backing out; she was going to say she couldn't get everything together on such short notice. Or maybe she got lost driving herself down.

Mario's voice came on instead, "Hey Ritzy, how ya' doin'? It's Mario."

"Jeezus, where are you?

"On my way down South, just like you said. But not to Mexico. All that passport shit takes days. Did ya' hear about Michael?"

"You mean Lazaro?"

"Yeah."

"What about him?"

"He got arrested."

"Mario. Hold on a minute. I'm going to call you back on my phone."

"Oh, right, but make it soon."

Nick's heart beat picked up as he punched Mario's number in. Lazaro might cave under interrogation. What if he spilled that whole plan for getting the bag? Nick had used the Ricky Montrose name. He had that safe-guard, but even still... The phone rang once.

"Mario, it's me. Tell me about Lazaro."

"I heard it on the radio this morning just before calling for a taxi."

"Where are you now, in a cab?"

"No, I'm at La Guardia, waiting for my plane down to Florida."

"Jesus. I don't believe this. What airline?"

"Delta. They've got lotsa' flights for down there. I got one for Ft. Lauderdale. It leaves at 12:05."

"Okay, that's great. But tell me about the arrest. What were the charges?"

"All they said was the FBI was charging him with fraud, somethin' about falsifying the company's financial records. So's he could keep the money himself. It's some kinda' backdating game those pin-stripers do now. I don't understand it all."

"Anything about Paula Metz?

"No, but the news guy said he'd be a strong suspect,

301

even though he claims to have a tight alibi. And ya' know what? He even pleads not guilty to the other stuff about covering up the company records. You can read about it in the papers."

Nick immediately thought of those other papers, the ones in her bag. They must have proven he was covering up stuff. Yeah, that was it. Metz was gonna' blow the whistle on him.

"Mario, does Lazaro know my name? I mean that you called me from Grand Central that night?"

"No, no! He thought I killed her, that I went up there to Darien. But I did just like you said, Ritz. I got off at 125th and went home. They got no evidence I was ever up there. All they know is I worked at Comp part-time for Michael."

"That's it then? No more about the gun?"

"Nope. Nothin' I've heard about."

"Jesus, what a screwball situation. The sooner we get out of here, the better. I'm headed for Puerto Rico. Nobody's following you, or anything, are they?"

"Naw, not that I've noticed. And Ritz, remember. I never mentioned your name. Not once."

"You're my stand-up guy Mario. Always have been. Give this about a week, ten days, and then we'll catch up. Are we good?"

"Sure thing Ritz. See you on the beach." As soon as he flipped close his phone, Mario sat back in his seat gazing through the windows at the planes outside with a look of satisfaction on his face. It lasted until two men in suits came up on either side of him and sat down on bordering seats. The one to his right asked, "You planning on going somewhere, Mario?"

Mario looked at him, "What the hell?"

"We're FBI agents. You're under arrest."

"Jesus!" he yelled, "What for now?"

"Keep it down Mario. You are charged with obstructting justice. We want you to stand up and walk calmly with us back to the concourse."

"This is a fuckin'..."

"You have the right to remain silent. Anything you say can be used against you....." Mario yelled, "Don't give me that crap!"

"If you make a scene we'll have to get rough. Then you'll be slapped with another charge - for resisting arrest."

Mario sank back, his arms limp at his sides and his head hanging low. "Why me? All the time it's me."

*

First thing Nick did was to walk down the corridor looking for a news stand. There it was on **USA Today**. *"Former Comp-Coordinates Senior Accountant Indicted On Fraud Charges"*. He started to read the article, but then flipped it under his arm. He had to hit the men's room and then he'd go outside to watch for Clio.

The air felt good and it wasn't even that cold out. He spotted a bench some distance down to the right, but it still gave him a view onto the zebra walkway leading out of the parking garage. He said excuse me to two women and they slid sideways to give him some room in the middle. It was 11:42. She'd be at least another fifteen, twenty minutes. He sat down and started to read the article, looking up occasionally toward the walkway. It described how the ill-gotten gains these executives had hidden were accomplished by selling stocks that don't reflect their true value. How did these guys figure such a scam? He read it again trying to figure out how they turned themselves into millionaires just sitting at a desk and applying numbers and dates to paper.

Maybe this angle of profiteering was cut from a higher grade of polish and maybe you needed a couple courses in finance, but he didn't see how it differed that much from **B**ig-**T**'s business dealings. What the hell's the difference between racketeering and extortion, besides a name like Wall Street? The part he didn't like was the FBI getting into Lazaro's house and taking possession of his computer and papers. The ten grand would show up going through Western Union to Ely's Variety. He told himself to relax. It'd be a good couple of weeks before they connected the Ricky Montrose I.D. to his flight charges with Spirit. He'd be long gone before then.

*

They'd made good time getting up to Central Terminal and parking their cars. Clio and Gemma's mood began to charge upward with Steve's energy. The five of them were gathered in the garage as he pointed out how they'd take up their positions.

He and Gemma staked a place inside, close to Spirit check-in. The lines were getting long and the crowd thicker, but so far no sign of Rizzo. Hernandez stood watch at Air Tran, the next airline down. This way he could scan the people stepping off the escalator or those lining up for the gates to Concourse B's security line. Steve called Blake to check on their set-up. He'd found a good spot near a garage pillar for Clio but didn't think it gave him close enough access to taxi drop-offs. He wanted to walk across to the central island. Steve said to go ahead but tell Clio to stay put and maintain eye contact with each other. Steve was pleased that they'd been able to get set up before one of those FBI chargers whizzed onto the scene. They had ten minutes left till noon. So far, so good.

Less so with Nick. He was beginning to wish the benches weren't made of metal. His butt was getting cold. He'd wait a few more minutes, then go in to warm up. With all these taxis pouring through, it occurred to him that Clio might have decided to take a cab or limo down instead of driving her own car. He was pulling out his phone to give her a call when he spotted Clio step out from the garage. She stood for a moment watching the traffic and cabs doing their drop-offs.

She shook her head. What was she waiting for? Or maybe she was just confused. Nick zipped across the street to avoid oncoming traffic and entered the garage one section down, weaving his way through the cars. He punched in her number. He would slip up behind her and gave her a hug. The bip-bip/bip-bip from her purse startled her. Maybe it was Steve calling to say they'd nabbed him inside. She fished her cell out of her shoulder bag and put it to her ear.

"Hey, lady," Nick joked, "need some help with your bags?"

She couldn't pull her voice up to say anything. It sounded like Nick. Should she even answer him? Finally she managed, "Who is this?"

"It's me, honey. At your service, just like I said."

"Oh! Are you here? Now? Inside?" She hoped her voice didn't sound as desperate as she felt.

And then from behind and to her left his figure appeared as he crossed through the last lane of cars in section C. He waved and laughed when their eyes met. She returned a half smile but then stepped onto the walkway, turned right and raised her arm in a wide downward wave. But to no avail. Blake was facing the concourse.

"What are ya' trying to do, hail a cab?"

"Uh, no. I was...I don't know. Everything's happened so fast today. My mind's in a spin."

"Well, here. Let me take your suitcase for you. Now just take a nice deep breath and leave everything else to me." He waited while she did as he instructed. "You see? We're here, we've got lots of time, and we're on our way for some fun in the sun." He put his free arm around her shoulder and they started across to the center island. Blake was just turning back to check again with Clio, but there she was, stepping onto the island only six feet away. A man with his arm around her was leaning in, giving her a kiss on the cheek. This must be Rizzo! He looked like the guy Gemma described earlier.

Clio stared hard at Blake, her forehead creased in a frown. He gave Clio a quick nod. His first instinct was to stop them right there. He took a step forward to block their way, but then let them pass. Too many people around. He'd need help. As they stood waiting for the light to change, to let them cross, he called inside. "Hansen, we have a 10-14. He's holding Clio. They're heading across now. I'm right behind."

Ritzy stopped midway to look at Clio. She wasn't keeping up. "Something wrong, honey? You seem a little uptight." She shook her head but looked behind for Blake. Nick followed her glance. That same man from on the island was watching them and now he had a cell to his ear. Nick suddenly realized he'd heard the guy say Clio's name. Nick pulled her arm tight against him. "What's goin' on here!"

He looked left then right and back again. Out of the sliding doors came Hansen at a run.

Clio gasped and pulled away from Nick.

He yanked her arm back and pulled her tight against his body. He let go of her bag and pushed her forward. "Move! I'm gonna' kill ya', I swear." One hand grasped the back of her neck forcing her to run through crowds of travelers getting in and out of shuttles and cabs.

Steve started after them yelling at Blake, "Call Hernandez! Tell him to get security to block the exit. FBI, anyone! Now!"

Nick was pushing her so fast she almost fell forward on her face. Just beyond that same bench he grabbed her arm again. "Come on! Run!" They raced across a stream of oncoming cars. The air filled with honking and the screeching of brakes. Next a siren went off somewhere. They were in the parking garage now in a crouch, threading their way through the lanes. "Where's your car?" he demanded.

She just shook her head. She had no breath.

Keeping low, Nick turned around to see if anyone was following. He caught sight of Hansen standing at the entrance with his gun out scanning the sea of cars. Then another one ran in. It was Hernandez. "You go that way!" Steve ordered. "I'll head to the right."

Nick crouched down, yanking her with him. "This was a fucking set-up, wasn't it." She said nothing. "Wasn't it?" Still no reply. "I should just break your fucking neck."

Pretty soon they'd be surrounded by cops. They had to get out fast. Where's your car!"

"I didn't drive." He shoved her hard to the ground.

His only chance was to car-jack someone who was pulling in. He skimmed down one lane toward the far end where cars entered in search of parking spaces. He saw a silver Audi pulling into a spot one lane over. The driver turned off his engine, got out of the car, and walked to the trunk to get his bag. Nick leaped on him from behind and grabbed his keys before the man knew enough to yell. He jumped into the driver's seat and took off for the exit.

Leaving Clio behind was better. She was just one more piece of shit to handle. He was glad an E-Z Pass tag was mounted on the windshield. If he was lucky, he could get over to the hotel before they could track this car, and then he could take off on his own.

From his rear view mirror he saw Clio with both arms waving and pointing in his direction. He was slowing down for the exit when way off to his right he caught sight of two men running toward him, their eyes on the Audi. Christ, plainclothes men!

There were no cars in line at the exit. Great! They'd never reach him in time. He stopped at the gate. When he saw the man in the booth, it hit him. He needed a ticket for the toll reader. Frantically he scanned the dashboard and cup holders. Nothing. He gunned the accelerator and crashed through the barrier. He was out and away. With no cars in sight, Nick steered directly into the merger lane and then on up the slope curving to the left and the airport exit. Yeah! He was on his way out, ahead of them.

Until he reached the top. Three cars in a line were held to a stop. Just beyond he saw why. A white, FBI police car parked horizontally across the entire lane blocked their way. The drivers sat waiting and wondering what the hell this was about. A drug bust? Two agents in navy FBI jackets flanked both sides of the lane. They stood poised with their holsters open and hands on their guns.

As soon as they saw him in the silver Audi they drew their pistols and started the walk down. Rizzo looked into his rearview mirror. Those other two were on their way up. This time there was no fuckin' way out.

Rizzo sat in place waiting for them to order him out of the car. By the time Steve and Hernandez reached the scene, Rizzo's hands were on the car roof and one of the Agents was doing the pat-down. Steve and Hernandez held up their badges and described the assault and theft below; Hansen said he'd write up that report. Before Nick was taken off, Steve couldn't resist an impulse. He took two steps forward and pulled Rizzo's sleeve back to see his right wrist. There it was, the iron cross bracelet. Steve nodded his head and smiled. They put him in cuffs and took him away.

Hernandez and Steve began the walk back down the ramp toward the garage. Steve was proud that they'd done the job without anyone getting hurt. He knew his boss would get a full account starting with Dana's call from the rink right down to today's arrest. Halfway down he received a call from Minicus. "Okay, we just got a report on Rizzo. The arrest is for Assault and Battery as well as attempted auto theft, right? We want him on your warrant as well though. How'd you get this lead on him last night, Hansen?"

"I'll give you the whole bit once I get up there. But now I've got to see to these ladies. They're somewhere down in the garage with Blake. We've got to get them back home, and then I'll drop off that package. Has Lazaro talked yet? Mentioned Rizzo's name at all?"

"No. We showed him the bank records from his computer. Also the Western Union confirmation sheet with his money transfer control number. It came by e-mail from Ely's Variety this morning. That, along with some five hours of questioning wore him down. He admitted to transferring the ten grand to some guy by the name of Ricky Montrose who was supposed to send him some important documents. But he claims the whole thing is a frame-up, and he swears he never heard of the guy before. Said he never got the package; he'd been blackmailed. Can you beat that?"

"So this Montrose must be his fake name."

"We figured that too. Spirit Airlines checked their 601 flight list. Rizzo made his reservation under the name of Ricky Montrose. We'll see what Mario has to say about that part."

"Why Mario?"

"Oh. That's a good one. Our tail followed Mario to La Guardia this morning. They sat right behind him at a Delta gate listening to him talk to someone he called Ritzy. Most of the conversation was about Lazaro's arrest. But here's the funny part - his good-bye was, 'See you on the beach.'"

"Steve smiled, "This is all coming together, isn't it."

"Yeah, we'll get 'em. I'm going down to Ely's Variety now to get the form "Montrose" had to sign as rightful recipient. We'll have a writing sample from it. And you'll be coming up with the package. Good job, Hansen, He pulled in a long breath and let it back out. "Okay then. They'll be bringing Rizzo up here to Stamford, and we'll be back at the station within the hour. See you there."

Hernandez was on a glow chattering away about the arrest and asking questions about the call from Minicus. "Hey man," he said, "Darien Police are gonna' hit the news big time now."

Their eyes had to adjust to the dark once they entered the garage, but they spotted Blake leaning against their squad car. Next to him Gemma was holding Clio in her arms, "Are you sure you're not hurt? Let me check you over again, just to make sure."

"No honey, I'm all right. I'm all right. That fuckin' son of a bitch better get put away for good or I'll do it myself."

Blake was feeling a little awkward, not knowing what to do with all this, but he came up to full attention when his pals came into sight. He was anxious to hear the results. He'd called Port of Authority Police to report the Audi theft. Then he gave its owner directions to their office inside. He had also retrieved Clio's bag and dispersed the gawkers. Once again it looked as though travelers were back to their normal comings and goings.

The Ride Back

Each of the three was lost in thought. Steve's attention was focused on finding his way out of all the airport ramps and locating the exit for 678. This time Clio sat in front. It had taken her some time going from furious hysteria to suppressed rage. Gemma leaned forward a couple of times while they passed through Queens to pat Clio's shoulder. It pleased Steve to think about the call he'd be making to Dana. He thought she'd probably want to thank Gemma and Clio for doing their part.

Gemma spoke up. "I'm insisting that you stay with me, Clio. Don't go back home. He was bad enough to live with before. What'll he be like now?"

Clio's voice was close and louder, "You can bet your sweet ass I will. I'm not going near that cheater. Soon as I can get to a bank I'm taking out half of every account we've got. If he gets fined, it's his debt, not mine.

"Well, you can give it a try, but you might have to clear it with the FBI first. They've taken possession of all his records. The SEC will want them too. And you better check with a lawyer about emptying out any checking accounts."

Clio thumped back against the car seat. "Oh great. That's just great. And here I was, Gemma, all set to get us to Miami Beach for a good time."

Gemma turned and said, "We'll do it, somehow, honey. We'll do it."

Steve smiled and gave his head a slight shake. Yeah, they probably would.

Stamford Police Station - 5:15 PM

He waited until Rizzo finally confessed to the Metz murder before making the call to Dana; Steve was riding a high, "You can enjoy your vacation, worry-free, Dana. We caught Nick trying to leave the country. He's here at the Stamford station under arrest."

"Oh, thank God!"

"It took over two hours of interrogation, but we finally wore him down. I wish you could have heard Agent Minicus shouting at him. I was on the other side of the glass. He yelled out, 'In cold blooded murder you gunned down a good woman who was trying to perform a heroic act!'

Rizzo kept saying no, no it wasn't like that. He insisted that he was just trying to get her bag and they got in a struggle when she wouldn't let go of it. He swore that the gun went off accidentally." Steve chuckled, "The best part though was when Minicus started firing at him with one blast after another. 'Does this mean Nick, that you blew every single job because of a woman doing you one better? Does it? Does it?' And that's when he finally broke down sobbing. Think about it - first was Paula, you were next, and then Clio. Oh, that reminds me. She and Gemma helped us identify him at La Guardia. I thought you might want their number to give them a call before you go away. Clio risked her life, just like you did. *And* with this confession, there'll be no trial. I'll bet that's something you wanted to hear, huh.

ABOUT THE AUTHOR

JILL SAWYER received her B.A. in philosophy and psychology at Sarah Lawrence College, an MAT at Manhattanville College, and an MA in English Literature at West Conn. She taught at New Canaan High School and lives in Norwalk, CT where she gained certification as a volunteer for the Domestic Violence Crisis Center and serves as a volunteer tutor at the Center for Global Studies.

Several of her essays have been published in The New York Times and local newspapers. Her recent interest has turned to fiction: short stories, poetry, and this, her first novel.

Finally, thanks go to the exemplary staff at the Darien Library who provided me with ongoing support.